COUNTERPUNCH

CAROL ROSSEN

COUNTERPUNCH

E. P. DUTTON NEW YORK

Published in the United States by E. P. Dutton,
a division of NAL Penguin Inc.,
2 Park Avenue, New York, N.Y. 10016.

Published simultaneously in Canada
by Fitzhenry and Whiteside, Limited, Toronto.

Library of Congress Cataloging-in-Publication Data
Rossen, Carol
Counterpunch / Carol Rossen. — 1st ed.
p. cm.
ISBN 0-525-24635-5
1. Rossen, Carol.   2. Rape victims—United States—Biography.
3. Rape—United States—Case studies.   I. Title.
HV6561.R67A3   1988
364.1'532'0924—dc19

[B]   87-30469

Designed by REM Studio

3 5 7 9 10 8 6 4 2

*In memory of William Goyen
with gratitude to Shelly Wile*

a chronicle of how it is for us

PROLOGUE

I swear to God, I'd played the scene before. I don't know if any of you remember but in the sixties there used to be all these melodramas on TV, and I was in all of them, "Kildare," "The Fugitive," "Naked City," "The Untouchables," and if you were a young leading lady in those days, your job was to be mugged, or doped, or raped, or roughed up by some guy who really didn't mean it, you know? I remember at one point there were a slew of rape shows. I think I did three within a space of six months. Anyway, the last one I did was on a "Dr. Kildare"—Dick was held down while Brad Dillman invited his pals to gang-bang me. You know how popular rapes had to be if Dr. Kildare got held down to watch one. The networks were so scared of it that they refused to air the show. *That* was a very expensive rape, by any standards.

1

Anyway, I walked on the set the day of the scene, and wouldn't you know it but the actor who'd been hired to rape me was the same boy-chick who'd raped me in two previous shows. Can you imagine what it's like to be hired all the time as "the rapist"? It's a great deal more flattering to be "the victim." And this creature was a real banana brain. I mean, he really got into the part, you know, he really took the job very seriously. It's these kind of retards who give Method acting a bad name! This guy had left me black and blue the last time around, finger marks on my arms and scratches on my body.

So I walked on the set, was introduced to my rapist, and went straight to the director and told him this creature had raped me twice before and to watch him because he was a nut. I said I was glad to earn my money screaming and yelling and writhing on the floor, I'd act it any way to Sunday, but if the cretin put a real hand on me, roughed me up even this much, I was gone, it was a wrap, I'd see 'em all in the commissary.

Dennis Hopper once kissed me so hard in a scene—this one was about murder, not rape—that my front tooth slashed his upper lip by accident.

And we were only rehearsing . . .

THE DAY

FEBRUARY 14, 1984
Valentine's Day

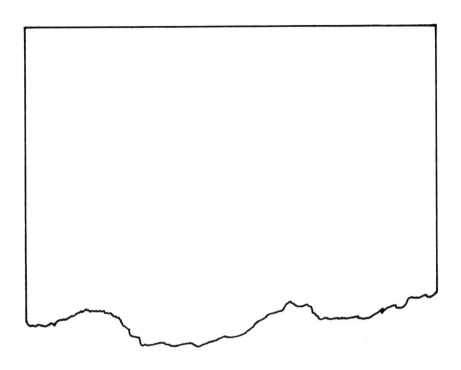

Morning begins
7:10 A.M.–7:30 A.M.

"Cream of Wheat or hard-boiled eggs? This can't go on forever. A decision has got to be made, Eve!" The big blond broad, the almost fourteen-year-old, the Harlowesque preppy punker, my daughter, was late for school.

"Haul ass, sweet baby. Your options are up. You can have *my* hard-boiled egg."

Intercoms blared, bounced sounds against beamed ceilings, barn siding, brick fireplaces, pine floors, intercoms echoing through our New England–style Texas ranch house in West L.A., California. Rise-and-shine sounds. Mother-daughter sounds. There was no need to whisper. Eve and I lived alone.

I was in the kitchen. She was in her room. Now she was in the kitchen. "And take your vitamins, and drink your juice

5

and, oh damn, the car pool's here. Take a banana, I'll eat your egg," I said. She grabbed banana and books and the purse jammed with makeup. "Here, don't forget your lunch," I said.

"Happy Valentine's, Mommy . . ."

"Happy Valentine's, beauty." I was trailing her to the front door. "And tell Daisy to come up to the house after car pool. I have the grocery list for her, tell her."

"You don't have to walk me to the door, Mommy!"

"I like to! Okay, I won't. Tomorrow."

"I love you, Mommy."

"I love you, Eve."

"See you later."

She was out the door.

Manageable chaos
7:30 A.M.–8:30 A.M.

"Get out of my way, Rags, will you?" White dog never moved, and today was no exception, seated as he was in the center of the kitchen, neck extended, chest thrust forward, his limpid eyes staring skyward, mutely singing Italian arias. *Comme toujours,* I wasn't swayed by his courtship. We coexisted, he and I, this ornery avocado-eating giant of a poodle who believed he was everyone's lover.

"Move, Rags, move! I'm not kidding! Go outside!" The Jack Benny of "dogdom" stared on. Black dog Jebediah, Jebbie for short, loped past the kitchen table, not waiting for further instructions. Jebbie was a dog-dog, Jebbie was my favorite, Jebbie could be relied on. He came and he went and he ate and he hugged and he understood the English language perfectly.

Rags spoke only French, an archaic form at that, and his refusal to attend drove me crazy. Endlessly needy, leaning on guests, laying muzzle on all available laps, he wanted to marry and become the homebody and do dishes and arrange the flowers. But if you needed protection on a walk at the beach

6

or up a trail or even down the block, he'd dance around in circles and pull the leash from your grasp, or play hide-and-seek in sand dunes or behind trees. He wasn't *there*, like my ex, Hal Holbrook by name, who had found Rags and left, a strange twist on a going-away present. He reminded me of Hal, it was something in the eyes, or perhaps it was Mark Twain I envisioned. Either way, the dog was charming but a pain in the ass. Twain and Hal had come back to haunt me.

"Listen to me, Rags, you're not coming on my walk today, you're not going up to the park and that's it!" I would watch the morning news and listen to Diane Sawyer, and drink decaf expresso in peace!

The phone was ringing, it was ringing already, the daily dialogue with the East Coast had begun. My friend and accountant of fifteen-plus years was calling from New York City. The keeper of numbers for Hal and me, he tallied who owed whom what and why. Today Hal owed me money, reimbursements for horse fees and lessons incurred, Eve's passion and her parents' delight.

"How *is* Eve?" he asked.

"Taller than I am and twice as menopausal." He laughed, he'd been around at her birth. "No, it's true!" I said. "I'm hopeful we *both* make it through adolescence by the time she's twenty-one."

The other line rang, an astrologer friend, calling from Washington, D.C. Her life was a shambles, she hadn't time for my stars, she was canceling this morning's reading.

"What reading?" I asked. I'd quite forgotten. "Don't worry, Janie, take care of *yourself*. I'm fine, just fine, my life is on course, the seven-year plague seems to be over. And you remember Mr. Wonderful? Well, he's dropped to second place, a mercy given all the stresses."

"That's good, very good." Janie was generous. We were spending her dime on old news. "As I told you," she said, "if we have his hour of birth and the chart is working, he won't know up from down until summer."

"I know, I remember, we'll speak, Jane, when you can."

A moment's respite before the dash. I stared at Rags, he stared at me, the news had glazed, my coffee was tepid. I missed him, Mr. Wonderful. Was I still in love? Perhaps. I couldn't remember.

Diane Sawyer works hard and she doesn't have babies. How much time does she have for a life? Thoughts as I walked from kitchen to bedroom, today's news on hold until the night. Two cats, my cats, screeched and scratched, warring under the dining-room table. My home is a jungle! I must like jungles. "Rags, get out of my way!"

"Carol, it's me!" she hollered from the entry, and slammed the front door. "Rags, stop it, get out of my way!" Daisy, the mother's helper, had returned from Wednesday car pool. Out of breath at nineteen, in the fast lane to Mars, Daisy managed with more or less grace. She drove a car and spoke the English language, which met most of my expectations. I needed wheels, I needed savvy, I needed youth on my side, a bit risky but worth the effort. Six child-women have passed through my kitchen portals and only one had done me in and robbed me blind. The creature had stolen my diamond wedding ring. I tried never ever ever to think about it.

"Daisy!" I hollered; it was too early to holler. "The grocery list is in the kitchen. My check's on top, and you're picking up the kids after school?"

"Right!"

"Well, I'm gone," I said. "I'm going up to the park. I'll take the truck, I'm gonna walk the trails."

I was "white rabbit late," on my way to a life, unemployed but terribly busy. Unwashed hair but clean skin, Aida Grey–cared-for skin, I'd wash the hair when I showered later. It was a bright day, a clear day, it would be hot on the mountain. I was fair. Creams and lotions were called for.

Lavender sweats and my favorite pink tennies lay waiting in a heap in the bathroom. I grabbed white wool leg warmers—I'd pull them on at the park—as I whirled through

8

the bedroom at top speed. I was late. Where's my watch? Where's my hoops? Where's my purse? I gotta make the chiropractor by ten.

I'd give it a shot. The odds were with *me*. I was strong. I'd walk fast. I'd get there.

"Dogs, stay outside, don't come back in the house, but if you do, stay off the couches! Check out all coyotes, and I can't find my keys! Watch the door, white dog!" And I was gone.

Looking for posies
8:40 A.M.–8:45 A.M.

Horse smells, tree smells, white double fences, Kentucky farm double fences, morning. I sat on a tree stump pulling up my woolly warmers as Teresa, the assistant to my daughter's trainer, exercised a bay mare in the riding ring.

"Hey, Teresa! What a day! Happy Valentine's Day!" She was passing on the rail at the canter.

"It's my birthday." An aside, her voice calm and cotton soft. The horse was high, it was no time for talking.

"Well, happy birthday then! *And* happy Valentine's Day!" Damn, they don't make sweat pants with pockets! What am I gonna do with the key to the truck?

I held it tightly in the palm of my right hand.

"Well, Terese," I said, rising up off the stump, "I'm looking for flowers!" She nodded. Mythical posies, armfuls of roses, Valentines laid at my doorstep. It was a minor fantasy, not enough to spoil the day, an addendum to my belief in Santa Claus.

Teresa and the mare circled the arena as I jogged some thirty yards to the right. There a sign read INSPIRATION POINT TRAIL: NO SMOKING.

The path commenced. I began my walk.

Set Piece

Christ, I saw him three times that day. Just a glimpse, first really, football fields away, but still it counted, in the name of something. I saw him as I was rounding that part of the hiking trail that hangs low but well above the riding rings and horse paddock. It was eight forty-five, St. Valentine's Day, or more precisely St. Valentine's morning. I know because I tripped over time that Wednesday. I hadn't time to take time for such pleasures.

I was exercising in the park, Will Rogers State Historic Park, his homestead at the crest of the Pacific Palisades, where Los Angeles drops off into the sea. It was *my* park, *my* playground up through town above the ocean, a variant on the neighborhood watering hole. The Rogers's ranch house was its centerpiece, full mooned by rolling lawns, picnic grounds, a polo field, a tennis court, and riding stables where Eve trained and boarded her show horse. I was on intimate terms with this parcel of land. Every eucalyptus tree was known to me.

For the record, I *never* hike and I hate to jog—I see no reason to bounce breasts in quite that fashion. What I like to do is work out in a dance class and study my alignment in a mirror. But there I was climbing the lower terraces of the Santa Monica Mountains because Shirley MacLaine had suggested one must in a book; hiking because I had pulled a muscle in my arm, which was aggravated by a masseuse, adjusted by a chiropractor, and paralyzed by a poodle who runs the marathon when leashed; hiking because the six-hour-a-week stretch class had been forbidden and I had to exercise or go mad from excess energy and cellulite.

I needed the exercise. I raised my arms to some god and pulled upward in a stretch without breaking my Western stride. I let my head fall back, elongating my neck, and it was then that I saw him, from below, gazing up, a stick figure tucked into the sky. I saw a man, standing alone, on the tip of a minimountain, a stubbed spot known as Inspiration Point. Will had dubbed it years ago and the name stuck, for good reason, the view more than fulfilling its promise. The epicenter of my wilderness, the Rome of these palisades, all roads led to its green, graveled grandeur. It was in fact my ultimate destination that morning, before returning to less lofty adventures.

The sun, on its way over Hollywood freeways, backlit man and mountain, two-dimensional against a Technicolor sky. Milk-white Dresden light drenched "the everywhere" the eye might see, not a teardrop of smog fudged the picture. Surely there was a camera rolling in the area, buried in the grass hugging white fences or hidden in the tail of a helicopter. Any ad man worth his scotch could sell a Chinaman Russia flashing footage of this heaven as a teaser.

This is it! I thought. This is grace! What clarity! How peaceful! I love living here in the West!

Other voices, other accents haunted the moment, hissing "folly!" from over the Rockies. "That's all you ever talk about, you know, you *do* know, you people in California, that's all! The weather and the weather, that's all you ever talk about, it's the main course of conversations! Occasionally it's spiced with tidbits about cars, but really breakfast, lunch, and dinner *is* the weather. Your brains have been blanched, your curiosity baked, and you've died in a fruit cup of health!"

I'd been having this bicoastal dialogue for years, and its fascination lay only in its obsessiveness. These were the pale and grimy comments of darling pals in New York, reflections from The City, the Big Apple, the unsolicited comments of discriminating urbanites who practiced geographic bigotry via telephone. Long-distance lines burned with "When are you coming back? Aren't you bored? How's the weather?" We also sometimes talked about boys.

I was born in California. I'd returned to California. I cut short the morning's three-minute fantasy.

11

It *was* unusual weather—this was February, after all, typically flooding season in the West. Last year's rains had decimated the California coastline, drowning houses, piers, the very edge of a continent. This year was fall-brisk and sparkle-plenty, New England clean in texture, terrifying the natives who understood summer's water-crunch, delighting tourists thawing out from winter freeze. The yellowy gray crust of pollution had lifted, and greens and blues startled the eye. You could see Catalina, "sunny Catalina," L.A.'s island of penguined romance.

So could he, my man, the man way away, hummingbird poised to the left, then the right. Where was he, who was he, this blur in the sky? I refocused, sharp-shooting the image. Standing on a ledge that rimmed the point, hot-footing its twenty-foot perimeter, a cock on the walk, primed to punch out the world, the man oozed with locker room fervor. Or not, I thought, perhaps not at all. Perhaps we've a prince from Beverly Hills on a hike surveying Daddy's domain. The tip of suburbia and all of the coast would be his when the old man knocked off.

The red redness of his shirt and the blue blueness of his shorts shimmered in the higher altitude. Primary colors. Maybe he's an Indian. I continued the climb at pace.

In the mode of the eighties, I marched up the mountain-side modeling faded lavender sweats and pink seven-star tennies. Tiffany hoops, a silver watch, a scattering of rings were as always the accessories of choice. Gray-tinted sunglasses framed in a matching mauve cast completed the I'm-a-girl-but-I'm-hiking attire. I liked my look. It was for me that I dressed. My cheeks burned. I'd forgotten my hat.

I'm not alone, I thought. There are creatures about! Hidden behind barriers of sage and chayote and wild oak brush, birdies back-fenced a stereophonic hysteria. Reserved seating, those high perches in the canopies of eucalyptus that bordered the parkland below, was unavailable for gossip at these altitudes. A snake crunched in the chaparral that carpeted the ravine falling away to the left of the trail. A rattler, I thought. Well, the birdies don't mind and neither do I! I'd lived with their slitherings since childhood. Grammar schools of my youth had taught the mechanics of snake fear and how to tend to a bite or kill if necessary, and I'd done so once, when I was ten or eleven, riding alone on the Palm Springs desert. Dismounting a horse in the middle of nowhere, I'd heard a rattle and saw a snake midway into coil some six to ten feet away. The horse and I had violated cactus sanctum, and there was no time for polite excuses. I'd hurled a large rock and struck its head, killing *him* before he sprang at me.

There would be no repeats of that desert incident here in the Santa Monica Mountains. This snake was on *his* turf and I was on *mine*, and we both lived in the world of the eighties. This hiking trail, so called by residents and the state, was in fact a ten-foot-wide road of pounded gravel and earth, the park ranger's private drive through quasi wilderness. Our mountain trails and pathways had been civilized and were maintained with regularity. Today's rattler knew that. I knew that, too. "King's *X*" was the modus operandi.

I heard footsteps prancing toward me somewhere nearby ahead, and they were close and they were closer and I was startled. Bird-brush harmonies jammed to the back of my brain and the symphony of silence stuttered. All senses focused on the who and the what and the dammit, I didn't come for the company. He appeared, quite suddenly, a stocky gray-haired gentleman in white shorts and no shirt, jogging out of a deep twist in the trail. I hadn't seen him approaching, I couldn't see him approaching, an eight-foot road cut masking his presence.

"Good morning," I said, as I smiled and sniffed him, continuing my walk up the incline.

"Good morning," he said, gasping and dripping and staring the glaze of the faint. And he passed on his way to heart-attack heaven, or at the very least a bout with double pneumonia. But he'll be fit when they take him to the hospital, I thought. He'll look swell in those cute little smocks!

Other footsteps were dancing down the mountain toward me, out of sight, twenty yards ahead. It seemed I'd discovered an entrance to the freeway and was headed into morning traffic. I glanced at my watch, as if time provides insight, and clocked the hour at 9:05. This would never have happened to Shirley MacLaine, Shirley has much better timing. She would have bought the mountain by selling Warren to a stud farm in West Virginia.

Neatly tailored blue shorts and a red Polo T-shirt looped toward me, shoving Shirley aside. The man on the mountain, a young man in his twenties, gently jogged his way down the trail. I had guessed correctly, he *was* an Indian from either North or South America, if genealogy can be read with any certainty; his cheekbones were high and broadly spaced, and heaps of healthy brown-black hair combed à la John Travolta framed his olive-skinned face. A blue backpack, sparkling clean or perhaps it was new, embraced a muscular middleweight frame. The blue of his high-toppers matched the blue of his shorts. He was neat. He was upright. He was graceful.

I wished him good morning as I passed on the right, the polite gesture offered fellow travelers. He smiled a startled smile.

"Morning," he said.

He was gone. I continued to climb.

I had arrived at the Y, a split in the trail, midheaven in the natural arc of the mountain. One of its arms reached up toward Inspiration, the other led downward to earth. Hugging the mountainside, I took the right toward the point. I'd push on up the hundred-yard sweep.

Here the trail became steep and arduous, requiring muscle to maintain an even pace. I walked steadily, evenly, long confident strides, dance disciplines held in good stead. Fifty yards up and only fifty to go and then a park bench with an ocean view! A Valentine's gift from me to me. I felt good. The sun was shinning. The sky was blue.

Footsteps again, this time from behind, someone else heading for the point. I glanced over my left shoulder and saw him, my Indian friend, the red-and-blue kid, trailing by twenty yards. Hunched, deeply curled in a starter's position, sprinting up the incline, his face was drenched with that intensity of purpose that afflicts the sporting world. He hugged the mountain, as I had done, the easier route in an unnamed course, and seemed to be racing against himself, his own time, squeezing the distance between us. I smiled. The white heat of a jogger's mentality always struck me as funny and crazed. They're nuts! I thought, and laughed out loud as he bolted like a shot out of hell. Only five yards or so behind me now and I was standing in his chosen pathway. I turned away from him slightly to adjust my position and give him the right of way.

And suddenly I felt it, I felt a bash to the right side of my skull, and it was prickly and buzzing and warm. What the hell is *that*? What the hell is happening? I turned in the direction of the blow. He was there, the young man, standing on a diagonal, just above me, outlined against a vibrant blue sky. He was poised, feet apart, his hands together above his head, holding something dropping down behind his back. Something long. Something half-hidden and hard to discern. I hadn't seen him pass, I never saw him pass. He was just there and it was beginning again.

He hit me, he hit me a second time. What the hell is happening? What's happening? *What's happening?* I bobbed and weaved, a prizefighter against the ropes, my hands palms up, my hands palms down, my hands butterfly flitting about my skull, trying to fend off the blows. My face turned away, I would save my eyes, my nose, my mouth, my senses.

No! No! No! echoed through my brain. I'd not spoken a word, a sound. My back was to the mountain, I still hugged the mountainside. There was no place to run but down the hill.

He'll follow! He'll catch me! I can't escape! He hit me a third time and then a fourth. Unrelenting, consistent, three-second intervals, I wondered at the precision of each blow. He never missed my skull. *He never misses my skull!* or glanced my shoulders or my arms or my neck.

15

What's happening? *This can't be happening!* I was conscious, still conscious, my mind computing. I turned to face him—perhaps the challenge might work. I pivoted and he bashed me at the top of my skull, and the gravel of the trail scattered every which way under my shifting weight. I slipped and fell backward into the ditch lining the base of the road cut. Ditch cradled spine as both legs karated upward, catching him midchest or midsection. Let him fall, give way, somehow stop the onslaught!

And he stopped. He had stopped the action.

Our eyes met in the pause, his face speaking surprise that I fought on, that I fought back even now. He stood rigid, head held high, arms raised over head, the heroic worker pictured in a thirties mural, a three-foot sledgehammer pointed skyward in his hands. He was perfectly balanced. My kick had meant nothing. We did not speak. It began again.

The sledgehammer arced in a downward motion. I heard a buzz and a sting in my ear. Where'd he hit me? Didn't feel it. Doesn't matter. I get it, what's happening, he wants to kill me. This is about murder. I must die for him. I must die for him right now.

I stopped fighting and rolling and shielding my head and slumped as if lifeless on my side in the ditch. It stopped, he stopped, and it was silent and still and I was limp, a dead weight, my eyes closed play-acting, and alive, conscious, listening.

I heard the sounds of gravel crunching under footsteps and felt two hands around my ankles pulling outward. He was straightening my legs and turning me face upward and pulling me over the road. My body slumped into the dragging action and we crossed the trail and I felt leaves and branches. Brush scraped my back and then combed through my hair and he was pulling and I was moving with him. Tree limbs crackling in front of my face, and I'd been levered to the sun and now lay flat on my stomach, head downward toward the ravine. My right cheek was pressed against the earth, my head twisted back to my shoulder.

16

I felt hands, gentle hands, tug at my pants and I cracked my eyelids to see. He was squatting by my thighs, pulling down my sweats.

Does he see that I see? Does he see *me!*

Closed eyes once more, blind eyes, birds chirping, bathed in silence, covered with brush.

It's about fucking, that's what it is. *This is all about fucking!*

And there was nothing. No hands. No touch. No tugging. My eyes opened.

He was gone.

I lay face-down in the four-foot California wild oak brush that coated the mountainside. I lay face-down in the wild oak at an eighty-degree angle, blood dribbling from my mouth, or was it my head? I couldn't say. I lay limp, twenty-five feet down a mountainside, pretending to be dead. Bright morning silence scanned my body. The bees in my brain hushed the birds in the brush. The all of me screamed, toneless, in my ears.

Stay conscious. Stay conscious. Think your way out of this.

Someone sobbed. It was me. My heart grabbed my throat. Heat ravaged my temples, mind exploding.

Eve, my baby . . . she's down at the bottom. I'm getting off this mountain. She's waiting for me.

About being speechless

You know how a bad actor, when he's playing the ghost, the dead king, in some jerk-ass production of *Hamlet,* actually I've seen it done that way on Broadway and in London, too, you know when the ghost first meets Hamlet and needs him to draw close so that he might whisper what's rotten in the land of Denmark, a bad actor playing the ghost will raise his hands in front of himself and sort of flap his wrists inward like an old lady bathing in the ocean off Coney Island? It's sort of the reverse of a baby saying "bye-bye."

17

Well, that's exactly what I did when I came down off the mountain and was standing in the horse paddock trying to talk to Jimmy. Actually kids do it sometimes when they're trying to be scary, you know? They spread their fingers like a Frankenstein monster and wave their arms in slow-motion counterclockwise toward their bodies, and they usually pop their eyes, as well, just to make a really big impression. Well, that's exactly what I did when I was trying to talk to Jimmy, only I wasn't trying to be scary. I just couldn't talk. It's just that my voice would not come out of my mouth, no sounds came out of my mouth. All I was saying, if I'd been heard, was "Jimmy! Jimmy!" and hoping he'd come to me and grab me before I passed out. I just suddenly let go and I thought for sure I'd pass out if he didn't grab me.

I mean, there I was standing with these two old people, and they were scared shitless, and of course I didn't know how bad I looked. I was just glad to be off the mountain and with my friends.

Come to think of it, *that's* an interesting choice for an actor to make when he's playing the ghost in *Hamlet*. It's not that he's some authority figure beckoning his son to get his ass over there close to his father. It's that he's rendered speechless with relief now that he's *with* his son and *finally* has the opportunity to get a few things off his chest. And he's hoping that maybe he'll get an embrace from Hamlet. After all, it's been a long time and a lot of things have happened!

In the barn
10:05 A.M.

TRANSCRIPT: JIMMY TOWNSEND, HORSE TRAINER, MARCH 10, 1984

. . . it was a great day, okay, that's the first thing I remember when I think of what happened to you . . . everything was going so well at the barn. I came around the corner to do my usual thing and somebody, one of the kids, said "Jimmy," like you'd better look, you know, and I thought, what is it this time? And I looked up and there were these two old people standing there with a lady in between, you being the lady, but I didn't know that at the time. They said this lady was in an accident. She asked to be brought here to her friends. I looked at you and I thought, you know, I didn't know it was you, I really didn't, and I looked and then you stood there real quietly and you beckoned to me with your finger, and it was really an eerie feeling, because you're covered with blood from head to toe and you raised your hand up slowly and with one finger just beckoned, just up toward your face and just motioned. And you know, I got kinda—it was really a weird scene, two old people, this lady. So I started to walk over, I guess, I don't even remember the walk over, and look at you, thinking, well, I don't know what . . . and then I looked into your eyes and I remember thinking, God . . . first thing was, I know that face, and then, Carol! You know, I couldn't believe it. . . .

TRANSCRIPT: TERESA HUGHES, ASSISTANT TRAINER TO
TOWNSEND, MARCH 20, 1984

. . . Well, I first saw you when you first were in the barn and you were beckoning to Jimmy and I remember realizing that he didn't know who you were for a minute, . . . and I knew because I'd seen you go up the trail 'cause I remember I said hello to you that morning, and you told me you were going to get some flowers and go for a walk, and so I recognized you I think more from that you still had your sweats on and 'cause I'd seen you before and remembered, and you beckoned to Jimmy and I sort of looked at Jimmy because I didn't think he realized who it was and then he realized and I remember thinking what happened? if you had fallen, or what had happened.

19

. . . I remember thinking, God . . . first thing was, I know that face, and then, Carol! You know, I couldn't believe it. So I went over to you thinking, my God! First thing in my head was that you'd got into a car accident down the street and you asked to be brought up to the barn 'cause you didn't know where else to go. And so I said, were you in a car accident? And you couldn't speak but you just shook your head . . . you shook your head, and then the old people said, she had an accident on the trail. They wanted to get out of there, you could tell. They just wanted to give you over to somebody and do their thing and get out. They were scared, like you told us later, but you could *tell* they were scared. So I just, you were standing there and you were like motioning to me to just go sit down somewhere, so I took you in the office, . . . but you looked just awful. Really seriously like, just like you were, just what happened, bludgeoned . . . blood all over your face . . . this is what scared me . . . you had a clot of blood, like this, about this big, about like a tablespoon just laying on your sweatshirt, a clot, I mean you know the difference between just blood and a clot. You had a clot of blood coming from, I didn't know, 'cause you know you had blood everywhere but there was no open wounds 'cause the big one was under your hair, which we found out later. So I thought maybe it came out of your mouth, that there was some injury I didn't see and that's what scared me at first was that clot of blood. There was blood on your pants but mainly on that sweatshirt, and in your hair and your face, all over your arms and hands and everything and there might have been a little bit on your pants but not as bad. . . . But I'll tell you the worst, the most significant thing was when I first came out of the barn you were standing there with those two old people. I mean if you could just have a picture of that you would just die. I mean it was so weird, eerie, the way you were standing there and holding yourself up, and they were not too close, but they were near you. They weren't holding you or really helping you, but they were just next to you, and the way you beckoned to me, and the way I realized it was you.

. . . well, you were a little bit hunched over because you were sort of shocky and you were beckoning and your face, you know, there was blood all over the side of your face and you just looked, you know, it was a picture of somebody who's really been hurt and is frightened and kind of like when you think of an animal hurt, you know, and how they're kind of frightened but want help, you know. . . . . I remember just trying very hard to realize that it was you underneath that blood, that this is Carol, this is someone I know, and I like and I care about and that's just blood, that's not, you know, that's something that happened and that doesn't affect the person. It's strange to think that you almost have to do that, you know, you have to remind yourself that the person isn't somebody to be scared of, you know, this is a friend and this is a friend in trouble and you have to remind yourself at the time because it is frightening to see someone like that because they use blood, that kind of look all the time, you know, in TV or movies to frighten you.

    . . . And so I think you learn a lot about the things that they do wrong in TV movies in a situation like that, and that you know it's bad the way they condition us to things like that, 'cause there's no reason to be afraid of someone you know and care about when they're hurt I mean, that's a silly reaction, but I think we all feel that way.

The old people
9:20 A.M.—9:40 A.M.

Reprise

I lay face-down in the four-foot California wild oak brush that coated the mountainside. Bright morning silence scanned

21

my body. The bees in my brain hushed the birds in the brush. The all of me screamed, toneless, in my ears.

Stay conscious . . . stay conscious . . . think your way out of this!

What time is it now?

I lay face-down in the brush, arms up, stick-'em-up arms, twisting my left wrist slowly, slowly, not to make a sound, not a leaf must crunch, twisting my wrist slowly, as I had done before, how many minutes before? when he left, when he was no longer there, what time is it now?

Nine-twenty. Five minutes. Five minutes since then. I'd looked then, when he left, twisting my wrist slowly, watch face in focus, marking the moment, no longer there. I'd lain "dead" for five minutes, never moving, hardly breathing, listening, listening for him. I'd heard nothing, no footsteps, just birdies going crazy and my heart going crazy and my mind going sane.

The next move. The next move. *Now* is the next move!

I was bleeding from my mouth, or my head or my ear. Five minutes alone. Five minutes without him. It's not good to be bleeding from your head upside-down. Gotta sit up. Gotta chance it. Now!

Bare ass to ground cover, I swiveled around, facing the ravine and a back road below. My sweats were at my knees. I pulled them up. My hands hurt. They were swollen. Turning colors. They still worked. They were shaking. My sweats were all baggy. Flopping sweats. Falling down. Where's the string, the tie, the cord? It's broken. It's gone. Doesn't matter. I'll hold 'em. Next?

Next move. What's now? I could climb down through the thicket to the ravine below and then up the other hill to the back road far away. Pass. No good. Too hard. Too shaky. I'd never make it, except I would, I could, if I had to, if he came back I'd have to, if he came back . . .

Next move. Keep thinking! Next move. What's next? No move. I'm staying because maybe he's waiting, where is he now? No, I'll stay till noon 'cause I'm frightened I'm scared and Teresa knows she saw me and I told Daisy I was going and my truck's at the stable so they'll look and they'll find me because maybe he's waiting why did he go? Why didn't he fuck me?

Got to keep thinking. Got to stay conscious. Stare at the rocks. What's new about rocks? Bleeding. Blood. Dribbling. Down my neck. Dribbling. Off my chin. Blood.
 I touched my cheek, my ear, my head all over. Again. Once more. An ear filled with blood. Clogged in one ear. Deaf in one ear? Bleeding from my head. What to do about bleeding? Put on a thing, a thing, name please—a tourniquet.
 I tied a white wool leg warmer around my head.

I hear sounds. Voices. Cutting through silence. A woman. A man. Two voices. Not one. Where? Over there! Through the brush. On the back road. On the other side, the far side of the ravine.
 Echoing laughter. A canyon between us.

Nine-forty. Twenty minutes. A canyon between us. Now! Do I dare? I'll stand up and they'll see me. I'll wave and they'll help me. Just "Hello!" and a wave. No screaming for help. I don't want him to hear me. I don't want to scare them. *Now! Stand up!*

I stood up into space, open space, killing space, head and shoulder cleared the brush, and I saw over there a man and a woman, nonathletic, not youthful, walking and talking. A Valentine's stroll.
 "Hello!" I waved. "Hello!" again.

They walked on. Pretending. They were old. They were frightened. They'd stopped talking and seeing. They walked on. A little faster.

I knew they'd ignore me. I knew they wouldn't come.

I was running through the brush, up the hill, through the thicket, twenty-five feet to the road where he hit me in the sun. And I was there and it was easy, and I was running down the mountain forty yards to the Y, to the intersection, to the old people, where the roads meet, where they were headed.

"You have to help me! I've been attacked. Please help me!" I said.

When I asked Jimmy what had happened to the old people, I wasn't surprised to hear that they'd disappeared without leaving their names. They hadn't expressed a lively interest in my problem.

To be fair, the woman was terrified. When we'd met up at the Y, she looked at me as if I'd materialized from Saturn and if there was any possible way for her to escape to Vulcan, she'd pay cash and book passage. She actually ran from me, but stopped some twenty feet ahead. The man was mesmerized, or paralyzed, but he stayed in my vicinity. Eventually he took my arm, but the woman, she kept her distance.

Of course, I had no idea what I looked like.

Exhaustion

Jane Fonda made a movie called *They Shoot Horses, Don't They?* and this flick began with a few shots under the credits of a beautiful horse running wild in natural surroundings, and ended with the same shots or some quite similar of a horse running wild in natural surroundings. I don't remember if, in the end, the horse was killed, but if the horse was not killed, it would have been in the very next frame. One was left with that impression.

24

The picture, however, was not about horses. It was about marathon dancers in the 1930s, and how they danced till they bled, how these beautiful people, within the context of economic and social despair, persevered with a special tenacity, an almost tiresome tenacity, or something like that, all in the name of a couple of bucks. They had to complete the action, they had to stay in the competition, or die in the attempt, which is exactly what happened. It destroyed most of them. Or that's what I remember.

To tell you the truth, I never understood the title. Wild horses could not be equated with marathon dancers, not by any stretch of my imagination, and the simile of *they* who might shoot them if only they had hearts resembling Hoover's administration or Wall Street bankers or capitalism or whoever was responsible for the Great Depression, whoever was responsible for the exploitation of human beings and poverty with a capital *P*; all of it stuck in my craw.

It seemed a bit artsy-fartsy to me. But we needn't milk a dead cow. Suffice it to say, I got it in my head but not in my gut. What I got in my gut was the exhaustion of the proceedings, the exhaustion of the dancers, and the exhaustion of the viewer bearing witness to this gavotte, this marathon, this horrific odyssey.

I just thought, Those poor fucks, they need a massage.

Do you have any scotch?
A Keystone cop blip
10:05 A.M.–11ish

"Do you have anything to drink?" I asked.

I wasn't hurt. That is to say, I wasn't feeling any pain. I was hunched, bent over like Quasimodo because I was very busy holding up my sweats so they wouldn't fall down as well as holding my head in some sort of fixed position, on the off chance of cracks, in case of concussion. Neither inconvenience had cramped my flight off the mountain, yet now I hunched. A person, I thought, ought to be cautious.

They'd walked me into the office, the one in the barn, filled with leftover saddles and pictures of horses and riders jumping over tall fences at competitions. It was just me and Jimmy and Teresa and another woman, a woman named Pip, a woman they had recently hired to answer the phone. Thank God, because no one ever picked up the phone in the barn. I'd only met her two or three times before. They sat me down in a chair.

"Do you have anything to drink?" I asked.

TRANSCRIPT: TERESA

. . . yeah, and we gave you some water, we got a drink of water, but your hands were shaking, you had a hard time, you weren't so sure about whether the water tasted so good at that time and you had a hard time 'cause the one hand was so badly bruised it was hard to bring the water to your mouth, and of course you were shaking. . . .

They were sweet, my friends. When I asked them for something to drink, they scurried about and found me a clean cup and water, which let me tell you isn't easy in a barn where everything's always messed up and about horses. I tried to drink the water but it wasn't exactly what I had in mind. I wanted something to *drink*. Like scotch. They didn't have scotch. They weren't the type of people to have scotch. If they had had anything it would have been wine, and I didn't feel like wine. So I didn't ask for scotch. I drank the water.

TRANSCRIPT: TERESA

We brought you into the office and I remember you seemed to be drifting a little bit—you know, you weren't quite sharp but you knew you had to try to stay sharp and remember the

26

details. It seemed it was an effort for you to stay real sharp and remember to say things. . . . Pip didn't realize who you were, you were giving her the name of your doctor and when she called your doctor's number, she asked you your name in order to tell the doctor and then we said it, "It's Carol! it's Eve's mom!" and she was shocked, too, she hadn't quite realized.

TRANSCRIPT: JIMMY

. . . and you said, "Get me my doctors! Get me my doctors!" and Pip said, But who are you? She had no idea. Do you know how long you were in the office before—you were there ten minutes, I'm not kidding, you were there ten minutes, and she said, . . . "Is this a mother from the riding school?" and I looked at her and I said, "Pip, that's Eve's mother!" And she just, then her face was just . . . and then I could tell from her face that . . . she just couldn't believe it was you!

There were no mirrors in the barn. There used to be a Coke machine where you could catch a glimpse of yourself if you squinted and concentrated hard on the glass part that covered the cans, but it's been gone for over a year. So when I came into the office and sat down on the chair, and my friends were so busy doing about me, they never stopped and stared, never reflected in their eyes, or the set of their mouth, or the way they were breathing that I was a walking train wreck. If they were having a tough time with blood, they weren't letting on to me. Even if they had, I would have read it differently. You see, I was so filled with the *story* I figured the world must be, too. I figured they almost knew already, by osmosis. That kind of horror blankets an area. Why wouldn't they be horror-stricken?

I was aware, however, that there were no mirrors in the barn.

So then, anyways, then when you got in there, you all of a sudden—it was like you took a deep breath, we asked you what happened? and you wouldn't even let us speak, you wouldn't even let me interrupt. You just told us the story. I mean, you were really thorough, but you didn't like me even asking you the questions, but I just kept asking them because I was—I didn't know how alert you were, if you could remember, and I just thought, well, I got her talking! Because I was afraid you were going to be hysterical any minute, because I couldn't believe you could even speak, after looking at you. You see, that's why I tried to keep asking you the questions and you would be—you would push your hand out, like let me alone, let me talk. . . .

Of course I remembered every detail! Jimmy really pissed me off asking me all those questions as if I'd leave out a detail! I remembered everything, because that's what the walk had been about. It had been about really seeing and hearing and smelling and sensing the moment, not just rushing through experiences like so many chores on a list! Life had felt like so many chores on a list for too long! I'd been busy with chores when my marriage had busted! I wished to savor each day and never again program joy for tomorrow. I wished to taste the present and deal with later when it happened. That's why I remembered every detail, because I was committed to being there, to taking in every detail, and Jimmy really pissed me off asking me questions as if I'd forget!

. . . and then you kept going on, and then I asked you did he rape you, you know, in order—Did anything happen? is, I think, the way I asked it, but I figured we needed to know. 'Cause I didn't know if you were going to even stay, I thought maybe you were going to go out [faint] or something, the way you looked. And you said no, and I knew you were being honest because of the way you are, you know. I mean, if the guy raped you, you'd say the guy raped you, you know; but you said no, the asshole pulled my pants down, or something, whatever you said—I don't think you used that word—and then you . . .

It was odd that he asked if the guy had raped me. I'd tell him, tell anyone if it had happened. I would never withhold that. It just felt odd when he asked if the guy had raped me.

TRANSCRIPT: JIMMY

. . . but then, you see, then you went over it again to make sure. I mean you were so disciplined, self-disciplined to make sure we got the facts. And you—but the second time you went through it you said I don't want to have to say this over and over. And it was like you knew what was going to come. You knew that the paramedics, you knew the police were going to come, you knew the reports you gave the hospital and then I started to know, you know, she's exactly right, they're going to be real idiots, you know how they are, they're so unorganized . . . and basically they're very nice and everything.

TRANSCRIPT: TERESA

. . . you were trying so hard to stay in focus, and you were looking and focusing at me or at Pip or at different times, you know, and you would look right at me, like you were looking right into my eyes to try to stay in focus. . . .

I wasn't hurt. I wasn't feeling any pain. I was tired, I was limp, bone-melting drained, not to be refreshed by a good night's sleep. And Jimmy began to ask me questions, and I *wanted* to tell him every detail of the story so that they might catch this man, this person. But really what I wanted was to capture the *story*, because I couldn't find a place in my head to put it. It had happened and I could tell it, but it couldn't possibly have happened because those things can't possibly happen. So I stared at Teresa and Jimmy and Pip but I wasn't staring at Teresa or Jimmy or Pip. They were screens on which to project a movie. My movie. My re-creation. They were walls on which I visualized pictures. They weren't even in the room when I was telling the story. I wasn't in the room when I was telling the story. But pretty soon a lot of people were in the room and I was telling them the story.

Can you imagine anything so rude as asking a girl like me, bashed up as I was, asking a lady how old she is? I refused to answer the question. The cops asked and I refused to tell them! We were all of us squished into the office: two cops, two paramedics, one ranger, Pip on the phone, Teresa holding my hand, me answering questions, and Jimmy! Jimmy was standing there! Jimmy is my friend and he's gorgeous and twenty-eight and he knows more or less how old I am, but I didn't see any reason why he should know *exactly* how old I am. Life's tough enough without that information being publicly disseminated. This is Hollywood, for chrissake!

And I said so! And I could tell they all thought it was terrific my being so funny in the middle of attempted murder and *I* thought it was funny, but I wasn't *being* funny. I meant it! I had no intention of answering that question! One of the paramedics, on his knees at my feet, taking my pulse with an inflatable armband, looked up into my eyes and said quite gently, "You have to tell them, you know, you gotta tell the cops." Him I liked. I liked his friend, too, the other paramedic. They were guy-guys and they made me feel like a girl, not a statistic. I could tell him, I thought, and I whispered in his ear the date of my birth and then said out loud, "You'll have to subtract it from today's date to get the exact number!" I figured by the time they did that, on the back of the report, nobody would be interested in the answer.

———

Pip had called the park rangers right after she called the doctors and the hospital. I'd told her which hospital and that I wouldn't go elsewhere. She'd phoned down to the rangers who policed the park, found them in their office next door to Will's house, and two of them showed up at the barn real fast. Cal, the main man in charge at the park, was sort of a Dick Tracy type if you can call a ranger a Dick Tracy type, which you can't because they're just not that angular. Cal's assistant, Ranger I—it said so on his chest—was softer, less severe, more like a kangaroo. He told me his name was Tucker, and I knew I could ask him if he had any scotch. I didn't, at least not right away.

When Tucker first received the call to hustle up to the stables because someone had been hurt, he thought the "geek game-show host" had struck again. He thought the weird guy who attacks people with horses, tries to run people over with horses, one Captain Dick, was back.

"Yeah, he's kind of a strange dude. He's attacked some of the riding lessons and stuff in the park occasionally over the years, tried to ride people down with his horse and things like that."

"Jesus Christ," I said some time later, "does he keep his horse at Will Rogers's?"

"No, he keeps it in Turkey Canyon."

"So he just rides up?"

"Yeah, he assaulted one of the rangers here one night, attacked him."

"With the horse?"

"No, with himself."

"Yeah, two guys jumped him, two other rangers, so we went to court and got a restraining order against his being in the state park for the next three years. So I was really surprised when I walked in and saw you with blood all over your head."

Cal, the head man, was asking all the same questions again—what happened, where did it happen, what time did it happen, color of eyes, color of hair—all those questions, and I was sitting in my chair answering his questions but I was concentrating on the blood that was dripping off my chin. Little beadlets of blood were dripping off my chin, and I was flicking them away as they dropped. I got 'em, all right, I got all of those drips as they dropped, but they kept coming! Finally Tucker went and fetched a first-aid kit and put a gauze pack on the wound he'd found near my left ear, under my hair, which was where the blood was coming from.

"I guess I'm not deaf," I said.

Tucker cleaned me up again, although Teresa had already cleaned me up before, but Tucker said, "Do you have any water? We'd better clean her up a bit." And Teresa said, "Yes, but I *did* clean her up a bit." That didn't stop Tucker. Cal left to go check out the trails and wait for the police, and as soon as he disappeared Tucker pulled out his tape recorder and started asking me all those questions again! I couldn't figure out why I was being asked all those same questions over and over, but I answered them anyway and my friends listened again.

Not too much later the paramedics arrived and they checked my eyes for concussions and cleaned me up a bit, although Tucker and Teresa had already cleaned me up a bit and Tucker had checked my eyes for concussions. They all agreed, everyone said I was fine, "It's amazing!" although perhaps they were lying and not telling me otherwise, but in my heart I didn't think so. It took me only five or ten minutes after the paramedics settled in to ask "Do you guys have any scotch or something?"

"We don't, but that's a good idea, we ought to stock it," one said and the other agreed. I knew they knew what I meant.

I didn't think the office could hold more people but I guess there's always room at a party because when the police arrived, as they did, quite suddenly, they found a space and began asking all those questions again. First they asked me my name. "Carol Eve Rossen," I said, and Christ, I started to cry! "Eve," I'd said, "Eve," "Eve" my middle name,

"Eve" my daughter's name. I thought of my daughter and I started to cry. I could see from Jimmy's face he didn't want me to cry.

"Don't worry about Eve," he said. "We'll take care of Eve, we'll pick her up after school."

"No," I said, "but you know you told her to lose weight, Jimmy, and she's lost weight and she looks beautiful, she is just beautiful. Now you tell her, you make sure you remember to tell her she looks beautiful."

"I will," he said, and I stopped crying. The interview resumed. There were many more questions.

"What color was his backpack?"

"Navy blue," I said.

"What color was his T-shirt?"

"No, no, not a T-shirt, it was open at the neck."

"Polo shirt?"

"I guess."

"What color?"

"Bright red."

"About what time did this happen?"

"Around nine-ten. Nine-oh-five."

"Can you describe the weapon?"

"It was . . . it was. . . ." What was its name? "It was wood on the bottom with a thing on the top."

"Was the thing made of rubber?"

"No, it was metal."

"A hammer? Was it a hammer?"

"No, much bigger than a hammer."

"What did the thing look like, on top of the wood?"

"Like a brick, long and short, many-sided, flat across."

"A mallet? Like a mallet?"

"Like a mallet but not." I couldn't remember, my mind wouldn't work. I couldn't remember the word. I couldn't. I could see it in the air, dancing on the desk.

The mustachioed policeman flipped his notebook. "That's okay," he said. "We'll catch up with you later over at the hospital."

"You'll be at the hospital?"

"Yeah," he said, "after we look around the area."

"I don't guess you guys have got any scotch?" I lost the laugh. They left, without answering, to join up with helicopters circling the park.

Let's *go*, I thought, let's *move*, I thought, I'm tired, I'm tired, let's go, I'm tired. The hospital was stuck, the paramedics were stuck, the world had got stuck for no goddamn good reason.

"An IV must be given," the hospital had radioed.

"No IV is required" was the answer transmitted.

"An IV *must* be given," they radioed back, glued to procedure, grounded in process.

"You don't need it," the paramedic said to me. "Just tell them you won't take it; they can't force you, you know."

"I won't take it. I don't need it. I won't take it, you tell 'em!"

All hospital procedures were waived at once. Now was the time to *adios* this party.

"Teresa, will you come with me in the ambulance?" Teresa was soft and strong and calm.

"Yes," she said.

"I'll follow," Jimmy said.

"I need my purse, Teresa, will you get me my purse? It's locked in the truck near the riding ring."

"Do you have the key?" She needed the key. I unclenched my fist. It was in my right hand.

About my dog
10:30 A.M.–11ish

Black dog Jebediah was a black-and-white border collie, the kind usually found in Marlboro ads herding sheep or other livestock. Although raised as a house dog on eyelet bedspreads and feminine laps, the cool earth was his comfort, out in the sun or under Western bright stars as he rolled in

34

high grass or raced beside horses, cars, children, and avocado trees as if they were cattle crossing a landscape. His breeding had stuck to his bones, it seemed, for the moors of Scotland were in his paws. God was kind when He presented Jebbie with Rags as a brother, for Rags, in his reincarnation as a white standard poodle, very much resembled a sheep. Sheep were to Jebbie as the moon to the tides, every movement sweetly intermingled. Heaven was the search for herds yet unfound, in the driveway, down the road, under shadows, in his dreams. Heaven was reflecting on the day becoming night.

I spoiled him. He was my favorite.

That Valentine's morning, somewhere between the hours of 10:30 and 11:00 A.M., Jebbie heard the sirens of the paramedics rounding the road, heading through town and then to the park. He and all the other dogs who prowl the neighborhood, some seventeen fruitcakes in all, let out a howl. This was not unusual. Something to do with the frequency of pitch.

Fifteen or twenty minutes later Jebbie and all his friends heard the same siren's scream as the paramedics drove back from the park and rounded the road on their way to home base, St. John's Hospital, and the dogs began to howl, as they had before, which was not unusual. I was in that ambulance, of course, deep-breathing oxygen, the very best in the larder, which would do quite nicely in lieu of scotch.

After a proper interval, the sirens long gone, the dogs stopped their wailing and went about their business as usual, guarding the grass and peeing on flowers. Everyone but Jebbie, who continued to wail for at least ten more minutes, a dog aria of sorts, splitting eardrums and muffling the birdies. A young man down the road who was tending a lawn wondered what was the matter with the dog.

Hearts and flowers

When I was a little girl in my twenties and living in New York City with my husband before we married, he and I found

35

a ground-floor apartment in Greenwich Village on Minetta Lane, right off Sixth Avenue, between Fourth and Bleecker. The real-estate agent called it a two and a half, but actually it was a rectangle with a raised dining area, a thumbnail kitchen, and a half-moon bath, and it was all we could afford. I thought of it as a semibasement apartment, somewhere in between the pavement and the sewer, which meant that when one looked out on the street, one saw people's feet and occasionally a bum watering the window. But what did we care? We were in love! We provided the charm and a Castro convertible and a scattering of oak pieces found in the area.

We were both actors. I was working on Broadway at the time, and Hal seemed always to be working on a part he was about to perform, for he was in repertory at Lincoln Center Downtown. We were as honeybees drowned in the sweetness of theater by O'Neill and Arthur Miller and Tennessee Williams and Albee and Sondheim, as well as giant directors Kazan, Hal Prince, Mike Nichols, Guthrie, Ulu Grosbard, Bill Ball, José Quintero. Our life was a rush of sweat and language, with no time to shop for eggs and bacon and cans of tuna and toilet paper. Eating, however, was a priority, and so it happened one day that I was forced to drop my prima donna status and plan an outing at the A&P. It was either that or eat *The New York Times* for breakfast.

It was drizzling. I found my beige umbrella and my grocery cart and trundled down and out the half-lit hallway into a noontime world.

New York is odd. You never know if the streets will be crowded or the streets will be empty and you don't think about it and proceed with your life. That day, as I was pulling my clanging cart down Sixth Avenue, the streets of the Village were almost empty and I didn't think about it at all. I was thinking about my list. Suddenly a man appeared in front of me, walking toward me, north on Sixth Avenue, and he looked just like your average lost person. He might have been thirty or forty or fifty, stocky, a bit taller than I, your average character out of a Dostoyevski novel. As we passed, I moved slightly to my right, as one does in New York City when you pass a loser, on the theory that a little distance never hurts although a lot of distance is better.

We passed, and as we passed he hit me in the stomach. If I hadn't moved to my right the moment before, he would have doubled me over and knocked me cold. Without pausing I smashed him with my open umbrella, smashed him about the neck and the head, wherever one hits with an open umbrella.

"What the hell's the matter with you?" I said, leaning into his face. "Do you want me to call the cops?"

"Do!" he said.

It was time to rethink my strategy. I looked around the street and said to myself, Now who's going to be my witness? Who's going to say he hit me in the gut and then I smashed him with my umbrella? I saw one man, about ten feet ahead, a black man lying on the sidewalk with his back propped up against a school fence. Somehow I didn't feel he'd bear witness for me. I figured I was fucked. With flair and panache learned from Margaret Leighton, I turned my back on the weird one, adjusted my umbrella, rearranged my cart, and continued my clanging walk down Sixth Avenue toward Bleecker Street and the A&P. I was shaking.

I shopped for the groceries and waited patiently in a check-out line while three old ladies tried to cut in front of me. Having stacked my cart smartly with five overflowing brown paper bags, I walked north up Sixth Avenue the few blocks to our building. I found my keys in my purse and unlocked the outer door and rolled down the half-lit hallway, finally reaching the apartment.

"Hal, do you know what just happened to me?" I said as I walked through the door, and I told him the story.

I cried. And he embraced me. We put away the groceries together.

I was well rehearsed. And I *was* in control. In the first place, an ER is an ER is an ER is an emergency room, and most of them are green except this one was blue, which aesthetically speaking was a very nice sign. I'd spent a great deal of time in emergency rooms, on "Dr. Kildare" and "Ben Casey" and "The Nurses" and all over Western Europe and New York City with my father, who'd been ill throughout my adolescence. Experience had taught that with the exception of room color, something no one controlled, the sense of the action was entirely up to me. And I *was* in control. I was feeling very cocky. Lest anyone forget, I'd saved my own life.

I knew that ERs were a study in compassionate hysteria. I knew that if, as a patient, one was conscious and willful and quite a bit wary of the medical profession, a description that fit me down to my toes, it was wise to stay awake and monitor the interns who were high on enthusiasm but raw on experience, in order to ensure that my doctor of choice would make with the needlepoint and any cross-stitching. Quality work was what I was buying. My doctors hadn't arrived. A directive was issued.

"Call my surgeon, Gareth Wootton. He's connected with this hospital."

"Do you know him?" I was asked by a creature in white.

"You bet," I said. He's *fired*, I thought.

I was left with the nurse, left alone in a room, my first private moment, to primp and prepare and reconstruct me, with the help of a she, a nurturing presence. She removed my clothing, gently, slowly, and suggested I might slip into a blue-and-white-flowered three-quarter-length smock that was clean and hospitable, the blue-room nightie. The nurse, my dresser, whose name was Terry, unclasped my jewelry and removed my rings and hid them for safekeeping in my change purse. I lay back on the pillow of my portable bed as she bathed and dried me for coming encounters. The laying on of a woman's hands felt safe, lifegiving. She asked if he had raped me. I wondered what I looked like.

When Les, my real doctor, my everyday doctor, the one for sore throats, first arrived minutes later, he handed me a giant red all-day Valentine sucker and asked, "What the hell happened to you?" It was then that I knew that I wanted to marry him and bear his children and make his breakfast at any hour requested for the rest of my life. I might also consider becoming his nurse. I would suck that sucker for the next three hours down "where are we going?" corridors, under "this position isn't natural" X-ray machinery, through "please wait in this corridor the technician will be with you" intervals. I sucked that sucker as I retold the story to doctors and policemen and was tended and observed. As I wept to myself, deep silent heavings, in the in-between moments, before and after procedures.

The only other lollipop I craved at the moment was my husband. Since we were divorced and he was about to remarry and I could never remember a foreign phone number—and by foreign I meant anyplace he was living that wasn't with me—locating him required major thinking. Thinking was not my strength at that moment. Sucking on a sucker was working to capacity.

I needed my husband. He was, after all, my only husband to date, the one and only in my life, my husband the divorced person, just as the lady of his first marriage, the one prior to ours, had been known and referred to as his wife. Fifteen years into our marriage and the phone would ring and like a relay runner I'd hand off the message, "Your wife is on the phone, it's for you, your wife!" Who *he* perceived to be his soul's tender mate was a question for gurus, high priests, and Talmudic scholars. The fact was that he was *my husband* and the father of my child. That was important. I might have to stay the night.

I could not remember his phone number. I did not *know* his phone number. The only number I remembered, wheeling into Emergency, was my girlfriend Leila's number, a casting director in town who could get, if required, any actor's phone number from any actor's agent by threatening future unemployment for half the Screen Actors Guild. Might is right, particularly in Hollywood, and if it was working for me who gave a flying fig? A second directive was issued as I rolled through Admissions.

"Jimmy, call my girlfriend Leila, Leila Johnson at her office, tell her what happened, tell her not to worry, tell her not to talk about it, tell her please to find Hal!"

Jimmy managed the climb over three secretaries' backs before finally reaching Leila, who promptly put him on hold and went into shock. Her secretaries, however, ransacked the office, the index, standing files, and old booking sheets, all of this while Jimmy hung on hold, looking for Hal's number. They must have Hal's number, where was Hal's number? They didn't have Hal's number. What they had, however, was Hal's girlfriend's agent's number, and while Jimmy hung on hold, Leila phoned said agent and importuned. "This is important, gimme Hal's girlfriend's number." Leila importuned and the agent acceded, fearing unemployment for half of his actors. Leila relieved Jimmy of his on-hold position, gave him the number, and went back into shock.

Jimmy then phoned Hal's girlfriend, but he didn't get Hal's girlfriend, he got his girlfriend's machine, which was not what he wanted, but he proceeded to leave an important message hoping Hal's girlfriend would check her machine. Hal's girlfriend was listening, listening to her machine, and she picked up the phone and started to cry. Jimmy told and retold her the story twice, she was so upset, so disbelieving. When she calmed down she gave Jimmy Hal's number.

Jimmy then phoned Hal, but he didn't get Hal, he got Hal's machine, so he proceeded to leave an important message, but Hal was listening to the machine, to his machine, for he picked up in midsentence and he was stunned. There was a silence. "Okay. I'll be there."

"You don't have any scotch, do you?" I said to Terry,

my nurse, my lady-in-waiting. I was the director and star of this production. We were out on location in an emergency room. She'd shot the X rays already, we had 'em "in the can."

"No, I'm sorry, no scotch."

"Why not?" I asked.

"I don't think Mother Superior would look kindly upon it." I'd chosen a Catholic hospital in which to stage this production. The consequences of choice are ever present.

Hal entered through the door, stage left, through the audience. I was stage center, raised high on the bed, sucking my sucker, in charge of production. Hal entered the room and stood behind Les. I turned in his direction. We stared at each other. What are my lines? I'd forgotten my lines.

After all, I thought, I *am* in control. I don't need him particularly. I've got this one taped. We'd spent fifteen years together and six more of not knowing, and then four months ago the divorce, the finale. I had learned not to need him, minute by minute. If there was any residual doubt still clogging my nervous system, it had just been shattered into billions of pieces. I had saved my own life. That was definitive. I didn't need him particularly. He was here for Eve.

I looked into his eyes and saw his blue eyes, and under his blue eyes I saw his rage, and under his rage I saw his tears, and under his tears I saw his blue eyes. "Don't worry, I'm all right, I'm all right," I said. I couldn't bear his pain. I couldn't bear his rage. I was in control. He was about to remarry.

The room was crowded with medical personnel. Les, my doctor, was talking to me. He had never met Hal. I did not introduce them. I was busy, very busy, maintaining control.

Gareth arrived, my surgeon, my friend, Hal's friend from other times of couples and parties and parent/teacher blowouts at our children's grammar school. They nodded a greeting.

"What happened?" Gareth asked. I told him the story. Hal was listening. ". . . and I never did a better acting job in my life because I knew my life was at stake and really, I was proud of my acting!" No applause. Hal said nothing. "I don't think I could have done it if I wasn't an actress, a good actress, I mean. I don't think I could have pulled it off," I said.

Gareth had begun to examine my head, and Hal was staring, lost to the moment. He'd forgotten to give me an Academy Award for best performance by a leading actress in an attempted murder. I wanted that award and I wanted *him* to present it, but he was busy, too busy maintaining control. Too busy fantasizing the death of the killer. Too busy kicking and ripping and gunning him down. When you've lived with someone, you know what he's thinking.

I looked into my husband's eyes and I knew he was frightened, I knew he was raging. I knew that he cared. I looked into my husband's eyes and I knew he was my husband even though he was to marry, even though we'd divorced, till death do us part.

Or not.

Whatever.

It was Valentine's Day.

"I don't see any fractures," Gareth was saying, "but I want you to come into the office tomorrow."

"I can leave?"

"You can leave, but don't wash your hair." I won't be spending the night after all! Notwithstanding the bloodied vision I'd presented, there were no cracks, the head wound was superficial, a one-inch gash above my left cheekbone was threaded together and on the mend. Head wounds have a way of making messes. With the exception of my hair, I'd cleaned up pretty good.

Stitched and analyzed, all questions answered, the dissection was over, I'd been pickled for the day. We were left alone, Hal and I and nurse Terry. A time for leaving, and Hal would drive me. The drama was over. Exit stage right.

There was a silence. Cue the nurse, for chrissake!

"Would you like to change back into your clothes or

would you like to stay in the smock?" she asked. "You can keep the smock or return it tomorrow."

"Oh, I'll change!" I said and sat up in my bed. Hal stood at my feet, she at my side. I lifted the smock well above my head, hiding my face, exposing my breasts.

"It's all right," I said from under the nightie. "He used to be my husband."

Terry held up the sweat pants at bed height so that I might slip into the legs with ease. They were broken and bloody. I'd completely forgotten.

"Christ, I'm losing my mind! I'll stick with the smock." Tears filled my eyes. Everything quivered. "I'll be all right. I really will be. I know I will be. I'll be all right."

"Oh, Carol," Hal said.

"Oh, Hally," I said, "but what am I going to do with my rage?"

He left for the car. She wrapped my head in an oversize white towel and pinned it in the back with a giant safety pin, à la Ann Sheridan, a swollen fat-faced Ann Sheridan playing a nun. I'd be nunlike for some time. I mustn't wash my hair.

"When you come back tomorrow to see the doctor," she said, "go to the third floor and talk to the social worker. There's a place that can help you, I used to have their card. I've lost it. I looked. The social worker knows the place."

It was that casual.

My daughter
3:00 P.M.–5:00 P.M.

Eve was born in 1970 in New York City, at the dawn of the Age of Aquarius, or perhaps it was noon by that time, I'm not sure. Certainly it was the stuff of most conversations, although I understood not a word of those conversations. As a graduate of Sarah Lawrence College, I understood nine-teenth- and twentieth-century European literature and nine-

43

teenth- and twentieth-century political science. As a graduate of some thirty years on this planet, I understood working my buns off as an actress and making my mark in a killer business. I understood I was married to a chocolate-kissed actor who was very successful and away a lot working, and that I had housed if not raised one female stepchild, the other male visiting on regular occasions. I understood I was drenched in a budding drug culture and I'd never smoked a joint or dipped into angel dust, and I'd waited to have my child until the drugs and their culture had moved on to college. I did not have time for the Vietnam War, for I was far too busy fighting personal wars, and I certainly hadn't time for astrology because I was far too busy cooking dinner.

It was with some confusion, then, on the evening of my daughter's birth, as I held her in my arms for the very first time minutes after her arrival, that I looked into her eyes and thought, My God, this kid has been here before! She's an old soul! She knows a whole lot more than I do now! My father's soul has returned and entered the world through her body, this time at peace with what he knows! It was a very private thought, whose origins escaped and frightened me, but nevertheless I thought it as her gaze met mine. I quickly counted fingers and toes to make sure there were twenty.

Old soul she was, my instincts had served me, an old soul clothed in the rags of a child, traipsing through life, educating her mother not by word so much as by attitude. Hers was a special humaneness, a compassion often played at by the overanalyzed who pretend understanding but possess no mercy, an open-armed vulnerability centered in strength. She shied from nothing but neither was she shattered. Fourteen years later, on Valentine's Day, I was startled once again by this quality of grace.

Hal and I had managed to return to the house before Daisy and the car pool left Eve at the door. Betoweled and puffy, I lounged on the sofa, Hal distraught, pacing the room. How exactly were we to present today's horror without jarring the psyche of a young girl at the edge of adolescence and experimentation and loving and learning how to trust? We'd fought already, between car ride and couch, over how to preface the telling of the story, we two fractious adults vying for control, projecting *our* fragility onto a child.

It was Hal's desire to wait outside on the porch and meet Eve personally when the car pool drove up. It was my desire that he not do so, for I thought his presence might alarm her, layering drama on top of drama. He said it was hardly proper, it was in fact unfatherly, not to wait outside and greet his daughter. I said I understood his feelings but he mustn't say a word and must let *me* tell the story because it had happened to me. It was less traumatic coming from me. I would rather die before I scared my daughter and if Hal told the story, actor that he was, *I* would be frightened and Eve might catch it. There was no need at all for pith or pathos. We reached a truce just as Eve drove in.

Hal escorted her into the living room, my baby she-swan weighted with books. I lay on the couch propped up with pillows.

"Hi, darling," I sang. "I've had a little accident."

"What happened, Mommy?" she asked as she sat down before me, proudly self-possessed but very much in the moment. Hal sat beside me on the couch. I began the recitation, the PG version, the bare bones of a tale stripped of carnage, interspersed, appropriately, with reassurances. "And of course, you can see I'm all right! I'm telling you the story so of course I'm all right!" I had sketched a line drawing without coloring it in. If it worked for Picasso, it would work for me.

When I finished my monologue—Hal never interrupted—Eve smiled. That was it. Eve smiled when the story was over, an enigmatic, Mona Lisa, Renaissance smile, but never said a word. And I thought how human and how nice she feels free to be, how human to smile a nervous smile upon hearing a horror story, a smile that reads, "You're kidding, you must be kidding!" And I smiled, too.

45

"I don't see any reason why you shouldn't go up to the park and take your riding lesson now, do you?" I said, acting the mother. We'd passed through the storm. Life sludges on.

"No, Mommy," she said.

"Daisy can take you, where is Daisy anyway? and I'll be here when you get back and we'll be together." Nurse Terry's towel was falling off my head.

Daisy was on the phone but Daisy got off the phone and drove Eve up to Will Rogers's in uncharacteristic silence. It seemed Daisy felt very sorry about what had happened to me, very sorry and very frightened about me *and* her father. He'd just called to say he'd had an accident on the freeway, she must come quickly and pick him up *off* the freeway. She was very frightened. "This is not a good day," she said as she left.

When Eve arrived at the barn, she found Teresa and Jimmy and hugged them and thanked them for taking such care of her mommy. Then she rode her horse for forty-five minutes, not a brilliant lesson, albeit the horse was perfect, but Eve, Jimmy thought, seemed slightly distracted, mulling other matters and sifting her thoughts. After the lesson there was a birthday party for Teresa that the grooms had planned the week before. Today was *her* day as well as St. Valentine's. Eve phoned down and asked if she could stay, "at least until they cut the cake, Mommy, and then I'll come down. I want to be with you."

It was five o'clock when Pip dropped Eve at home. I was alone. I had missed her. She walked over to the couch and sat down beside me and kissed my face where it wasn't blue.

"I want to talk to you, Mommy." She was the mother, sitting in a pool of pink-white light, elegant but demure and always joyful. "Is that all that happened? Did you tell me everything?"

"Yes, I did," I said. She stared into my eyes with infinite patience, unhurried, relaxed, awaiting the furies. "Do you mean did he rape me?" I finally asked.

46

She nodded a yes.

"No, he didn't rape me." I hadn't explored the man's intentions and those bloody moments hidden in brush, for I'd thought, After all, she's only a child! The truth might damage a reality of roses.

"No, he didn't rape me," I said to my daughter. "He pulled down my sweats but he never touched me."

She sat for a moment and gazed into my eyes and then wrapped her long arms about my body.

"I love you, Mommy," she said to me. "I'll go fix the dogs' food. What else can I do?"

"Tell me, Evie, if you don't mind, why did you smile when I told you the story?"

"Because it was funny," she said. "I smiled because you were lying here with a towel around your head and all kinds of bruises and stitches and your thumbs were fractured, and you were telling me you were all right. That was funny. You're the one who's hurt, Mommy. I'm all right."

Knock, knock, who's there?
4:00 P.M.—12:00 A.M.

When Daisy drove Eve up to the park, Hal and I were left alone together, left alone in the house, *the* house, our first home in California after having gotten up the courage to leave New York City. We'd rebuilt the house after a fire had burned it to the ground while we were in escrow, an improbable scenario because it was true, and we'd lived in it as a family four months before separating.

Hal and I were left alone without Eve's protection, without the presence that bound us together. The house was silent. The walls were listening.

"How are the beams doing?"

"Just fine, Hal, fine."

"You have any leaks?"

"Oh, there's one in the attic but I just put down a bucket

47

and let the thing drip." He looked at the beams. I watched him looking.

"Do you mind very much if I use the phone?"

"Not at all. Go ahead." He made his calls and rearranged his appointments. I lay on the couch and smoked a cigarette.

"Have you got a beer?"

"Sure, Hal, help yourself." He found himself one in the refrigerator. I lay on the couch and smoked a cigarette. We were alone. We didn't look at each other.

"It's all right, Hal, you don't have to hang around."

"Will you be all right?"

"Sure. I'm gonna call some friends."

"Well, if you're sure it's all right, I'll speak to you later."

He crossed to the sofa and caressed my face and patted the dogs and walked out the front door, the one he'd designed with the special lock. This wasn't his home. He wasn't my husband. I lay on the couch and smoked a cigarette. I'd call my chiropractor. He was a friend. I'd missed my appointment with him this morning. I'd call and apologize and explain the situation. I felt nothing at all. I was short on air.

I called Mr. Wonderful. I called him after I called my chiropractor and if the order of calls should have told me something, I wasn't listening to my head. The only voice I heard growled up from my gut, craving a man who'd put his arms around me, and hold me, and rock me, and make me safe. My chiropractor cared but his arms weren't available.

I called the *old* Mr. Wonderful, who'd dropped to second place, rather than the new who was currently married and committed to no one, neither me nor his wife. I phoned Patrick, who'd saved me once before. We'd not spoken in over a year, which should have told me something if I'd been listening, but I didn't care who'd said what, why, and when. Surely he'd cross that moat and rescue me now. We'd been friends, after all, good friends before lovers, a pattern, it seemed, repeated by others in my life since the separation, by dinner dates and talking dates and touching dates and late dates—

old chums who'd been waiting in the wings to make an entrance, cued to wipe my tears and fondle my heart. It was nice but out of sync with the world as I'd known it, the world of babies and breakfast and dreams to be shared.

Patrick was different. Patrick was special. I dialed his number. My mind was numb.

"He's not here," she said, "he's out of town, away on business" in news, national news, the world of illusions. When I told Patsy, his secretary, what had happened so that she might tell Patrick when he phoned in, she cried. She sobbed into the speaker. *That* surprised me. No one else had done *that*. "I'm sorry, Patsy, please don't cry," I said. It was just a story. Nothing had happened. I'd not meant to cause anyone pain. I'd just wished to get hold of my own Prince Charming to make sure he brought home the other glass slipper and held my hand for the rest of my life. I wondered what he'd do when he got the message.

The sun was drooping behind Inspiration, a respectable time to pour myself scotch. Two more friends, lady friends, had cried when I called them. I wished they hadn't. It made the telling so difficult. It made me feel there was something the matter.

Leila didn't cry, at least not in front of me. Leila insisted on spending the night, for she was sure that someone should stay with me. That's what she thought, and as a rule of thumb, it's best not to argue with a casting director, but in fact I felt fine, except for my hair. I desperately wanted to wash my hair.

Daisy cooked fish that was indescribably dry, and we all ate it and watched the Olympics from Sarajevo, wherever that was—Yugoslavia, Czechoslovakia, Alsace-Lorraine.

I wasn't frightened until I went to bed, and snapped off the light and closed my eyes. I saw him, then, running up the hill, running up behind me about to strike.

He didn't. I slept. Fatigue won the day. I held myself hard and slept through the night.

THE
FIRST WEEK

FEBRUARY 15–FEBRUARY 21

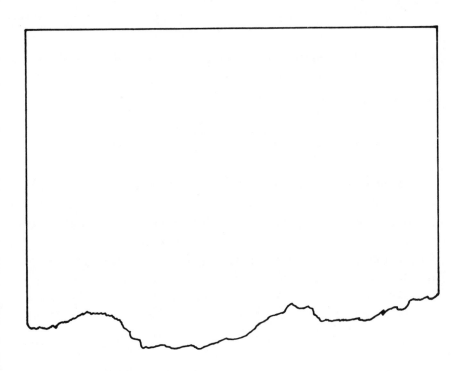

A couple of miracles and two Tylenol please
February 15—day and night

Who knows what direction my life might have taken, what
fires, at the very least, might have been lit, what interests
kindled if I'd been exposed to a decent, semithoughtful course
in biology while in high school? I had not been. My biology
teacher at Staples High in Westport, Connecticut, was a man
by the name of Mr. Pynchbek, and he was a pervert. That
evaluation is not the result of hindsight for I thought so at
the time, then the early fifties. It was not hard to notice.
When we, his captive audience, arrived at that part of the
textbook that dealt with human reproduction, Mr. Pynchbek
demanded all the girls in the classroom stand at their desks
and one by one measure the distance between pelvic bones,
assessing the probability of an easy carriage. Our grade for
the term was on the line. The boys crunched into balls of

jellied laughter, assured they'd not have to measure their parts. The ladies flushed and then blanched, all of them virgins, confused, humiliated, too fearful to disobey. Mr. Pynchbek stood before us, smiling sickly.

I finished out the term and received an A, but I'd stopped listening to his lectures months before. All of my class time had been spent working out the details of Mr. Pynchbek's execution. I chose not to take chemistry the following year for I feared a demand for a urine specimen. I didn't trust his science department and that was my loss, for my body and most of nature remained a mystery. I'd been raised by urban, ghetto-made intellectuals; I dug dialectical materialism and noodle pudding laced with guilt, the dominant themes in a Jewish Marxist upbringing. Class struggles were the issue in life as we lived it, not the tides of our bodies and the tides of the sea. Mr. Pynchbek hadn't supplemented my education.

It was the morning after and I was stunned. Nature's revelations were not my game! I sat alone in my kitchen, just me and the dogs and the two pussycats, gathered together to offer up prayers. Leila had left, she'd gone off to work, Eve had car pooled off to school, and I sat alone in my kitchen drinking decaf espresso.

I was stunned. I'd gotten my period. Right on time. I'd not thought I was pregnant, I knew I wasn't pregnant, but I was stunned by the *fact* of getting my period, by the very insistence of that life-force within me. It could not be withheld, it hadn't needed to hibernate, it was oblivious to circumstances that included sledgehammers. That seemed miraculous. That was the first miracle.

And I was *alive*. That was the second miracle. I had lived and not died. I'd survived the encounter, although the word *survival* somehow revolted me, conjuring up lifeboats and the *Andrea Doria*, a dumb-shit happening that might have been avoided, but survival was the word that defined the experience. I had known something I hadn't imagined I'd known, something in me, not in the world, something unseen that might inform my life. I needed to talk about it.

Les, my doctor of the all-day sucker, made time for my ramblings over the phone:

"Listen," I said, "I've been thinking and I don't know why I'm still alive. But what comes out of my head, what I think is that I've heard of women who when they see their child under the wheels of a car summon up the energy to lift that car. Or people who don't feel needles and nails driven into them, and I think that's what happened to me. My positive energy to live was as strong as his negative energy to kill, and that's why I *lived*, that's why I didn't die. Because I knew in that moment, when I knew I must die in order to live, I knew in that moment that I knew everything. That I was connected to all living things. I knew about him, that man, instinctively; it had nothing to do with book knowledge or even street smarts, I just knew, like an animal knows. I had to belly up or die."

"Carol . . ." Les said, but I hadn't finished.

"Have you ever seen two dogs fighting and suddenly one knows he's going to get it, so he turns over on his back, making himself totally vulnerable, giving up his defenses. And the other dog just stops fighting because, what the hell! there's no fun in that, it's too easy, and they just stop fighting and walk away?"

"Carol . . ." Les said.

"The urge to kill is in the confrontation. It doesn't occur when faced with passive resistance."

End of thought.

End of miracle.

Christ, it was hard to describe how it felt to be one of two yolks in the same egg.

"What do you think, Les?" Now he could speak.

"I think you're right. I think you would have died two years ago if this had happened to you then. But you were strong and ready, and listen, Carol, nothing that anybody ever throws at you again can get to you, do you understand? Don't let this get you, throw you back, beat you."

I didn't understand, not a word he was saying.

Well, damn! I thought. So much for miracles! I have to have surgery.

We stood in the middle of a hospital corridor at St. John's Hospital talking with Gareth. Kitty was with me. Kitty was twenty. Kitty would be my baby-sitter. She'd worked for me as a mother's helper, but she was more than that, she was like a daughter. The very first day, when the news splashed the street, Kitty appeared and offered her services. I'd pay for the gas. She'd do the driving. She'd fix my bandages and pin my towel. She'd helped me bathe that very same morning and buttoned my buttons and unbraided my nerves. She was my friend. Her presence soothed me. Kitty had driven me to the hospital.

Well, damn damn damn! I have to have surgery! I don't want to have surgery!

"What kind of surgery?"

"An open reduction of the zygomatic arch."

"What's that in English?"

"Your cheekbone is fractured. If we don't fix it now, your face will be lopsided."

"That's not a good thing. When do we do it?"

"When the swelling is down. Next Wednesday. That's a week from today. My nurse will give you the information."

"Okay. You're on."

"Come see me on Friday." He was walking away. We'd been standing in the middle of a hospital corridor.

"Gareth!" I said. My head was hurting. "Why didn't the X rays catch this yesterday?"

"They didn't shoot the right angle. I needed more pictures."

———

His nurse needed data. Yes, I want a private room why not? that sounds like a nice idea. Yes, I can make it anytime on Friday my dance card is sparse and I've hours of time. Yes, I have a little headache and yes thank you I'll take two Tylenol and water. No hard stuff, no codeine. Yes, I've filled that prescription but I don't want to get hooked I've seen that happen. Yes yes yes yes I am amenable I am the sport please let's finish and steal away in Kitty's Jeep into the sunlight and over the freeway to get some booze and buy gobs of gauze and wash my hair because I have permission and watch the Olympics and toast health and fortitude. I have my list. I have a schedule.

I wanted to see the social worker on the third floor of the building. I wanted the name of that place Terry mentioned. I was *seen* right away by a slice of white bread, a puffy, dry square kind of female person, without a hint of caraway or a wisp of wheat.

"Is Kitty your daughter?" she asked for no reason.

"No, my friend," I said. Don't fuck with me, I thought. Do what you do but don't get personal. I was shaky and tired and I hated her office. When I told her what had happened, she became very angry, not with me, of course, although I winced when she raged, but rather with the ER for not giving out information, for not doing what they were supposed to do.

"They were busy," I said. I couldn't bear her rage severing my nerves into string cheese.

"I know they are busy," the social worker said, "but they're supposed to call us whenever there's a victim!" Okay. She had a point. I didn't like the word *victim*.

"Do you have the name of the place that's supposed to help me?" I asked. She handed me a brochure. The words were fuzzy. "Kitty, read me the front, I've forgotten my glasses."

"The Center for Victims of Violent Crimes, a Coordinated Approach to Meet the Needs of Crime Victims."

"Is that what it says?"

Kitty nodded a yes. Words without meaning. Mumbo-jumbo. The social worker lady continued her lecture.

"The center will put you in touch with the City Attorney's Victim-Witness Assistance Program, or I can give you their number if you prefer."

"The what assistance?"

"They do all the paperwork when you apply to the state."

"For what to the state?"

"For medical reimbursements. For all monies spent over your insurance coverage."

Christ almighty! Mark it. Mental note. Items for the list. Money. Call my mother. Insurance. Surgery. "Thank you very much." I was tired. We left and rode the elevator down in silence. The shopping could wait. I was exhausted.

Eve hadn't encountered *any* miracles that day. Eve had had a rotten day. She sighed a great sigh as she walked in from school. She needed to talk. I was the mother. I was at my post draped over the sofa.

"What happened?" I asked. Confront! I was ready.

"Karen and I had a free period just before lunch break and Karen had forgotten her homework so we decided to go back to her house and get it," she said as she sat down beside me.

"How'd you get back to her house?" I asked. I wasn't aware she'd developed wings.

"Her housekeeper picked us up" was the whispered answer set aside along with her books. "And so we got the homework and while we were there we had some lunch—"

"Some lunch?"

"And then we came back and the whole school was going crazy. No one knew where we were, and they were all out looking for us."

"Who all was out looking for you?" *That* was the question.

"Mr. Fatutto, the dean of girls, and so my friends said,

'Run and hide!' but I didn't and neither did Karen, but the other girl, Janie, she did, they didn't see her, and we went up to the office—"

"*What* other girl? Why did she run? Never mind. What did he say, what did—what did Mr. Fatutto say?"

"That this was serious and that they are responsible for the kids while they are at school and that we are not allowed to leave campus without permission and that we knew that. I swear, Mommy, I forgot that. I just forgot that. I'm not perfect. Everybody makes mistakes."

"Yeah. What else did he say?" The point was at hand.

"That these were grounds for suspension and where is my mother?"

"Where is your mother?"

"So I told him you were in the hospital."

"In the hospital?"

"And he said what do you mean, so I told him you were attacked yesterday by a man with a sledgehammer, and he said oh, my God, this always happens."

"This always happens?"

"Yes. Then he asked to have you call him tomorrow. I really do understand, Mommy. I realize I must be more responsible. And Mr. Fatutto said he wouldn't suspend me but that I would have to do work detail, pick up milk cartons and stuff for the rest of my life. I'm sorry, Mommy."

"*Do* you understand what you did?" I asked.

"Yes," she said.

"Do you understand that *anyone* could have been in that car, that they *are* responsible for you and that they are *right* about your not leaving campus during school hours?"

"Yes, Mommy," she said.

"Okay. I'll call him tomorrow. Give me a kiss, you gorgeous blond chicken." The bleached-out dinosaur kissed me gently. I closed my eyes. I'd rest for a moment. Eve needed a mommy. I needed a wife.

———

That evening, at 7:00 P.M., Hal picked Eve up for a sleep-over date. They'd planned the date before I'd been hurt and I saw no reason why they shouldn't be together. It pleased me to see them enjoy each other.

One of the ladies who'd cried the day before dropped by with flowers and Chinese food, and Leila checked in and said she'd be glad to stay over, but I felt tired and I had company and I didn't think that was necessary. My girlfriend and I would watch the Olympics.

Curt Gowdy and Jim McKay had finally stopped talking about how much snow there was in Sarajevo. The downhill had been canceled once again. It was late by the time I walked my friend to her car and watched her disappear down the circular drive. The crickets were screaming. The dogs were asleep.

And then I couldn't breathe. And then I was shaking. I was alone in the middle of the night and I ran into the house and locked the doors and turned up all the lights inside and out and screamed for the dogs and put them on leashes and forced them to run with me everywhere, run with me past all the French windows, I saw his face staring in at me through the French windows, and into my bathroom and he was there, too, I saw his face staring in at me through the window, and then into my bedroom and thank God it was shuttered and the dogs hugged my sides and tried to cuddle, and I closed my eyes and he was there inside staring in at me through the lids of my eyes but I held my dogs and breathed deep breaths and fell asleep without his staring eyes.

I did not cry.

A bit of American history for the record

I was born in Hollywood and alternately raised on the East and West coasts, and sometimes in Europe. I was *always* sent to public schools, a philosophical statement on the part of my parents, except during sojourns in France or Italy. That's when *I* drew the line. There'd be no rubbing up against unfriendly natives and learning their lingo in creepy-cold halflit postwar classrooms. It was either English-speaking schools, and they were private, or if they should prove unavailable, funny/sad tutorials with foreign college students. And the Champs-Elysées was for socializing. And the Via Veneto.

I missed California.

Surely we sound like military brats, my brother, my sister, and poor little me, or the maladjusted children of the diplomatic corps who spent most of their time wandering the streets of the world in search of a hamburger and a chocolate shake. We didn't belong to either group, nor were these trips conceived as part of an eighteenth-century Grand Tour of the artistic edifices of Western Europe. That was not their intent, although it became their pleasure. These sweeps were more spontaneous burstings of fate. During most of my pubescence and early adolescence, the family Rossen was on the lam from the Feds.

Admittedly the chase was rather high falutin'. Political refugees aren't always impoverished—and I refer you, for example, to Charlie Chaplin—not if they are lucky, and we were lucky. My father, Robert Rossen, was a much-admired and successful triple-threat man, the writer-director-producer of such American films as *All the King's Men* and *The Hustler*. He was thought of as an artist; he called himself a moviemaker. He was also a rather influential member of the Communist party in the late thirties and early forties. So was my mother. That was not a popular stance after Yalta, when *pinko* and *red-bastard* infiltrated the language, and when J. Parnell Thomas and Richard Nixon and Joseph McCarthy infiltrated the Constitution. So the family Rossen was on the lam from subpoenas and hearings and restraints of trade, and unsolicited visits from the FBI. We were crossing borders in search of work for Daddy. We'd been kicked out of Eden, known as Hollywood, California.

(Point of order, by way of clarification. We're talking about HUAC, the House Committee on Un-American Activities, and its efforts to cleanse the artistic community from 1947 to 1953. We're talking about my childhood and adolescent memories.)

It *was* a witch hunt, a miniholocaust-in-process in which hundreds of men and women were fractured by the crunch of terror, humiliation, ostracism, loss of work. No one felt safe as lives were savaged and families stood by and watched it happen. Some survived. Some did not. Each fared differently for many reasons; there are those who've voiced them and those who've refrained, and many are dead and some live on, nurturing hate. But that's *their* story. It's not mine. Better *they* tell it than Victor Navasky. Beware, social historians, toe the mark! No matter what your momma says, you may not be Plutarch.

As a kid of a commie, I spent a lifetime struggling to overcome my distrust of the cops, and by cops I meant anyone in a position of power, anyone who might hurt me if I turned my back, anyone sanctified by any society, anyone representing social authority. I'd witnessed too many transgressions of human rights, hands and feet squashed like stewed tomatoes: plainclothesmen knocking at our front door, hoping to subpoena my daddy at midnight; movie cameras hidden in a neighbor's window photographing everyone who paid us a visit; "click-click" taps on our telephone, bugging all calls, including my boyfriends'; FBI agents assigned to the case who knew every detail of *my* personal life, "Oh, you're Carol, born in August, your eyes are really hazel!"; invitations to visit the director's office, Dr. English of Beverly Hills High School, who demanded an explanation of my father's "position"—the First, the Fifth, the upside-down, constitutional amendments used in defense. Dr. English explained he must respond to an irate parent body who feared my presence might toxify the campus. I suggested he go down to the L.A. courthouse and check out the files for that information. And I lowered my head and blushed and died.

I was thirteen years old. I'd handled it beautifully. I wanted to kill him. I sat on my rage. *There* was the rub. That was the double whammy. Anger was a no-no for my generation. Anger wasn't fashionable. Anger broke the rules. Anger wasn't the favored emotion among nice girls brought up in the forties and fifties, not that any of us were virgins in that department, or any department, if the sun came up. It simply wasn't to be revealed. It wasn't to be acknowledged. It wasn't nice. It wasn't girllike. It wasn't kosher.

It was ballsy.

And we all knew what that meant.

Tears in lieu of . . .
Thursday, February 16
6:30 A.M.–8:45 A.M.

Usually I cry when I'm angry. I've done so all my life.

Six-thirty. The clock read six-thirty. It was early Thursday morning, it was Thursday morning, and I was sobbing. I must have been sobbing for some time in my sleep because my pillow was wet. Drenched wet. Slippery wet. The dogs were nuzzling the bed. That's what woke me up. The dogs. Probably. I was lying on my back looking up at white beams and a chandelier and I was sobbing. I couldn't stop sobbing. It had nothing to do with bad dreams. I hadn't had a bad dream. It had to do with my forgetting something. What? What had I forgotten? I'd forgotten an appointment. I'd forgotten an appointment with the detective "on the case." He'd called the day before, on Wednesday, the day before, and asked if we could meet at my house this morning. Thursday was this morning. This morning was Thursday. He would bring a sketch artist who'd make a face based on my description of the man who'd bashed me. I didn't know this detective, I'd only spoken to him briefly, on the phone, the day before. On Wednesday, yesterday. I had an appointment this morning at nine o'clock with two strange men who were coming to my home. I was alone. I didn't trust them. I couldn't let them in. They might hurt me.

63

I sobbed as I called Mary, my friend in New York City, and finally located her in Florida on vacation. She was a therapist. I told her the story. I told her I was frightened. I couldn't let them in. "Call a friend, there must be someone, to come over and sit with you." I hadn't thought of that. We talked for an hour.

It was seven-thirty. People were awake now in California. People rise early in California. I called Eve's best friend's mother down the block and asked if she had time to drop by before work. I told her about the detective and the sketch artist coming. I told her I was frightened and I broke down again. She said she'd come, of course she would, if I couldn't find anyone else to help me. She was a psychologist and she'd patients to tend.

I called Kitty's mom and Kitty. They lived a few miles away. I told them about the detective and the sketch artist coming and they said they'd get here as soon as they dressed. Kitty's mom, however, must leave for work by nine-thirty.

I left a message on Hal's machine. I sobbed through the message. I hadn't meant to do that. I asked him please to call me after dropping Eve at school.

I called the victim center and I reached an answering service. The operator asked if this was urgent. "I think so," I said. I left my name and number.

It was eight-thirty. I stopped sobbing. It was time to be a mother and call the dean of girls.

I dialed the number of Eastbrook School for Girls:

"Mr. Fatutto, this is Carol Rossen, Eve Holbrook's mother."

"Yes, Miss Rossen, how are you feeling?"

"Much better, thank you very much. Mr. Fatutto, Eve told me what happened and that you wanted me to call you and I just want you to know that I support you completely, I support the school completely in your point of view about this incident, and I really do think Eve understands what she

64

did and that it won't happen again and I wanted you to know that I appreciate your not suspending her."

"Well, it's very serious, you know," Mr. Fatutto said.

"Yes, I do know, and I just wanted *you* to know that I support you completely," I said.

"Well, even though we didn't suspend her it is as if we suspended her, because if she gets into any more trouble, it will be as if we suspended her . . ."

"Yes, I understand. I wanted you to know that I appreciate your not suspending her."

"Yes, well, there are a few other things I'd like to talk to you about."

"Yes, Mr. Fatutto, what would that be?" Get on with it, please! How long will this take?

"Well, we feel that Eve and her friends, how shall I say, set themselves apart from the others, that they, eh, feel different than the others, the other girls in their class, that they, eh, that they're, eh, how shall I put it, that they, eh, eh, travel in the fast lane." He didn't know his ass from a hole in the wall.

"Mr. Fatutto," I said, having paused for five seconds, "I do not take positions on color of hair. If my daughter and her friends, and I won't talk about her friends because that's not really my business, if they're acting out adolescent behavior *during* their adolescence instead of waiting until they're thirty-five to do it, then I support it."

"Yes," he said, "but we feel that perhaps their parents don't really *know* what their daughters are doing . . ."

"Mr. Fatutto, I have worked very hard as a single parent over the past six years, and so has Eve's father, as it happens, to establish a close relationship with my daughter, an enviable one I might add among the Eastbrook parents, and there is nothing I don't know about what my daughter is doing, including what my daughter doesn't *think* I know. But since you've brought up some of the problems *you're* having, I think you should know what it feels like to be a *parent* of an Eastbrook daughter who comes home everyday with stories about

65

the elitism, the bitchiness, the drugs, and the general shit that's going down in your school, and if you tell me that's not true then you're lying."

"Well, yes, we do have some problems . . ." Mr. Fatutto said.

"And so, Mr. Fatutto, although I'm sure my daughter is participating in the general rottenness that goes down between teenagers, unless you can tell me something real, like disruptive class behavior or bad marks or something, I really don't think we have anything else to talk about."

"Well, no, Miss Rossen."

"And I *do* want you to know that I support you in your actions yesterday and thank you for not suspending Eve under the circumstances."

"Thank you, Miss Rossen."

"Thank *you*, Mr. Fatutto."

I hung up the phone and burst into tears.

What are pennies made of? Dirty copper!
Thursday, February 16
8:45 A.M.–12:00 P.M.

Fortunately for me, the police arrived later than originally planned and I wasn't to be compromised by puffy eyes. I'd accepted the bruising and swelling and small hand fractures as one does a blister on the big foot of life, a great discomfort soon forgotten, but puffy eyes were totally unacceptable, puffy eyes meant I'd been crying, and it was graceless to invite guests into one's home and appear, as the hostess, with great puffy eyes. They might wonder at my tears and guess at my fear and x-ray the inner workings of my mind to discover it was they who were scary to me. That was unacceptable. That might give them the edge sometime in the future.

It was brunch, after all, a happening, a tea party minus

tea and anything to eat for I'd no instant cake mix or muffins from the bakery. Kitty and Barbara, her mom, had arrived just as I finished my call to Fatutto and Hal appeared sometime soon after, prepared to husband the morning with me. Barbara brewed coffee while Kitty helped me dress. I apologized to all for not pouring the cream and putting out cups and saucers on the kitchen table, doing my part of party preparations, but the splints on my thumbs made politeness impossible.

I'm quite sure the strangers had no idea I'd been crying by the time they appeared an hour later. They'd been detained. Detective Fullerton had called twice to tell me he and his friend might arrive a bit late because of a delay at police headquarters. It was decent of him to let me know. Decency counts. I'd remember that, if indeed he was telling me the truth, if he really was a member of the LAPD.

I was nervous. The dogs ran in circles and barked when the car drove into the circular drive and parked twenty yards from the front of the house. Barbara had left and so had Kitty by then. Hal was with me. Two against two.

I stood out on the porch and clearly observed them walk the few yards up to the house. The dogs were at my feet. Hal stood behind me.

Their car was unmarked, beige, a sedan, an American car of some make or another, an unmarked car without insignia. They wore civvies, not uniforms; one wore traveling salesman clothes, polyester threads in a light-colored tweed—a proper suit and a tie. The other wore slacks and an open shirt and carried a portfolio. He was the artist.

They looked their parts. They were well cast. The man to the left, the man in a suit, resembled detectives I'd known in my youth or in the Glenn Ford half of a double bill. But then the man on the mountain had looked like a jogger.

The dogs wagged and panted. The strangers nodded and smiled as they walked up the steps. The dogs gave their approval and I held with their instincts, committing myself to believing they were lawful creatures in the performance of duty. The variable of the equation was how they'd behave. Hal was with me if hell broke loose.

"Hi," I said.

"I'm Detective Fullerton." He flashed his badge. "Are you Miss Rossen?" The man with the tie was asking the questions.

"Yes, I am," I said. His eyes went funny.

"I'm glad to see you're up and walking." When the call had come into the police station on Tuesday and Fullerton had been assigned to the case that day, the first thing he asked, after hearing the details, was "Is she dead?" When he discovered I wasn't, he assumed I'd been taken to the hospital, but the hospital informed him I'd been released and sent home. He was shocked. That's not the way it went in his business often.

"I like your dogs," said the man in slacks with portfolio. "My name is Frank Ponce." He offered his hand. He spoke with a South American accent, the same accent the man on the mountain had used.

I invited them into my living room but they preferred to sit at the kitchen table. Frank needed the space to lay out his materials. I offered them coffee. They preferred water. Rags offered himself. He was not denied.

Rags had married Frank on the front porch. There'd been no ceremony but I'd read his mind. Rags had married him as soon as he heard that this new guy in town had a sweet tooth for poodles. After all, Frank had said, "I like your dogs."

Rags lay his muzzle on Frank's lap and stared up at him lovingly for the entire two hours the interview lasted. Hal tried a couple of times to detach Rags from Frank's thigh, but Frank demurred and took the time to caress his buttermilk curls.

Neither man could have been more gracious and kind at this a proper gathering of consenting adults. Gary, the detective, began asking me questions about what had happened and how it happened, and I launched into the retelling with force and focus, for I wanted them to know every single detail. They listened quite carefully and took their notes but never with that sense of barbed-wire urgency that makes a human feel inconsequential, placing the event before the person. Gary listened but then he paused to comment on the design of my kitchen and its rough cedar siding and the smell of forest that perfumed the room. Frank mentioned the wildness and beauty of the greenery framed in the windows and French doors of the kitchen, as if we'd fled the city to some far-off glen. They didn't mind, for a moment, when I took a call that rang through for me in the midst of our conversation. It was a Melody Dunne, the lady in charge at the victim center. She could see me that day at one o'clock.

It was Frank who brought up the shape of his face, but only after we'd chatted a chunk of time, perhaps we'd chatted half an hour. He said there were square shapes and ovals and rounds and heart shapes and each of our faces fall into a category, with certain adjustments to account for differences. "Let me show you some diagrams and then you tell me which of the shapes fits the man who hurt you." He spread before me a layout of faces, outlines, shapes of empty faces, shells without eyes or noses or mouths or hair, shells of faces yet to be found. I picked one, the one closest to what I remembered, and I told Frank what was and wasn't the same, what wasn't on the page that was in my mind. He began to sketch the shape of a head, the lines of the face I saw in the air.

We repeated the process for the eyes. "His eyes were oval and not heavy lidded, unbagged, set apart." I could see them before me. We repeated the process for his nose: "Not thick or thin or hooked or smashed, it was nice, regular, nothing special." We repeated the process for his mouth, and his cheekbones, and his hair and hairline and the thickness of his hair and the texture of his skin. I viewed dozens of diagrams of parts and pieces, and as they were mulled and chosen and eventually discarded, they reappeared before me as Frank would sketch them and erase and readjust and shade with charcoal. A face had emerged in black and white, drained of color.

Frank asked about his ears. I hadn't thought about his ears. I didn't know about his ears. Perhaps his ears weren't so special. His ears worried me. I was exhausted.

I looked up for Hal. Hal was with me. He was talking with Gary about guns and the law and whether or not you can shoot when you have to. We'd been at it an hour, the making of a face. My head was a washload of spinning images. I was tired and anxious and I wanted it right. I wanted it perfect, the fast-food version, I wanted a Polaroid, not a drawing.

The questions had stopped, I hadn't asked that they stop, but both Gary and Frank had stopped asking the questions, and we chatted instead about this and that. We spoke of killers and intruders and where to shoot them if one must, and how Frank had gotten into this line of work. As an artist who'd migrated from South America, it had been difficult to make a living in this country, so he drew four sketches a day of possible suspects, four faces of people who hurt other people so that he might afford to draw what he wished.

I never mentioned his accent was similar to the man whose face we were trying to capture.

"Given your experience," I said to them both, "do you think I survived because I wanted to live?" I'd barely finished the thought before they interrupted.

"Definitely," Frank said.

"Definitely," Gary echoed. "You know about women who pick up cars when they have to!"

"If a person has a great desire to live and this happens, they somehow are able to survive," Frank said. I thought that was interesting, given their experience. I myself wasn't sure of anything.

"Won't you change your mind and have a cup of coffee?" I said.

"No, thank you," they said. Hal poured himself one.

The focus had shifted back to the sketch. A box of colored pencils were now featured on the table, as Frank prepared "to set" this face I'd ordered up of symbols and lines and inadequate language. I stood behind him to watch the process, staring as I'd stared many times at myself in a mirror backstage in a theater, an actress readying to powder down, set the makeup, let go of externals and get on with the work, make an entrance on stage and say the words.

"Do you think you could move the eyes just a bit farther apart?" I said to Frank. "I know it's late to be asking but, eh . . ." He did, he erased, but that didn't help. Words strangled the image I had in my head. Watching made me nervous. It was not a mirror image. The makeup wasn't perfect.

He finished. I smiled. It was fine. Damn close.

Gary said they'd take a picture of the sketch and put it on a postcard-size piece of Kodak paper, and at the bottom of the card they'd write a description of the man, the event, the weapon used, and the type of investigation.

"What do you call what happened to me?"

"Assault with a deadly weapon," he said, and I nodded my head as if the words made sense.

Gary said he would send me some copies as soon as they were processed and he would phone me if any leads came in at all, and that I should phone him if I had any more thoughts about anything. Frank put away his materials.

Rags was disappointed. I walked them to the door. Hal was with me.

I don't think there was any question but that they were gentlemen.

Cactus flower
Thursday, February 16
1:00 P.M.–2:15 P.M.

The Center for Victims of Violent Crimes was located in one of the older medical buildings in Westwood Village, a twenty-one-story cement-and-glass structure smeared with an overlay of pebbly rock. The pebbly rock looked like cottage cheese gone bad in a dust storm. It cost $1.25 per half hour, $7 after three o'clock, to park inside the building, and you must eat at Monty's to get validation. That was outrageous. "Let's find a meter," I said to Kitty. How dare they charge that! I was born in the village! The day was too long. My mouth felt starched.

I thought the building was very ugly.

The brochure had said that a group of professionals had come together and agreed that victims of violent crimes suffered symptoms similar to the posttraumatic stress disorder of Vietnam veterans. Whatever that meant. It meant nothing to me. I'd never known a Vietnam vet. All I knew was they'd returned my call quickly.

The elevator was crowded. Kitty was with me. I pressed up against the side wall to avoid body contact and the possibility of anyone's standing behind me. There are too many people in this elevator! Why haven't they taken one of the others? People behave like herds of sheep! I shielded my face with my right elbow as I pressed forward and out onto the seventh floor.

Where am I now? I took Kitty's hand.

The corridor was paneled with three-foot by nine-foot sections of walnut veneer that abruptly cut off as one turned the corner. I knocked on those walls as we walked to the office. Plasterboard covered in greeny rice paper! The ceiling reflected the cottage-cheese motif, hopscotched with squares of neon lights. Who thought this up? Gone are aesthetics! Maybe they'll treat me like I belong here.

The room was cantaloupe. That was the color. It took time to decipher but I finally got it. I'd painted a living room cantaloupe once. It's a great mistake, cantaloupe color. It turns to an orange, depending on light. The reception room was painted this cantaloupe color. There were four plants and two love seats and a table and chairs and a sign hanging next to the sliding glass window that separated the outer office from the inner sanctum. The sign read NO SMOKING PLEASE. I wanna smoke, I thought.

I tapped the partition. A blond slid it open.

"Hi. I'm Carol Rossen. To see Melody Dunne?"

"Hi, Carol, I'm Melody. Is this your daughter?" She was freckled and fair, a spirited young woman.

"No, this is my friend. This is Kitty," I said. What was so odd about younger friends?

"I'll be with you in just a few minutes," Melody said, "but first I need you to fill out some forms." Papers were passed through the sliding window. "One is a medical history with the obvious information, and the other has to do with how you've been feeling."

"How I've been feeling?" She couldn't have said that.

"Yes. It's really very simple. You just check the appropriate box—number one through five—after each question to indicate the intensity of your feelings in various situations. You'll see. It's very simple. We like to have a record of how you were when you first came here to measure against your progress later on. Do you have a pencil?"

"No." And I don't want one. Fuck the social sciences and their obsession with data.

"Here. Take mine. Make yourself comfortable. I'll be with you in ten minutes." She slid closed the glass window.

We sat on a love seat. I stared at the papers. Sweat beads pimpled my upper lip and under my brows. I tasted salt.

"Look at this stuff! I can't do this stuff!" Kitty sat mute as I rifled my purse. "I can't do this stuff! I forgot my glasses! Two days in a row. I forgot my glasses!" My arm thrust forward across the room, clutching papers at a distance I hoped might help. The words jiggled and blurred in a mud pie of print. "What does this say, Kitty? Read what this says!" I'd try, with Kitty's eyes, to accommodate science.

" 'In the last seven days have you been crying (1) not at

73

all, (2) a little, (3) off and on, (4) every day (5) all the time?'
and then there's a box where you enter the number."

"I'm supposed to put a number in the box?"

"Yes," said Kitty.

"They must be kidding. I'm not going to do this."

Papers in hand, I walked to the window and knocked on the glass. Melody opened the partition. "How can I help you?" she said to me.

"Melody, I'm having a problem with this. First, I've forgotten my glasses so I can't see the words and my hands are mucked up so it's hard to write. Second, this says"—I was shaking the papers—"in the last seven days, on a scale of one to five, have I been feeling up or down. Well, this doesn't really apply to me since I was just attacked two days ago and didn't wait forever to call this place. And anyway, I came here to make human contact, not to be treated like a robot and if you can't do that for me, I'd better go somewhere else."

Melody invited me into her office and we sat for half an hour while I was verbally tested. She made arrangements for a therapist to call me on Friday, someone she thought I'd get on with well.

I liked Melody and I appreciated her efforts, but no one was going to treat me like shit, a statistic, a lump in a crowd of weeping weirdos.

Men, guns, and booze
Thursday, February 16
6:30 PM I2OO AM

Tom Clayton was a robust cowboy sort of fellow who owned the concession, who leased the stables up at Will Rogers from the State of California, and he hadn't been around, he was away buying horses, or with a woman, or rustling up business when I had been assaulted on Valentine's Day.

When he heard what had happened, which was on

Thursday, two days later, he hopped into his Jeep and careened off the mountain and whipped through the town and swerved into the street on which Eve and I lived. He hit every goddamn pothole and scared two dogs and a puppy. Thank Christ the kids in the neighborhood were off somewhere drowning bees or growing pot or on the phone with their lovers. We heard him as he circled our driveway and stopped in front of the porch and front door. Eve and I went out to greet him. Eve recognized his Jeep. I stood beside her.

"I just got back, I was away, they told me up at the stable what happened to you, that goddamn son of a bitch," he said. "The cops haven't found him yet, have they? I hope they don't, I'd like to find him, I'd like to kill him myself. I hope to Christ he does come back 'cause I'd kill him, the son-of-a-bitch bastard."

"Hi, Tom," I said.

"I hope it's not too late, I had to come down, I wanted to come down. . . ." He hugged me. His voice was hard.

"No, it's not too late. Thanks for coming down."

"Now, listen, Carol"—he walked through the front door—"you're a woman alone here with a kid in this house, and you're isolated and I want you to get a gun. You should have a gun. The cops will teach you, just call them about it, or there's the Beverly Hills Gun Club."

"Beverly Hills has a gun club?" I was standing by the door and Eve was standing by the door and Tom was leaning on the piano.

"Yeah, and you get a license. You don't need a big one, just a small one that fits into your purse, and you carry it with you and you always have it." Hal had offered me a gun from off his boat. His was a shotgun. It could kill an army, or all the sharks he imagined encircled his boat.

"But somebody told me you have to have it showing," I said. "The cops said you can't carry a concealed weapon, that if you do you're the one who ends up in trouble." I wondered if the gun club was next to Gucci's.

"You shoot to kill, Carol, you shoot to kill," Tom said.

"You don't wait for those bastards, you can't live here with that kind of stuff without a gun."

"Yeah." I nodded.

"Will you think about it, will you do it? I hope you'll think about it, that bastard." Tom was on his way out the door.

"Yeah, yeah, I'll think about it." We followed him out. "Right now, Tom, I gotta have an operation, but when it's over, I'll definitely think about it," I said.

"I hope you do. I'm sorry if I bothered you."

"Oh, that's all right," Eve chorused. Tom was her friend. She knew him well.

"Don't be silly," I said. "It's very nice of you to come down."

"That goddamn son of a bitch. Lock your door!" Tom said.

He left. I was shaking. He was angry. It scared me. I didn't want to be with anyone who was angry.

Maybe I would get a gun.

My brother slept overnight at my home that night and we watched the Olympics and almost played Scrabble.

"Why didn't you call me when it happened?" he asked.

"You were working," I said.

"That was dumb," he said. "You certainly have a hard head. That's a joke."

When it was time for sleep I turned on all the lights, the outside ones and most of those inside, and my brother opened his door across the hall from my bedroom and Evie slept down the same hall from my bedroom and baby cat lay on top of my stomach and the dogs were in the living room and I was between • Wedgwood blue-and-white striped sheets from Bloomingdale's.

I was fine. Just fine. A little drunk from the wine and Dick Button's commentary, but that was fine, just fine. At least they hadn't let the kid from Van Nuys ski the downhill in a blizzard, that was fine, just fine. And the couple from

England made love on the ice, and the Germans were clods and the Canadians second rate and Alsace-Lorraine was not represented and my eyes were closed and he was there again, all hunched up, five feet away, his mouth set, a straight line, ready to get me. Open eyes, mustn't dream it, or he'll get me, this time he'll kill me this time I'll die. I thought of flowers and horses and animal babies and Dick Button skating out on the rink. I didn't think about guns. I didn't want to be angry. I fell asleep. He didn't follow. I made it through the dark.

I made it through the dark for a week each night. He would come and I would win by simply not being there. The Olympics helped and so did the scotch. I had switched from wine to scotch, single malt, Glenfiddich. It was winter, for chrissake. Fuck the sun. It was winter.

He stopped visiting me in my bed when I let go completely after the operation.

Random thoughts on love and beauty
Friday, Saturday, Sunday
February 17–19

There are certain matters in a girl's life that simply must be taken care of no matter what crises threaten her simple existence and I'd backed myself up against most every one of them: I'd run out of night cream and my legs needed waxing and my brows needed lightening and my nails were a mess. It was Friday, the day before the weekend, three days before Monday when most beauty salons closed across L.A., and I hadn't made appointments to tend to such business and must before entering the hospital on Wednesday.

Fortune rallied. My hair was perfect. I'd just had it trimmed the previous week, and I never dyed it or streaked it or rinsed it with henna so I'd slid in home free in the locks department. The trim was a mercy, considering karma, for no one touched my hair except Don the genius of Beverly Hills, my friend of ten years who snipped and styled, and I'd no intention of visiting Beverly Hills and spending an hour in a beauty salon surrounded by ladies of influence and power, show business ladies, wives *and* producers. I "weren't showin' up nowhere" in my condition, not in a town wrapped in cellophane paper, stocked with see-through lives labeled "private is public." Hell, no, this was Hollywood! I was a product. I was an actress in a soap-peddling industry where funky is cool and scatological interesting but all within the context of symmetry and beauty, neither of which standard applied at the moment. Being seen about town might lose me a job. I didn't need a haircut. The fates had been merciful.

Waxing my legs and lightening my brows were completely different matters, however, strategic maneuvers to be charted and performed before moving my tootsies into the hospital. Rubbing up against myself was depressing enough for there'd be no hanky-panky in the very near future, but friction caused by stubble was suicidal lying in a bed talking to the ceiling. Let the ladies of Europe or aging flower children flaunt body hair in some half-assed rebellion, but I'd be smooth and sleek between hospital sheets and my eyes would sparkle under lightened brows, and my eyes were an asset never unattended. I might want to flirt with an intern or busboy. I knew my priorities and called my beautician, who said she'd see me in an hour.

Halfway out the door on my way to Kitty's Jeep the telephone rang. I picked up.

"Hello!" I said.

"Hi," he said. "You're lucky he didn't give you another *schtup!*" which, translated into human, meant "Darling, I love you." That may have been the reason I hadn't called him myself but had asked a mutual friend to tell David the story. I knew I'd cry if I told him point-blank, and tears were not part of the bargain between us. "You're just lucky he didn't give you another *schtup!*" Thus spake Zarathustra, my latest lover, my melt, my crush, my married person. He called me on Friday as I was halfway out the door, on my way to find peace in baby-soft skin.

David had been an actor, now turned producer, and we'd worked on a film and become good buddies and he'd helped me get through some difficult times by calling around and promoting work interest. We'd lunch every fifth week and I'd give him advice on how best to handle a teenage vampire. He was the proud daddy of a girl-child gone crazy, the child of his wife's former marriage. Life was difficult. I knew about stepchildren. That was my gift in exchange for his kindness and we'd laugh and flirt and touch waists a lot and say hubba-hubba and wouldn't it be fun, the usual kidding on the square after forty. Good-bye, kiss-kiss, a gentle embrace, and we'd call in a month and be glad for the friendship.

One day he announced he'd come by in the morning, if I would be home, if that was okay and I said yes, which was trouble and I canceled the maid. I knew it was trouble when I canceled the maid. I bought quiche and watercress and chilled the champagne and made sure the daisies were freshly cut. I knew it was trouble. I was planning on lunch.

We were like children—that is, I was nervous. I was having difficulty forming a sentence. I showed him the house, I showed him the lawn, I showed him the dogs, and then I stopped showing and he took my hand and we found the bed, and we were in trouble because it felt right. Three years of lunches and never a tumble and now we had and it wasn't a habit I wished to encourage. I didn't play in this arena. I wasn't suited for the role of closet lover or clandestine meetings at another's convenience. I'd tried that once. I wanted more with my intimacy. I was strong now. I knew what I needed.

That coupling had occurred on January 30, two weeks and a day before the assault, and now it was now and I needed everything. I needed the intimacy implied in the lovemaking. I needed an intimacy we hadn't arrived at.

"They have to operate."

"When?"

"On Wednesday."

"I'll be there."

"You will?"

"I'll be there that night."

"I don't know if I want you to see me that way."

"Stop being so silly. I don't care about that."

"You really can visit at night like that?"

"I'll be there. I love you. I'll see you on Wednesday."

I phoned my beautician to say I'd be late.

My mother was absolutely desperate to do something for me, which was natural enough because she was my mother and I had been hurt and she wanted to do something. She wanted to drive me to all my appointments and I suggested she bake cookies instead. My mother was the worst driver in the United States of America. It had nothing to do with her age. This was a chronic condition. She was, had been, would be the worst driver in the United States of America. "It's not so much that I'm frightened of driving. I'm frightened of the other cars," she said, which meant she was the worst driver in the U.S. of A. I spent my childhood wondering which was worse: going through the windshield or being hit in the chest with my mother's right arm, as she tried to prevent me from going through the windshield. Stoplights surprised her. We'd be driving along and there they'd be and she'd hit that brake and karate my body. This happened as often as there were stoplights, which was far too often to suit my tastes.

Actually my mother was just plain scared of much of living. It was as if a speaker had been implanted in her brain that continually blared "But something might happen!" something disastrous, something she might not know how to handle, although she'd had to handle a great deal in her life and had made admirable efforts at maintaining sanity, which is all one can do, but she didn't see it that way. It was complicated.

Take, for example, holding one's breath underwater and swimming a lap without coming up for air. That, for example, was always good for scaring the hell out of my mother when we were kids and into lap racing, because "something might happen!" We might die. Never that we'd made it as mini-Olympians. We might die! and she'd press her heart.

Take, for example, when I had my baby. She left the hospital before Eve arrived because something might happen! a death in childbirth, and somehow by leaving it was better that way. Her fears were often mistaken for indifference, a horrific misreading but that was the reading. She wouldn't talk about her fears. *That* was too scary. She was in hiding. It was complicated.

The net result was a terrible lesson that all of us kiddies were taught on her lap: that fear was paralysis, not a natural thing, not something to work through on your way to your birthday; that courage was defined as the absence of fear, the absence of tears or the need for support. An inverse macho-ism taught by a lady, or that's what I got. It was complicated.

I didn't really think my mother was the right person to call when I was in the emergency room. I didn't call her at all until the next day when I could tell her I was fine and nothing had happened.

"Oh, Carol, I'm so glad you called and told me yourself instead of my hearing from somebody else. I would have died! Why *didn't* you call me when it happened that day? Oh, I know. I would have fallen apart, but I would have risen to the occasion, eventually, I always do. Why didn't you call me?"

"Mom, I didn't need someone I had to take care of."

Now the subject was cookies, or rather her driving. She wanted to help but what could she do? We couldn't hang out and watch the Olympics because Mom wasn't interested in the Olympics and hanging out didn't count, in her opinion. She wanted to talk turkey and scratch about in what I felt, but if I told her my feelings and all the gory details, she'd shatter a bit and wish I didn't feel them, and press her hand to her heart and hold her breath. We struck a compromise. She'd bake two dozen cookies and drive me the one mile between the manicurist ten blocks up back to my home. Two dozen cookies and one mile of driving. What could happen?

The appointment was made for Saturday morning at a local salon in the Palisades. I hadn't known a manicurist in the area for once every three weeks I'd frequent Frances, who worked for Don in Beverly Hills, but I wasn't going to Beverly Hills so I'd called Kitty's mom for the reference. Barbara knew a Louisa who "isn't very good but is pleasant and available even on Saturday. And Carol," she said, "I think you should know that Louisa was assaulted a year ago and would be most sympathetic if you feel like talking." I wondered how many people who'd passed through my life had been assaulted and hadn't mentioned it.

Talk is cheap but I only had a dime. I really wasn't interested in making conversation but I had to say something about my thumbs, so I told Louisa what had happened in a sketchy sort of way. She looked up from the bowl of sudsy water and her eyes turned to liquid and she paused for a moment before speaking softly in accented English. She might have been from Spain, or perhaps Brazil. She spoke of her assault and of the man who'd grabbed her purse and shoved her into the gutter, breaking her arm and bruising her badly.

"I don't go out much anymore."

"What do you mean?"

"Not after six. I used to walk early in the morning. I moved to the area so I could walk, it's very nice there by the sea, down by the beach, but I don't anymore. It's too dangerous."

"But you do go out to see a movie?"

82

"Not very often, and only with a friend. And then I don't drive because I am frightened of walking alone from the garage to my apartment door." She wasn't married and she hadn't any children or if she had they weren't in her life at the moment. She was forty-five or fifty and lovely looking.

"When this first happened did you go for help? There are centers and groups that specialize in this."

"Yes, I know there are but I didn't go. I thought about it but I didn't go." She lived in a box and she was resigned.

That amazed me. I'd been frightened of the cops and I'd had a couple bad nights but I was revved to hit a movie or go to a bar or some divine restaurant or fly to New York but I couldn't because I couldn't drive, or button my buttons, and I looked like hell, that's why I couldn't, but I would just as soon as the surgery was over and the swelling was down and my hands were my own. I'd driven that morning, I'd driven Eve to the park to watch her ride. I'd driven with eight fingers in defiance of thumbs, and I'd sat for an hour and watched Eve's lesson, sat fifty yards from the hiking trail and I hadn't been scared, I'd watched the lesson. I wouldn't go hiking, not alone, not without the help of the United States Army, but that was just sensible, that wasn't crazy. Nothing would stop me from having my life and going where I wished, alone or with people.

Everyone reacted so differently! Anne, my beautician, my waxing lady, my friend, a beautiful woman, a most together person, Anne freaked when I'd visited her on Friday. There I was lying on her blue leather table with strips of hot wax coating my legs and Q-tipped peroxide drenching my brows and Anne simply freaked. She hooked into the terror. She must have asked me ten times what exactly he'd looked like and who should she call if she saw him on Sunday walking the streets of Beverly Hills. Her fear was contagious and I didn't need it. She was drawn to the violence and horrified by it and I wasn't interested in either reaction. I wished to have my legs waxed in peaceful surroundings. I wanted to be quiet. I stopped talking.

Louisa and I hadn't much else to say. My nails were a mess. She scrubbed quite a bit. All that gravel and dirt from the top of the mountain had ground up behind them. They were difficult to clean. I wore pinky clear polish, never red. She *must* scrub the nails or the dirt would be seen. My thumbs were on another time schedule.

My mother arrived twenty minutes early, for time plus space plus car rarely meshed. She arrived without book and sat down beside me under a dryer and whispered disapproval of Louisa's efforts to cut my cuticles. Cutting cuticles was passé. I whispered I knew but it didn't matter. She whispered, "I'm only trying to help." She was doing her best. Her hair had been set and she had worn a print dress and baked butter cookies and remembered her license. She had parked next door at Kentucky Fried Chicken, but not in their lot, in the middle of their driveway, which was against the law and since she was early I thought it best she move her car and avoid a ticket. There was a spot in front of the salon, I could see it from my seat, in front of the door, but Mom shook her head, she wasn't interested. She didn't care for parallel parking. Mom found a spot across the street at Ralph's Market, which was swell but dangerous as we jaywalked that street dodging speeding cars. She wasn't a runner and I wasn't supposed to because of my head and all the swelling, but we ran as we crossed in the middle of traffic. It was just a small township in Los Angeles County.

We were off down Main Street twenty miles an hour. I hooked up my seatbelt. Mom never used one. We were fine until we got to the light—there were only two lights we'd have to contend with. She saw the light and hung a right down the road that led to the beach. My house was in the opposite direction.

"Mother, for chrissake, where are you going?"

"Oh, Carol. I'm sorry." She hit the brakes. "I'll make a left into this driveway across the road."

"No, Mother, don't make a left, just keep going straight.

84

And then you'll come to a corner and make a right, and then you'll come to another corner and make the right and we'll be on Main Street, back where we started."

We made it home and I ate the cookies.

It was Sunday and I was not pleased. "Single" Sundays are hard in any condition. I wished to do something gentle and sane.

A director friend called and asked how he might help to make me feel good, and I said I would like to ride out by the beach and find a restaurant with a view of the sea and have lunch that Sunday. That's what I wanted. My water-colored neck and yellowy skin would be camouflaged in chiffon and tinted glasses. And what was a demiblack eye between friends? I would thrill to be out in the world of pleasure. No one would know. Even I might forget.

It was a beautiful day. The beach was crowded. We drove and drove and then we stopped at Trader Vic's in Malibu, which was a bit too Polynesian for my taste but they served a late brunch with free champagne and we could sit by the window and stare out at the sea. Trader Vic's was dark, we were lost in a jungle, and as I wore sunglasses to mask my face, I managed to tumble into a chair. And then I managed to bump another. My friend grabbed my hand and stopped me from falling. I laughed and thought it all very funny.

We'd already ordered a drink from the bar, a giant Hai Tai or Mai Lei or something, something with fruit juice and plenty of run. The champagne they served was not from France or even from one of California's better vineyards but I drank it anyway, two or three glasses, because I love champagne, and then I drank rum.

I talked a lot about me, about strength in crisis, how I thought this incident had ranked my priorities, how connected I felt and how I'd saved my life, how flushed I was, did I look all right? And I thought I'd probably never act again, that my comeback was over and not even necessary. I didn't need acting to make me feel whole. I didn't need Hollywood to lend me importance. I didn't know what I needed but I'd know in the future. I ate some cold shrimp over lukewarm rice.

My friend suggested I needn't resolve all the major issues in my life this Sunday in Trader Vic's overlooking the sea. Before surgery. "Why not?" I said, and tripped on the chair as we rose and left darkness and reentered the light.

I was home by four-thirty. Eve wasn't home. I lay on the couch and gazed out the window and studied the oak tree on my front lawn.

Hal would be away two or three weeks. Away on the road. He'd left on Friday.

My sister Ellen would arrive late on Wednesday. She'd phoned that weekend from New York City to say she'd arrive just after surgery. She'd told them at work she was leaving to take care of her sister in California. Her big sister. In California. I didn't think the trip was necessary.

Before the ether
Monday, Tuesday
February 21–February 22

Ether was the drug they used when I was a kid and had an eye operation in New York because my eyes saw double. Ether made your mind go in and out like a busy signal gone haywire in a tunnel. No one used ether anymore, they told me. Now they used Pentothal. Mostly. Pentothal was the drug injected somewhere in my body when I was nineteen and had had an abortion way out in the valley on the back side of the Santa Monica foothills. I didn't know I was in the valley at the time, having been driven by a greaser blindfolded in the backseat of a four-door Mafioso black Caddy. L.A. in the fifties. Later Bill told me he had tailed the creep. My

86

boyfriend Bill was very courageous. Where was he now? Where was Billy? I needed him now. Who'd tail the anesthesiologist?

There was a man standing next to me in an elevator in Westwood on my way up to meet my shrink at the center. The elevator door closed. I couldn't breathe. The man to my left was free to attack me.

I sat with my therapist. We'd just met. Monday, this was our first appointment. The subject was surgery and losing consciousness. Consciousness had saved my life on the mountain. I wasn't about to give it away gratis. Who was this man, this Pentothal pusher? And who'd be me when I wasn't me, who'd sheriff the territory?

"I don't think my body should be floating around a hospital unconscious without somebody somewhere worrying about it getting lost. I don't trust doctors. I don't trust hospitals. My father was killed by bad medicine twenty years ago. It was a misuse of cortisone, and cortisone killed him. And we were always there, me or my brother or my sister or my mother, checking out everything when he was in the hospital, when he was in surgery. When he was unconscious. And still they killed him." The neon light overhead hurt my eyes.

"And later, when I was in labor with my baby and I arrived at the hospital and the hospital told me I had to sit in a wheelchair going up in the elevator, I told them I wouldn't. That I'd walk in on two feet and I'd walk out the same way. And I did!" I was crying.

"What do you want?" the lady said.

"I don't want my body to be alone in the hospital without somebody waiting for me to wake up." I was hoping she'd say she'd be glad to come along, or perhaps phone during surgery, or turn off the neon light.

The lady who was knee to knee with me in the semigracious office of three plants and a view overlooking a parking lot was named Margaret. Margaret and then a very long name afterward. Margaret the pretty. Margaret the intuitive. Tough-minded Margaret. The chemistry worked. She passed me the box of Kleenex on her desk. Margaret was really very pretty, with wavy shoulder-length chestnut hair, giant almond chestnut eyes, their downward slant outlined and shaded in browns and grays, a Lux complexion creamy white and clear double-defining a red-red cupid's mouth. A co-ed Theda Bara! She was really very pretty.

I rubbed my forehead. Something was pressing.

If she had looked like those principals of progressive schools I'd suffered, if she'd looked like Gertrude Stein with her creepy cropped hair and a creepy cropped soul, sternly humanitarian, no jokes no nothin', I'd have turned into a butterfly and Rorschached out the door.

I blew my nose and dabbed my cheeks. Pretty. Pretty. Someone had to look pretty! I'd tried, God knows I'd tried that morning for twenty minutes standing in front of my mirror waging a war against my thumbs. I had won! I had applied the "day" makeup, the "on-camera" look, plum eye-liner on the top lid, khaki liner on the lower, a bit of black mascara and a touch of pink blush, plum-colored lip gloss— a flash of panache. And voilà! My face! I looked like a clown. I'd forgotten my neck was a deep bluish mauve and my left eye newly ringed in the same color. The combination of the plums and the pinks and the khaki eyeliner had created an outtake from a Disney movie, or an undiscovered Jackson Pollock. "Pretty" would wait for another month.

A learning experience. Another one of those. If you're over forty and beaten up badly, it's best to go with the natural look.

Why did they call this the "victim" center? Cop jargon, I suppose. Shitty legalese.

"What do *you* want?" Margaret asked.

"I don't want my body to be alone in the hospital without somebody waiting for me to wake up."

"Don't you have a friend you could call, someone to go with you?" Of course I had friends but they were all working and my brother was working and he needed the money and my sister would be flying in from New York but later after surgery, later on Wednesday, which was sweet but I'd told her entirely unnecessary, I'd be fine, just fine, the surgery was nothing. And my mother would crumble. Be afraid. There was no one.

"I don't think so," I said.

"There must be someone," she said. I wanted my daddy.

Where were Prince Charmings? Where was my husband who wasn't my husband? He was out of town. He was working. And Prince Charming Number 1 was married and working and Prince Charming Number 2 was separated and working. And the other Prince Charmings had been married and separated and were frightened by that look in a woman's eyes that screamed "Help me, I need you, this is not about dinner!" They weren't ready for this, and they were all working.

I'd forgotten to take two Tylenol.

"I'll think of someone. I know I will. I mean, Margaret, I know I'm going to be fine. I *am* fine. I'm physically in the best shape I've ever been in my life. And I'm walking and talking at the same time, and I found my way here, I'm taking care of business. I mean, I have a lot of friends but it's such a terrible story, it's hard to tell your friends such a terrible story. Not that I mind telling it, I don't, I really don't. People seem to think it must be hard for me to tell it, but it's not, it really isn't. It's hard for them to *hear* it. *They*'re the ones who cry, and it brings up all kinds of stuff, and that's the part that's hard, that really scares me. And I tell them I'm okay, just a cheekbone broken, which is nothing, really nothing, when you think what could have happened. But I *can't* tell a lot of people. It's not a good idea. The press will pick it up. There's a murderer out there and he doesn't know who I am, which is good. I like that. And in this town, in my business, people talk. I don't need to be 'set' gossip, I don't need any medals, I don't need their pity. It doesn't help, it really doesn't!"

What were we talking about? I'd lost the thought.

"We have to stop now." Margaret said we have to stop. "But I hope you'll talk to your doctor. You are seeing your doctor before the operation?"

"Yes, tomorrow, Tuesday, I have an appointment tomorrow."

"Talk to your doctor about the anesthesia, and how you're feeling."

"Oh, I'll definitely do that!" I would do that definitely.

"Take care of yourself, Carol."

"Thank you, I will."

"And I'll see you in a week, a week from this Wednesday." She wasn't coming to the hospital with me. "And call me, if you need me."

I didn't think I'd call her.

I met with Gareth in his office on Tuesday. I did the talking, or most all of it.

"Gareth, I need to tell you something. I trust you. And I trust the hospital. But I don't trust that guy who's doing the anesthesia. Him I don't know. I need to talk to that person, to meet him, and I'd like for you to be there."

Margaret'll be proud! I did that just right. And he was more than willing to give me details.

"No, that's all right Gareth, you don't have to tell me what you're going to do. I mean, exactly how you're going to do it. Whatever you do, you do. It's a piece of cake, right? Well, it's not a piece of cake but it's nothing compared to what I've been through. As long as I see you when it's over. After."

What did he say about a rubber tube? I need to talk about double chins.

———

"And by the way, Gareth, while you're in there, if you see anything around the eyes or the neck that might need fixing, please, be my guest. We don't have to wait until the next time, you know."

My timing was off. I'd have to wait.

TAPED TRANSCRIPT: GARETH WOOTTON, M.D., F.A.C.S. (*Plastic and Reconstructive Surgery*), MARCH 28, 1984

CAROL (referring back to our appointment February 22, the day before surgery): . . . were you aware of the extent to which I did not want to hear what you had to say to me about what you were going to do?

GARETH: Oh, sure. You know, it was obvious you didn't want to know. You just wanted to be put back together.

CAROL: Is that par for the course?

GARETH: Some people really want to know what's going on and some people don't. It depends on the type of accident it is. An assault they almost never want to know.

CAROL: Really?

GARETH: Yeah, an automobile accident, they always want to know.

CAROL: Isn't that funny. Why do you think . . . ?

GARETH: Well, I think it's less personal. You know, an automobile accident, it's not a personal attack, it's just an accident. But a physical assault, it's really a very personal thing. Nobody wants to be personally assaulted.

CAROL: . . . was my attitude about going under unusual in any way?

GARETH: I wouldn't say that it was unusual. You had the feeling like you didn't want to lose control, you didn't really want to go to sleep if you didn't have to. Because it was sort of like, you had lost control once and you had been beaten up real badly and you didn't really emotionally want to lose control and go to sleep and have an operation.

91

CAROL: Right.

GARETH: I mean . . . it's a totally different emotional thing. An assault is an emotional loss of your own self-control, of your control over your environment, over your secure feelings with other people, with strangers. . . .

They took pictures that day, the day before. A blond Swedish woman, Miriam, one of Gareth's nurses, led me down the oatmeal tweed carpeting, through the cool white-walled corridors, past the high-tech consulting rooms, into a windowless oversize closet where I disrobed and she took pictures. They brought me right in, as soon as I arrived.

I didn't wait with the other ladies who were thinking they might need a snip or a fold sometime soon.

Miriam took pictures of the bash bruises on my face and in my head, eight of them scattered around, and of the bluish mauve neck and its matching left eye and of the five-inch abrasion on the right pelvic bone. They needed a record of how I'd looked before surgery.

TRANSCRIPT: GARETH WOOTTON

CAROL: . . . so ultimately the diagnosis—could you just tell me exactly what the diagnosis was that you made and what the procedure was in order to execute?

GARETH: Oh, yes, well, you know, first of all multiple contusions of the face and head. Number two, deep laceration, deep soft-tissue lacerations of the left side of the face, and number three, comminuted fracture of the zygomatic arch on the left side.

CAROL: So, in order to rectify that . . .

GARETH: I cut through the scalp, I cut back through the scalp over the temporalis muscle in order to get under part of the temporalis muscle, to get behind the bone fragments and lift them back out. And I also went—I just opened the cut back up to give me a direct access to the bones so that I could see when they were lined up.

CAROL: What was that rubber tube stuck in behind my ear?

GARETH: That rubber tube was placed in through the surgical incision to pack bone fragments out (until they set) and to let all the bad spirits out.

CAROL: Ah, now we're getting somewhere—to let all the bad spirits out. That I understand, bad spirits I can understand.

GARETH: I'm only kidding.

CAROL: I'm not. Listen, Gareth, one more thing. Did you really believe that I'd be in the hospital for just twenty-four hours, or were you not telling me . . . I mean, I was there until Saturday—what's that? three almost four days?

GARETH: Well, I thought, you know, from the surgical standpoint, you would probably only be in the hospital for twenty-four hours, but that was an assessment that I made taking into account only the physical injury—you know, the fracture, the cut, et cetera. I didn't really count on hospital time also including the disintegration of the defense mechanism. . . .

SURGERY
AND SOME

FEBRUARY 22–FEBRUARY 25

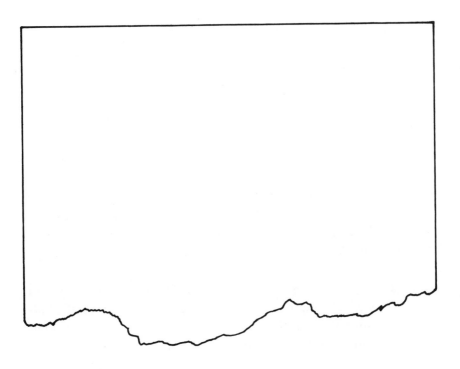

Sarah drove me to the hospital. Sarah, my friend and Hal's secretary, had offered to spend the day with me. She arrived at 6:30 A.M. Wednesday and stood out on the porch and spoke with the dogs as I tiptoed the corridor and entered Eve's room. Eve had asked that I wake her if she was still sleeping, and I kissed her good-bye as she kissed me good morning. I said, "Sarah will leave a message at the school after surgery and Ellen will take you to the hospital with her. Ellen will be here when you come home today."

"I love you, Mommy."

"I love you, sweet baby."

Hospital Admission Notice

PATIENT'S NAME: Carol Rossen
PLEASE REPORT TO: St. John's
ADDRESS: 1328 22nd Street, S.M.
FOR ADMISSION ON: 2-22-84 7 A.M.
SURGERY IS SCHEDULED FOR: 2-22-84 at 10 A.M.

Simple. There was nothing absolutely nothing that was going to stop me from getting out of that hospital, I would not die in that hospital, I would not drug-out in that hospital, I would not give in to that hospital, to hospital procedures.

SARAH: . . . you were calm, I remember you were calm all the way through. You know, we walked up to the admittance desk and you said, um, I'm having this operation, and this is who I am and I've arrived. . . . We were a little early and then they showed you to your room.

Room 332 was not what I'd ordered. Semiprivate. Shared television. Depressed bunkmate by the window. I'd asked for a private with a view from the window. She had the window. The curtains were drawn. Good money should pay for the room of your choice, not particularly subject to the management's discretion. Room 343 would vacate later that morning. I'd asked the head nurse after screening the floor. I wanted that room, Room 343, the one with the fishtank adjacent to it, the one that flanked the pediatric ward, the one catty-corner from the six-foot wall mural of Snow White and the dwarves playing on a hill. I wished to be in Room 343 with the very large window and a view of the mountains.

I wished for privacy and a space in which to cry. The head nurse agreed to move me later, after the presurgical "alphabet" workup, after EKG, and urine analysis, and CBC and bleeding time and chest X ray and taking my temperature.

When I returned from surgery, I'd be in that room. I asked if she'd seen my anesthesiologist. She shook her head and plugged me into something.

Daddy died hooked up to clicking machines and tubes and food clamped into his body, died in a hospital all alone early one morning when I was asleep and home for three hours desperate for sleep, wrapped in Hal's arms hiding from death. Once in a hospital somewhere else, he'd tried pulling the tubes and the strands of blood out of his arms, dangling in air, thrust them away in defiance of what? In defiance of death? In defiance of life? He didn't want to live as though he were dying, perhaps he wished for death as he wished for life and didn't know which he wished for more, self-destruction is such a personal choice. He never said. The machine was breathing.

Goddammit Daddy! My daddy is dead, my teacher my hero my always friend, who'd taught me to write, who'd taught me to bike, who'd taught me to swim, who'd taught me about that stuff in the Bible and said I must read all the Russian writers and screamed at the boy across the street who'd thrown a volleyball at my stomach, and held me tight when I fell off the couch, and danced about the room like he was Gene Kelly and jumped on the sofas and made me laugh, and told such wonderful Yiddish stories, where was my daddy?

And I his honey-haired ingenue princess predestined to marry his replica (whom I would understand far better than Mother).

Where was my daddy?
I was still looking.

I was my father. I was the hero/heroine. I was my strength, I would not die. I'd not be done in by celebrity doctors who'd forgotten the words to the Hippocratic Oath, indulgent ass-holes, kiss-up bastards collecting the rent as they passed the buck. No one would take advantage of me, I would not die in this hospital, I'd don my own cape and make my own sword and close my eyes and kill a few dragons.

SARAH: They put you on this corpse driver and wheeled you down a long hall and into an elevator and we went down to surgery and when they got to the doors of the operating room, that's when we parted and you were alone.

Parallel parked against the wall of a gracious corridor drenched in sunlight, amoeba particles sifting through rays that smother the floor and arced a body parallel parked across the corridor. Two feet from the tip of my mobile bed, a door ajar through which I could see two nurses wiping a steely surface, all eyes, no faces, all eyes are framed in bluey-white cotton hospital garb. Relax, deep-breathe, focus on breathing, two men walk toward me in caps and masks, a Lone Ranger Gareth and a white-faced Tonto, a Dr. Borden the anesthesiologist, hello, how are you, I'm fine, we're ready, we're early, we've finished an earlier surgery which is why Dr. Borden didn't visit your room before this moment just before surgery. An IV in my arm "Is that sodium pentothal?" Yes, he said, and then there was nothing.

White on white on white on white on ceiling on walls on sheets on bodies on corpselike bodies covered in white perpendicular bodies white necks white faces sleeping bodies walking bodies in white all white steel tubes all hanging or standing refracting the white on white on ceiling . . .

When I awoke I was in the recovery room, one of many corpses lying in a row, colorless, sleeping corpses strewn about like pickup sticks. I had awakened. The others slept. There were three nurses and an older one who was in charge of sleeping death and it was she who realized I was awake and came over and said, "This one is awake. Put this one over there." Time cobwebbed somehow and I got stuck and later, minutes later, the nurse returned and said, "What room are you

100

going to?" It was a test. I didn't know the answer. I froze and died because I didn't know my room, they were changing my room and I didn't know the number. "They changed my room," I said, hoping for kindness, prayerful of mercy. Was that a good answer or was I condemned to sleeping death in a corner of this room, lost in this room? "Take this one back, she wants to go back," the nurse said. I was "a this one," but I was free.

SARAH: You were conscious when you came back to the room but you looked awful, you looked so white . . . you were in great pain and you were barely coherent because of a tube. . . .

I got them to give you a pain pill. You did sort of drift off for like five, ten minutes . . . but every so often you said, "you don't need to stay" or "are you comfortable there?" or "what time is it?" You kept on waking up and instead of saying "I feel terrible," you were concerned that I was sitting there. "Are you comfortable?" you said. "Do you want to go and take a break?"

Beside vigils. Corridor cramps. Swollen hours after surgery. Thousands of prayers and pinpointed energies on Daddy's being, on life, on survival. He was my father. I'd wanted to be there in some hospital near him, beside him. She was my friend. Mustn't ask that of Sarah.

SARAH: You had collapsed like a balloon. That was why I stayed and you needed me to stay because, you know, we kept holding on to each other's hand, you know. I held your hand all the time. You just felt that you had to have that contact, like please don't leave me.

I just said I'm staying. I'll stay until Ellen comes. Every time I left or got up to do something, I came back and I held your hand again, because you needed to do that.

CAROL: How long did you do that?

SARAH: I think I was holding your hand for about two hours, even when you were asleep. You just kept on gripping me.

CAROL: . . . what else do you recall?

SARAH: Do you remember that your room was filled with flowers?

Eve brought me violets, a small potted plant of blooming blue violets. The other arrangements—there were five in all—the other arrangements in the room were yellows and oranges and browns, earth tones, tied to the earth, winterbound. Violets are blue. Violets are spring. Violets are Eve.

Later she said, "I thought you were going to be a lot more different than you were."

"What did you think I'd be like?" I asked.

"A lot more cheerful," she said.

"Your daughter really is a grown-up girl!" My sister had arrived with Eve in tow.

"Yeah, she wears the same bra size as I do," I said and closed my eyes. The room had tilted.

"Don't talk," she said and chatted on. Time for dinner. Mine was a milk shake. Eve was hungry. They should go. Eve was smiling and then she cried. "Don't cry, darling. I'll be all right." They left the hospital for Hamburger Henry's where Eve ordered a number 82, a hamburger heaped with peanut butter.

"Hi," he said. David walked into my hospital room at eight o'clock Western television time.

"Hi," I said. I'd forgotten he was coming.

"I brought you some chocolates."

"I can't eat them," I said. "Only straws fit in." My mouth was a slit. My words were slurred.

"Then *I'll* eat them," he said.

"Please, be my guest."

He sat down beside me, to the right of my bed, beside

102

the window, beside my bed. I reached out my hand. He laced my fingers.

"What are you watching?"

"I don't know."

"The ball game is on."

"Switch the channel."

The three-to-eleven shift nurse walked in. Blond and blowsy. Sensual. Lonely.

"Time to take your pills," she said, and she handed me water with plastic straw. I took the pill and sucked the water as she lowered her eyes and glanced at David. Her body leaned toward me over the bed. "Let me straighten this mess." And she ordered my table, spilling the water down my chest.

"Oh, gosh, I'm sorry."

"Oh, I'm okay," I said as I cupped my breasts, hoping to heat them. The outer edges of my palms brushed up against metal, metal tabs, bandage size, under my breasts, some sort of remnants of EKG, tarantulas trapped in between the creases. "What are these? Get them off! Please! Get me a smock!"

The room had become a landscape by Miró and Dali of breasts and David and dripping water. Order was reestablished, a drugged hospital order. The three-to-eleven watch nurse with blond hair glanced at David and closed the door.

"My wife always uses this hospital," he said.

"Yes," I said. "It's very good." Screams from the crowd. The Lakers were winning. Balls. Feet. Neon lights.

"I can't stay long." And he rose to leave.

"Yes, of course."

"I'll call you at home."

"Yes, thank you for coming." He opened the door. I switched the channels. The nurse reentered.

"He's very attractive."

"Yes, he is."

Midnight lollipop hit me up hit me gimme Demerol every three hours I'm barely inching to every three hours pain bashing my head haunting me why was the pain? Gimme a lollipop gimme the stick gimme sleep gimme gimme . . .

Morning's sun soaks the room. I'm awakened by waves of shaving cologne that drench my bed and make me smile. Les was there, reading my charts.

"You smell good."

"Go back to sleep."

My brother arrives for Thursday lunch. "You must walk. Have you walked?"

"No, I haven't," I said. I tried to get up.

"Not now, lie down, maybe later, Carol. Call the nurse later and walk down the hall." He left and I swiveled out of my bed and moved to the door and out into the corridor, tightrope walking, slowly, slowly. The seven-to-three shift caught me in her arms as my knees gave way in front of the fish tank. "You may not walk unless someone is with you."

Melting hours of daytime sleep punctured by nurses and nails of pain. "Is it time for my shot? I need some Demerol." My tears taste of salt. My tears taste of wrath.

There are flowers and phone calls and family in attendance. Mother is there. Ellen has brought her. Ellen chats on. Mother is horrified. I'm tied by a withered umbilical cord that nurtures me not. They leave soon after.

A new morning clamors with dishes and mops. Two days of dope. Two days without character. This morning I'd walk the pediatric ward, three strolls up and down the pediatric ward lavished in landscapes of rainbows and clouds and Snow White and fish tanks and crayon drawings. I'd hike a child's prairie and skate the slick floors and grab a bit more of daylight life.

"No, thank you, I'll ring when I want my shot," I say to the nurse at 10:00 A.M., but my head still burns with pain

104

from what? My tears are the fear of fear, of losing my medals, of owning the hurt and giving in to the notion that this experience was more than I'd begun to imagine. My tears are my rage swaddled in pain. Ellen is with me as I weep. "Two days of drugs won't make you an addict. Take the shots," she says, "and you'll feel better." I needed permission from my sister.

I was released from the hospital Saturday morning. Kitty came to fetch me in her Jeep.

I carried back with me the books I hadn't read and the nightgown and creams I hadn't used and Eve's potted plant of blooming violets and the remnants of David's box of chocolates.

He'd eaten the good ones, the ones with the nuts.

THE NEXT
EIGHT WEEKS

FEBRUARY 26–APRIL 19

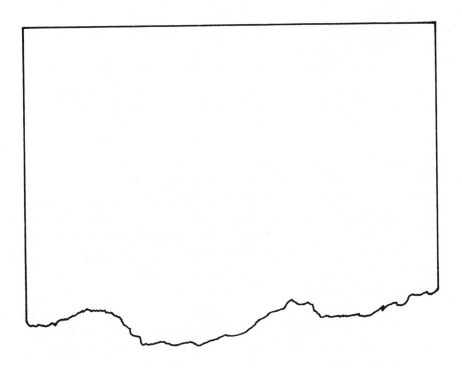

About getting your wings

Angels.

Angels in ties.

They used to make a lot of movies about heaven, which was a barren expanse just on top of the clouds and you could walk on it but you never saw the floor because all those clouds would cover the feet, midcalf to toes were smothered in mist, and there were usually one or two guys, occasionally three, chatting in the midst of this cotton-candy desert, and they were angels and they were terribly concerned about getting their wings. Which was odd. Because they seemed to be doing quite well without wings. They got around great—zap they were here, zap they were there—but even so they wanted those wings very badly and in order to get them it was necessary to come back down to earth and straighten out certain mortals who had suffered a loss of faith—in love, in commitment, in the order of things.

And they did it, by God, however grudgingly. Cary Grant (*The Bishop's Wife*), Spencer Tracy (*A Guy Named Joe*), Henry Travers (*It's a Wonderful Life*), Claude Rains (*Here Comes Mr. Jordan*)—those angels accomplished extraordinary feats all the while making it crystalline clear that theirs was a heavy schedule and they just might prefer an alternate lifestyle. Sighs of resignation accompanied most offers of help, a subplot to be sure but not without interest. It had something to do with celestial social climbing, a world-weariness linked with angel self-esteem—*X* amount of good deeds performed with grace and an angel was allowed to give up the ghost and play gin rummy for time eternal. And perhaps a little tennis to work out the cramps.

It was possible! That's what they did at the Beverly Hills Tennis Club where my parents hung out with clusters of show folk when I was a girl drunk on double features. Hollywoodians played tennis but mostly they played gin when freed from the chore of making those movies about heaven and angels and gangsters and Broadway. Heaven was new balls and going under with three.

For them. Not for me. For me heaven was heaven and angels were angels, and no one could bribe them with rackets and card games. My angels cared, however loudly they protested. (They were guys, after all, and mush was anathema.) My angels cared no matter what rules had been posted upstairs by divinities resembling Lionel Barrymore. I'd looked into their eyes and I knew that they cared and they'd be dropping on down ad infinitum whenever decent people lost the focus of feelings, lost sight of their humanity, wished to die rather than live with a loss of innocence.

Spencer Tracy was my favorite. An angel's angel. No magic, no ascots, no humble-pie ramblings. Just straight talk in a cockpit of a B-17. Irene Dunne was the earthling, he her dead lover looking over her shoulder, flying into the sun, an invisible presence, heard only by her, releasing her henceforth to feel once again, to care, to love, to live in this moment, to finish what had finished, to invent a new future.

How she was to do that completely eluded me, but the angel Tracy had done his duty. He had sung to her heart. He had fingertipped the truth. He'd released her feelings.

Released was the operative word.

Maytags never break down

I had folded them neatly and stacked them to the left of my white Maytag washer and dryer in the laundry room off the kitchen. I'd washed them the first time in cold water, gentle action, medium load, permanent press with Wisk, Clorox 2, and Sta-Puf for a seven-minute cycle. I'd used Clorox 2 rather than the Clorox Clorox of the big-bellied white bottle because they were lavender, after all, and Clorox worried me. I was fearful of white spots.

It didn't work. The bloodstains had not come out.

I had washed them a second time the very same day, the day after the assault, but that time I'd used warm water, regular action, medium load, permanent press with Wisk, one cup of Clorox, and Sta-Puf for a seven-minute cycle. I thought I'd experiment.

It didn't work. The bloodstains had not come out.

I'd refolded the sweats and stacked them to the left of the washer and dryer. I'd wanted to make sure that Pauline, my once-a-week housekeeper and entourage of three, saw the clothes the following Tuesday. Pauline would get them clean. Pauline understood Clorox. Pauline understood everything.

When I told Pauline what had happened the following Tuesday, that morning at seven-thirty, the day before surgery, she could barely speak. It was the first time she'd heard the story and she asked what she could do for me, which was strange since she never asked what she could do for me, she simply did for me, everything there was to do, everything I

111

couldn't imagine there might be to do. She was wise to ask. My sister would be arriving the next day from New York and the guest room did need to be done specially and perhaps the refrigerator should be cleaned that week rather than next as I wouldn't be around to oversee an evaluation of the ultimate worth of leftovers and lettuce. I forgot to mention my lavender sweat suit, and Pauline was preoccupied with more pressing business.

When Pauline arrived the following Monday (she worked in my home alternate Mondays and Tuesdays), I was up and about and making lists of the chores to be done that week with the help of my sister. Pauline changed my sheets and towels immediately in order to get the washing going, leaving me to the privacy of my bedroom and bath so that I might dress and be off to the doctor.

Someone knocked at my door.

"Miss Rossen?" she asked.

"Yes, Pauline."

"Your lavender sweats in the laundry room are badly stained. Do you want me to wash them?"

"Oh, yes, Pauline, if you would I'd appreciate it, I've washed them twice but I can't get them clean."

"Are the stains . . . ?"

"Yes, they are. My blood from that day."

"Oh," she said. And walked to the kitchen.

My sister and I were back home by eleven. I needed to rest. I was exhausted. Pauline and co-workers were finishing their chores.

"Miss Rossen?" she asked.

"Yes, Pauline."

"The stains on your sweats wouldn't come out. I soaked them and scrubbed them but I'm afraid they're ruined. What should I do? Should I throw them out?"

"No, Pauline. They were my favorites."

"They're drying, Miss Rossen."

112

"I'll take care of them later." She walked back to the kitchen. I went to my room.

I stood in the laundry room folding the clothes. The sweatshirt first, envelope style, avoiding the possible crease up the middle. The sweat pants hung loose, a pie-split rectangle. I would not replace the broken cord. I cradled the cottons in my arms and walked out of the laundry room through the kitchen into the living room and down the hall. I entered my bedroom and paused by the bed. Holy remnants. Where to store them? I walked to a closet half filled with dresses, Hal's old closet, now extra storage. An eye-level shelf had housed winter sweaters. Now it was empty. Good for the purpose.

I said to myself, one day they'll find the son of a bitch and we'll be sitting in the courtroom at a long table with his lawyer and his defense will be that he wasn't there or that he was crazy and didn't know what he was doing and then it will be my turn to give testimony and I will enter the courtroom from behind the judge's bench from his chambers or from another room someplace that will force him to see me coming and I'll be wearing everything the same, everything the same, except I will splash my clothes with make-believe blood and splash my hair and splash my face and I will paralyze the bastard and he will start to scream and everyone will know that he remembers perfectly and he'll be haunted forever by my bloodied image—he'll wake up in the night as I do crying and I'll be walking toward him and my figure will stalk him every night wherever he goes all his life. They won't kill him I know but I'll haunt him forever.

The next day I lay my gray-tinted sunglasses framed in a matching mauve cast on top of the stacked clothing. The police had retrieved them and asked if I wished to have them. "Yes," I had said, "they were my favorites." They were cracked, the right lens jarred loose by a blow. I'd wear them again.

When the time came.

113

Patrick O'Connell was one of this country's leading television news journalists. "Until tomorrow, ladies and gentlemen, God's speed and good night." He tucked America into bed every evening and then couldn't find his way home.

He had sent flowers two days after, to my home, from God knows where. His secretary Patsy had given him my message, had relayed the happening, and he had sent flowers immediately. There was a card. It read: Dear Carol, I hope this might be of some small cheer. With concern and love, Paddy.

They were extraordinary flowers. Stargazers, Gerberas, Festival lilies, Longa Florum, Amaryllis, and mauve Belgium tulips. I cried as I placed them on the dining-room table. They were the first flowers he had ever sent me.

He did not, however, call. I sent him a note.

February 17th

Patrick—

The flowers were stunning and indeed provided great cheer—although I really wanted you to know that within the context of a grotesquerie, I feel great. That not only do I not wish to be a victim, I don't feel like one, and that the message of that St. Valentine's Day was that I literally saved my own life. That's an extraordinary symbol which simply does inform one's life. I do have some surgery next week—a cracked cheekbone to be repaired or I'll end up a lopsided lollypop—but that's it— and then I'll be as gorgeous as ever. Confront . . . confront, a phrase echoes. I'm touched by your thoughtfulness and concern. I also simply adore adore adore beautiful flowers. Love to you, Carol.

King's X. Come back. It's safe. I need you. Echoes again. Unfinished business.

———

We'd met in college. He'd gone to Yale, I'd gone to Sarah Lawrence, a ninety-minute separation up the Merritt Parkway. His wife, then his fiancée, was my best friend, and they had a pal in the newspaper business and we'd meet in New York on "college weekends" and talk art and poetry and sip cappuccinos. After graduation we all moved to the city and he was working for CBS and she was painting and thinking of having babies, and I was a young actress hustling the theater. I'd drop by their loft on Forty-sixth and Sixth Avenue and make spinach salads every other night. They were my married friends. I was their gypsy. We were all the same age, but they seemed older. Or more substantial. I was still single.

He quickly moved into "on-camera news" and got his big break during the civil rights disturbances, after Kennedy's death when the cities caught fire, and she started to work in interior design and I got married and had a baby. They adopted a child a few years later and sometimes on Sundays we'd all walk in Central Park, trailing our toddlers and laughing at hippies.

Good fortune graced our families, demigods in residence, for both Hal and Patrick excelled at their trades, money and fame a natural consequence. We swirled in separate galaxies but kept the faith, dining together every two or three months.

We moved to California and so did Patrick part time. His marriage had crumbled, a terrible shock. She'd had an affair with the neighbor upstairs, or maybe it was because he'd been numbed by The News, by a boob-tube intimacy of two-dimensional feelings. I didn't ask. I simply nodded "what a shame" and thought if *that* could happen, no one was safe.

Paddy would visit with Hal and me, and I'd cook up a steak and we'd yak and laugh, which wasn't often given schedules, but always cherished and always special. His ex objected to these dinner visits. Given our history, she considered my friendship exclusively hers, a proprietary-rights issue that pops up in divorces, but she'd moved to Chicago and I was in California and he was in California except when he wasn't. It all seemed crazy. There was nothing to say.

My marriage shattered. Patrick called. We had dinner.

Patrick called. We'd talk. I had lost my way. The leperization of Carol. No job. No husband. Abandoned in Hollywood. Once as a child. Once again in my forties. I wanted to die. I did not. There was Evie. I wanted to die. I did not. There was Patrick.

His friendship was my lifeline to the other Carol, that shameless Carol who had lived with some dignity. I didn't know her. He assured me she existed.

"Patrick, look into my eyes. What do you see?"

"A survivor."

"How funny. You don't see fear?"

"No. Caution. Sizing up for the counterpunch."

We were as twins, joined at the mind. We were as siblings of shared times and places. We were each other's comfort and safety, and one evening as we stood chatting by the front door, he kissed me good night. I'd fallen in love with him. I hadn't known that.

There were two or three years of emotional hopscotch, a tear-stained passion soul-mating in purgatory, defined by frayed nerves and long separations and other wives, other husbands, night-riding ghosts, and beautiful children and hours of therapy. We couldn't let go. I wouldn't. He did, one day without telling me when. He had, of course, told me but I wasn't listening. I was too busy mourning a loss of continuity, too busy fixing dollar amounts to seventeen years of love and commitment, too busy dividing what had been a life.

It stopped. So it seemed. I'd write every six months and he'd call every nine, five-minute dialogues between appointments, caring connections, cautious offerings.

I really wanted you to know that within the context of a grotesquerie, I feel great. That not only do I not wish to be a victim, I don't feel like one, and that the message of that St. Valentine's Day was that I literally saved my own life.

King's X. Come back. It's safe. I need you. Echoes again. Unfinished business.

———

It was true it was only Wednesday but nevertheless the week was proceeding extraordinarily well. My jaw remained tight, and would for some time, but I was off all medication by Monday, five days after surgery, off all medication except two Tylenol every four hours for splitting headaches that rammed my brain, but then Gareth had warned me of that displeasure. "Six months," he had said. "Bones need mending."

I'd made plans that Wednesday. I would systematically eradicate all indications of my inertia over the past five years. I would fix things and sort things and clean things and replace them. My divorce cluttered the hearth of my bedroom fireplace: files, interrogatories, memoranda, threatening letters, the cat's favored hangout, Pauline's hidden shame. I had no intention of attacking that pile but it did represent an unsightly apathy. No more of that! Life was a gift. It was time to confront the major issues.

I made a list:

Restock wine and booze
Jewelers—have clasp on gold chain damaged in attack repaired
Find extra bolt of living-room couch material and bring to quilters
Call upholsterer. Need to cover frayed arms and pillows
Decide what to wear parent-teacher day Thursday
Get Datsun seatbelts fixed—jammed or something
Shoot the gardener
DO MAIL
Sort through vases
Buy new towels
Buy new place mats
Buy new rugs for bathroom floors (Eve and me)

The last three items caught me by surprise. I'd a pining for softness, a need for insurance against hard surfaces.

Ellen thought I was "overdoing it, don't you think?" but then what did she know? She was only my chauffeur and my nurse and companion and my very own chef of chicken soup and coddled eggs and minced and mushy delicacies to tempt my indifference. Bossy little Ellen, the five-foot-four shrimp, the youngest girl-child, the New York executive, forced her big sister into the sunlight, out of shuttered rooms and drug depressions ("I don't know why you live in California if you hate the sun so much"). Ellen served up meals on a proper bed tray and popped up pillows to support my weight as I watched the Grammys and laughed with strangers, guests, her friends, invited to the house to cheer and regale me with stories of personal intrigue and gossip and books and political nonsense and basketball scores. The Lakers had lost. The world was the same. My little sister had insisted on health. I had other plans. She'd have to adjust.

I released her from bondage on Wednesday evening, granting her leave to play with her buddies. I would dine that night on scotch and soup in a chop house overlooking the Pacific Ocean. I'd drive to my girlfriend's and we'd drive to the beach. "Yes, I can, Ellen, I can, the truck's got power steering. I'll drive with one hand. Go away, will ya?" My first night on the town! I was euphoric.

The only thing was I couldn't find my glasses and I couldn't find my keys and I had trouble with the bandage that covered my tube and I couldn't find my scarf to hide the neck bruises and I was late, very late. The phone rang and I grabbed it.

"Hello."

"Hi."

"Hi."

"It's me."

"I know, Patrick."

"I'm sorry."

"I know."

"Are you all right?"

"I'm glad you called."

"I've been working day and night. Network in-fighting."

"How are you?"

"Never mind. Tell me about it."

"Oh, Paddy, my God, you'd be interested in this. I bellied up, you know, it was an animal instinct, I saved my own life! It was incredible."

"Start at the beginning. Where were you exactly?"

"At Will Rogers, on the trails, walking in the morning. I saw him twice before, I passed him on the trails, and then I got to an intersection almost at the top, and I turned right up the mountain on my way to the point, Inspiration Point—you've been there, haven't you? You've been to Will Rogers? Patrick?"

There was silence.

"Do you know where I mean? Patrick?"

There was silence. The phone was dead. I was talking to myself.

I was out the next day, Ellen in tow, my first daytime gala, visiting Eve's school and partaking in classes. I dissected a pig's heart and solved algebra equations and bathed in the brightness of adolescent tomfoolery. When I returned, Ellen had driven, I'd let Ellen drive, "I'm driving," she said. When we returned home I found a message on my machine from Patsy, his secretary. It went like this:

> Carol—Patrick asked me to call you and say that the phones went out at the network last night and he waited ten minutes but still wasn't able to get back to you. He wanted to let you know. He'll call again.

He didn't that night. Nor the next day. I wrote him a letter Friday evening. I typed it myself, minus thumb splints.

Friday
March 2nd, '84

Dear Patrick,

What I don't need now is to be found babbling on the kitchen phone for fully three minutes about the most

119

intimate details of my psychic life before realizing that you aren't there and I'm talking to myself. That cuts just a little too close to a Red Skelton monologue about the birds flying down to Capistrano, or wherever the hell they flew to. . . .

And so, as I was saying—you asked how I was. . . . I once said to you I always know what I think but not what I feel. Not a very precise description. What I had meant to say is that I always knew what I felt but could not trust in its power, its direction, its reality. That twist in a knot has entirely unraveled, this experience providing the final pull, the final letting go of heady impositions—a lovely loss of control wherein lies real strength in vulnerability.

As they say on "The Phil Donahue Show," I would like to share with you some of the images and feelings that have poured over me in the last two weeks. I can only hope for and/or assume your interest, for it is a most self-serving gesture on my part. . . .

Nevertheless . . .

I need to talk about it—certainly with you—because I don't think I can be with anyone, in spirit or in fact, anyone with whom I have real history, without blabbing off about the wonder of me and my feelings. I suppose it's the "let me tell you about my operation" syndrome . . . and then we can talk about the third world war. . . .

And so, with the grace of God, I saved my own life by exposing my belly. . . .

And the other day I looked into the mirror and my hair was dirty and mostly straight because the doctor wouldn't let me wash it yet—and so it was in a kind of half-assed June Allyson page boy—and I had no makeup on, and I looked a little yellow around the edges, and I had a revelation about the forties' movies and how they had mind-fucked the country, 'cause I looked like Margaret Sullivan in a B picture melodrama in which she was dying "just a little bit" of cancer.

I cry when I can't find my glasses and at the same time I feel reborn.

I am touched by every single simple intimacy, from petting my dog to waving hello to a child on the block—and yet feel waves of incomprehensible shame at having been victimized—and panic when riding in elevators with strange men.

I know this man to be an abortion of humanity—and yet weep at how a man could do that to a woman.

I, a Leo person, spend tons of energy being courageous as I scare myself shitless being courageous—that selfsame person knows now that the soul and the spirit are the sum total of me—and although unseen is more real than what we perceive to be touchable, tangible—I caress King's phrase "I have been to the mountaintop"—there is nothing more to be discovered external to the self.

Lear says to Cordelia to quell her fears as they are both taken off to prison:

"No, no, no, no! Come, let's away to prison;
We two alone will sing like birds i' the cage:
When thou dost ask me blessing, I'll kneel down,
And ask of thee forgiveness; so we'll live,
And pray, and sing, and tell old tales, and laugh
At gilded butterflies, and hear poor rogues
Talk of court news; and we'll talk with them too,
Who loses and who wins; who's in, who's out;
And take upon's the mystery of things,
As if we were God's spies: and we'll wear out,
In a wall'd prison, packs and sets of great ones
That ebb and flow by the moon."

If they allowed middle-aged actresses to play old men in drag, I could almost play that role. Or that is my most current conceit.

And I, who assiduously avoided every aspect of the sixties—who steadfastly avoided the pain and the poli-

tics of the war and the civil rights movement, I, I'm quite sure, feel like a Vietnam vet—having fought a war no one cares about, left with feelings which cannot really be shared.

And yet, if you ask me how I am, I will say "fine." Because I am. It has been an extraordinary odyssey.

And now we can have dinner, in the sooner or later, and you can tell me about the heads of state and super-powers and network sensibilities and trade stories about the children who wander through our lives, and it will be such fun and laughs and I will enjoy the pleasure of your company.

Thanks, babe, for your friendship.

> *With love,*
> *Carol.*

He never called back.

I was sure we were still the very best of friends.

I was wondering why

Hal was straight-out about it. "I couldn't help thinking, my God, I wonder if in some way, you know, does a woman in some way provoke this? This goes through your head, it just does. I'm sure it went through everybody's mind, as well."

The line goes she must have been asking for it.

I was wondering about it, too. I hadn't before now, but now I was wondering about it. Now that I was out on the streets again, now that I passed men and women on the streets, or sat by them in restaurants, or talked to them in shops, and then only in order to buy something needed, strangers, un-knowns, the "others" among us, now I was wondering about it. Because anything can happen. Any one of them might at-tack me. Particularly the men. Only the men. And I was wondering why?

122

And I was terrified.

What had happened to me?

They were looking at me funny. They knew something had happened. They sensed it. They smelled it, my body perfume. My body stench. Electrical currents. Unseen energies. Giant rabbits they, encircling the cripple of the litter. Rabbits kill their weak. They might attack me.

What had happened to me?

Some were different. Some would melt and soften like Carvel ice cream and speak to me tenderly, newborn like, and not judge my shame and not hold their noses and refuse my eyes.

I decided that an eight-foot radius was the shortest distance tolerable when passing a large man, that is assuming presence of mind, for when I passed a large man my mind sped to amphetamine multiples and my eyesight blotched and my body raged and shook spasmodically. I had known large men to be the gentlest of men. Now I despised their size and potential power. Apes. All of them. Even the short ones. If they went for me now I would shoot them in the head.

If I had a gun.

The line goes she must have been asking for it.

What had happened to me?

I was wondering about me and my asking for it. Why had he picked me? Why had *I* been marked and chosen, an Auschwitz victim, tattoo numbered, pen punctured, and swollen? And why my shame? Why this toxic bloodletting? What had happened to me? What had I done? Why had he picked me?

Larry, my former therapist, a sixties person who'd migrated to Hawaii and given up the glitz of Hollywood neuroses in favor of family work within the penal system, in favor of psychopaths on "the island," which seemed extraordinary under the circumstances, Larry had flown into town and had called, on a lark, just to say hello. Naturally when I told him what had happened he wanted to see me, but the only time either of us could manage was on Wednesday, and then only if he came out to the house and picked me up and drove me back into Westwood for an appointment with my new therapist, Margaret. That struck me funny but he was game. We talked in the car about psychopaths we'd known:

"What do you think?"

"You looked into his eyes?"

"Yes. I said good morning."

"If you looked into his eyes you saw his devils, or he felt you did and he couldn't allow it. You were a threat to his survival. You must be eliminated or his secret would no longer be his secret. If he was a psychopath. And he sounds like one."

"You think?" I said. "He sounds like some directors I've known."

(I mean, shit. There's an interesting piece of information if you're interested in psychopaths, and I am not. I was interested in what I do with my eyes for the next twenty-five years and what I tell my daughter to do with her eyes as she walks through the world all liquid and marvelous. What's the fucking message? Assume all men are psychopaths until proven otherwise? Maybe that's a good idea. Never look a man in the eye.)

I could not figure out what had happened to me.

"Thanks, Larry, and perhaps I'll come visit you in Hawaii in a month or so. I think I need a rest." I opened the car door and stood alone on the corner. I crossed the street alone and entered the building, alone, and rode the elevator, alone, and walked the hall, all the while surrounded by people. Never once did I look up and into a man's eyes, and still my body raged and shook spasmodically.

I'd barely made it to the center. I'd never make it to Hawaii. And then I told Margaret this story:

124

When I was Eve's age, when I was thirteen or fourteen, all of us girls, the "good" and the "bad," wore Warner's brassieres under blouses and sweaters. They were cycloned stitched right to the tip, creating the machine gun I'm-gonna-spray-you look. That was a good thing. That was in. That was "it." Superhard tits under lamb's wool sweaters. But the rules were the rules. Over the bra you must wear a full-length slip, over the superhard tits that were cyclone stitched. Otherwise you'd look big, and if you looked big you looked sexy and if you looked sexy you were sexual. And that wasn't nice. That was bad.

I wore a 34-B cup, which was big, above average, the 34-A cup was considered normal. At lunch break one day, at Emerson Junior High, four "good" girls, four heavy-hitting "good" girls asked me to accompany them to the little girl's room. It seems they had been offended by my boob size for some time, and if I wished to be their friend it was necessary to strip. They needed to find out if I was wearing a slip, and if I was, and still they showed, I must be fronting falsies. I died three times and stripped to the waist. There they were, in glorious Technicolor, two fully developed B-cup breasts encased in a bra under a slip. I spent the next year and a half until I graduated walking with my chest pushed in, hunched a bit. The episode had been a very close call. I almost got to be a "bad" girl.

I wept for the rest of the session with Margaret. I wept for my breasts and my hips and my lanky long frame. I'd thought I'd brought my own Kleenex but I'd forgotten the packets. I used Margaret's instead.

Come on now, what happened, what happened, what happened, what happened? I'd skipped in math, I'd read all of

Tolstoi, I was on intimate terms with Camus and Martin Buber, and I was senior class president at Sarah Lawrence College. If I couldn't crack this fucker, what the hell good was I? What had happened to me?

1. A man committed assault with a deadly weapon.
   (is that what happened?)

2. A man tried to kill a woman with a three-foot sledgehammer and it wasn't a crime of passion and it wasn't an act of war and it wasn't a paid assassination, but rather it was a vicious, brutal, unfathomable act of violence, and the spoken and unspoken question in everyone's mind (including the victim's), the vicious, brutal, unfathomable question formulated in everyone's mind was: What did she do to elicit the attack, an attack that very likely had as its intent rape?
   She must have been asking for it.
   (is that what happened?)

Asking to be violated. Asking to be penetrated. Asking to play Jane to a meat-eating Tarzan, needing to know her female essence via the intrusion of a stranger's cock. Exploding inside her. Jammed up inside her. Hoping to know the power of maleness encapsulating the feminine by overpowering it.
   (jesus, sounds good to me)
Biological imperatives
   (fuck me, baby, come to me, come to me)
biblical references
   (she was somebody's rib)

a scattering of truths stretched to cosmic proportions,
      byzantine fantasies entertained at once,
      preempting other thoughts, all other considerations of
      what it is about the male of the species
      that when enraged
      or maimed
      or cracked in some way,

brutalizes a woman,
   violates her being.

And are not human beings the shame of the animal kingdom.
(I didn't get a B.A. for nothing)

Genesis 3:6, 16
And when the woman saw that the tree *was* good
for food, and that it *was* pleasant to the eyes, and a
tree to be desired and to make one wise, she took of
the fruit thereof, and did eat, and gave also unto her
husband with her, and he did eat.
   And the Lord God said unto the woman, I will
greatly multiply thy sorrow and thy conception; in
sorrow thou shalt bring forth children; and thy desire *shall be* to thy husband, and he shall rule over
thee.

In other words, be a good girl and wear a veil.

What had I done?
   I had taken a walk in my neighborhood park at 9:00 A.M.
on a bright Tuesday morning. I'd left the dog at home. I had
been alone.
   I'd passed a young man while I was jogging up a hillside
and I'd looked into his eyes and said good morning. I'd spoken. I'd acknowledged the day and his being.
   And I was attractive. A womanly woman.
   The line goes she must have been asking for it.

I'd send back the B.A.
   Nothing helped.
   I was terrified.
   What had happened to me?

———

The towels could wait. I'd shop for the towels next Monday or Tuesday. I'd been good this week, very productive, a proper normal person. My piano teacher would have given me three gold stars for this week. I'd bought the booze, I'd fixed the medallion, the fabric was quilting, the mail had been sorted, I'd seen Larry and Margaret, I'd visited Eve's school and sat through her classes, and this morning, it was Friday, I'd driven *alone* to see Gareth at the hospital. I'd parked, *alone*, in a four-story lot, next to Chevies and Mercedes and Rabbits and shadows and echoes and silence and empty spaces.

I was terrified. I ran from the lot into the building all the while checking to my right and my left and behind and in front, slow-motion ran for fear of jiggling my cheekbone or smashing my face against someone or something, a wall, a door, or tripping and falling.

The towels could wait, because the towels were at Robinson's and Robinson's was in the mall and I couldn't handle the mall and crowds of creatures coming at me like Hemingway's bulls.

I'd done enough this week. I'd done enough today! Gareth had removed all of the stitches, twice I'd had to sprint the Orwellian parking lot, and if that weren't enough, I'd had the seatbelts in the Datsun truck adjusted after the pit stop at the hospital. I'd stood six or seven feet away from the mechanic—he was a new mechanic, a stranger to me—and asked him very politely if he would help me with the seatbelts since I'd sprained a couple of fingers in a volley-ball game, and he said something in Japanese and then he did it. He didn't smile a lot and I was medium scared but we both managed the experience with a tiny touch of grace. That was good. That was productive.

The towels could wait.

The park couldn't wait. I wanted to go to the park today. I wanted to talk to my ranger friend, Tucker.

We sat under the pepper tree that fronts a white board-and-bat structure the park rangers use on their off hours. Tucker and I sat on the grass in that fifty-foot enclosure just below the riding ring and the stables. Teresa was exercising a chestnut Selle Française. Jimmy was at his desk in the barn. The birds and the bees dive-bombed our heads.

"Will you walk the trail with me some time, some time when you're free? I'd like to walk the trail again some time soon," I said.

"Sure," he said. "Of course. How are you feeling?"

"Oh, great . . . a little shaky, but I'm very lucky."

"The weekdays would be best. The weekends get busy."

"Whenever you're free is fine with me." And there was a silence. I sniffed in the park and feasted on peace.

"Do you mind if I tape it, the walk, when we do it?" I asked.

"No, not at all . . . how come? You a writer?"

"No, I just don't retain much these days, and I want a record of how it feels when I do it, and whether I remember the same things you do. About the day. Whatever. I don't know." And there was silence.

"Do you know about the woman?" Tucker said.

"What woman?"

"The police haven't told you?"

"Told me what? What woman?"

"He went for another woman twenty minutes before you."

"You're kidding."

"She's a regular around here. I saw her that morning. She stopped at the station, you know, just to chat. And while we were talking the guy went for you. Because we were talking about the same time you say he went for you."

"And she didn't say anything?"

"Well, he never really got to her and she wasn't sure."

TRANSCRIPT: TUCKER CHANEY, STATE PARK RANGER I, WILL ROGERS STATE HISTORIC PARK, MARCH 10, 1984

. . . the topic never really got on to what happened up on the trail that day, she just was telling me what a beautiful day it was and that she just came down off the hill. She had decided to take an early-morning run instead of an afternoon run. She never commented on anything else. It could be that it just slipped her mind, because the conversation never keyed it to remind her that something had just happened to her. But the next time I saw her, which was on the weekend, the next weekend, which was the first time she was back, I confronted her and asked if she'd noticed anybody unusual and before I made any more statements, she just butted in and said, before you ask me a single question about this, she says, the individual you're looking for was wearing a bright-red backpack, wasn't he? And I said, you tell us, you know. And she said, yes, he's athletic build, dark hair, had dark shorts and seemed to be a fairly young person, midtwenties to late twenties and light skin. She said she only saw him from a distance of probably seventy-five yards or so, not more. And she wasn't sure about the color of his shorts, just that they were dark and he had a red shirt and a red backpack and she'd heard that somebody was attacked. She said a red backpack. You said blue.

What had happened was that she got to the Y, just like you did, except then he was up on Chicken Ridge, just opposite Inspiration Point, and he was up there just walking around, back and forth, and he saw her, and she saw him, and she stated that his whole posture seemed to change, and he immediately started running down the hill, down Chicken Ridge, in her direction, down to the Y, at which point she thought something may be up. So she jogged up to the top of Inspiration Point because she said she was damned if she was going to miss out on the view, because that was what she came up for, so she came up to the top of the point and she just had this funny feeling about him, so she just, when she got to the top, she just looked around a little bit, at the scenery, at the view, and just continued on over the top and went down through the brush where there's no real trail rather than go back and confront him, because she wasn't sure of what was going on, but she just had a feeling that it wasn't

130

right. And later I found his tracks—you know, we were able to identify his tracks—I found his tracks—all around the edge of the point, between the two posts, overlooking the lower road. And obviously when she went over the edge of the point, he probably came up to the top, probably debating whether or not to follow her down through the brush and probably saw you coming up way down below, and decided just to wait for you. That's all speculation but it seems to hold. Because the time frame is about the same, because you would have been up here with him about the same time I was talking to her, right down at the gate, and it took her twenty minutes to come down off the top, and it took you twenty minutes to come up.

We had passed each other, the woman and I. She in the brush. I on the trail. He had watched her descent. And then he saw me. I had seen him watching. At the beginning. From the bottom.

That's what had happened.

The line goes she must have been asking for it.

What had happened to me?

Baby chickens and pizza

I really had no choice but to write. I suppose if my hands had been broken I would have found another way to say what needed saying and sort out my feelings, but my hands had not been broken. They were stiff and swollen and green and blue but they were of a piece and could be made to function and I knew I must write. A friend had suggested I might dictate my thoughts into a tape recorder but the idea wasn't appealing to me. I'd enough disembodied voices floating about my head and hardly needed another to add to the collection. I needed black print symbols on pink or green sheets of first-draft, second-draft typing paper. Heaven forfend I use the white. White paper implied a Broadway opening of printable products or definite statements. I preferred the pink or green sheets of paper.

I'd take the molded plastic thumb splints off my hands and sit down at the typewriter and finger my thoughts on my IBM Selectric, the portable model, which barely needed touching in order to speak. Its hum was my friend, a womb of electricity, the sound barrier that permitted my mind's ramblings to focus. I'd tell Evie to turn down the heavy-metal muzak and I'd close my bedroom door and shut my shutters and block the sun and the stars and the moon from being and turn off the lights with the exception of the one that shone down upon the celestrial Selectric, and I would write.

I'd write first to Patrick, and then I'd start a journal.

Friday night in a mining town, my father's favorite expression walked my mind. No, *Saturday night in a mining town,* that was the expression, I'd get it right. This was Friday, this Friday, this wasn't Saturday night, this was Friday in a night town he'd never known in the thirties or forties, his Hollywood then, a fun town on Fridays and weekend nights when strikes accomplished something of value and rebellion considered the highest art form and swell nightclubs on the strip blared big bands and funny funny men were backed up by girlies, a delirious time of love/hating father figures like Harry Cohn and Harry Warner and Louis B. Mayer. Or my father and mother and most of their friends might attend a scotch-and-soda Communist party—driving Buicks and Caddies and Plymouth Coupes—organizing support for the Lincoln Brigade, and the air was smogless and the town was honeyed and production was boundless.

A black-and-white time when Friday night was a hoot.

All that remained now were roasts and gay bars and the political event at $250 a crack and the occasional gatherings at the Universal Sheraton for network associates who booked sitcoms in Europe and Tallahassee. Pollution was a given. Production stuttered.

Friday. Saturday. Sunday. Monday. This "now" was not

132

fun, Hollywood style. Fun was my IBM Selectric of the evening, but only after I'd performed my motherly duties and provided the structures of fun and games, which in L.A. meant wheels and the run of the house for my darling daughter and her sleep-over pals.

I was the hen and they were my chickens. They had clucked and cluttered in the yard at Eastbrook the day before when I'd visited the school and attended classes. They had gathered around me and stroked my feathers and nuzzled my shoulders and neck and hair. They had phalanxed my movements, warding off other parents and high-speed students rushing at the bell to make it somewhere. Lunch break had been a love-in on a sunny grass knoll of compliments and sweet talk and bodies pressed closely: "Gosh, Carol, you look pretty," "No one would never know," "I don't mind your old glasses," "I love your suede jacket," "What can I get you, do you want some milk?"

Friday night in a chicken coop. I'd done worse.

TRANSCRIPT EVE HOLBROOK OCTOBER 25 1984

CAROL: Who else was here that Friday night?
EVE: Meredith, Dana, Catlin, and me. Karen wasn't here.
CAROL: What were your plans for the evening? When you planned the sleep-over date, did you have plans around those guys or some guys catching up with you, or what was your evening really about?
EVE: Well, I'm not going to tell you about the different feelings of each of the different girls because each girl wanted something else—but we didn't have any plans with any guys before you invited us to go have pizza.

I wanted pizza. I love to eat pizza. I especially like pizza when I wish I wore diamonds. It takes their place. They were huddled together, my cooped-up chickens, scratching and cack-

133

ling on a telephone down the hall, hungry as the devil and twice as fearsome. I'd play the Super Mom and invite them out to Maria's for Friday night pizza and Cokes. They'd be my mob and protect me on the street and join me in calories and later I'd write.

Eve rejected the invitation out of hand: "Please, Mummy, nobody wants to have pizza with you. I mean, thank you very much but my friends don't want to," and ten minutes later reversed herself, a touch menopausal but what did I care! I wanted pizza and I couldn't go alone.

Maria's Italian Kitchen is located in a U-shaped cul-de-sac straddled by stores. There's a Food Gallery, a sixty-minute photo, a deli, Baskin-Robbins, a florist, a bakery, Needle 'n' Knit, The Coffee Baron, a dry cleaners, a bookstore, a shoe repair shack, and a Shell gas station. It's called a village and that's what it is, a friendly place, all on one floor, predating monster malls and shopping centers.

Jammed between the gas station and the coffee bean shop is Maria's, a Mediterranean pink structure (never mind the cement blocks) with a white latticed entrance edged in gray that introduced a sheltered strip adjacent to a kitchen. This "patio" area boasted of an "in-order" counter and an "out-order" counter and a scattering of brown chairs and several wood-veneered tables built to seat four, which often seated eight. Only in America did such greasy spoons exist, an amalgam of Sicily and Armstrong linoleum. The red-brick-tile floor was chipped beyond description and the food was divine, the hot spot of these suburbs.

I was terribly happy to be there.

The girls were starving and asked me to order all kinds of dough goodies and diet drinks while they stood guard at the only free table. I made my way to the "in-order" counter. I ordered, and I waited, and I paid and turned around to ask one of the girls to come help with the trays and I was confronted by a vision of five mix-matched gangly stringbean subhumans often known by adults as adolescent boys hanging over our table, leaning on our table, poised on their knees at the foot of our table.

There was a lot of screaming and touching going on.

Try as I might, I could not capture the girls' attention and so made the first of three trips back and forth carrying sodas and pizzas and calzones and salad. And then I sat down.

"I simply couldn't touch a thing!" Dana said, and Catlin said, and Meredith said, and Evie said, and Evie always eats well. No one was hungry. Not anymore. I was the only one eating and no one talked to me.

And there was a lot of screaming and touching going on.

After waiting what I considered to be a respectable amount of time, I said, "Listen, boys, I'd be delighted if you would like to sit down and join us for dinner, there's plenty of food, but would you knock it off, you know what I mean, just knock it off!" And they did knock it off. For a while.

After I'd finished my dinner I whispered to Evie, "I really think we should leave now." The girls got up and the boys got up and we all walked out to the street. As the girls and I slid into the car, I was confronted with the vision of five mix-matched gangly adolescent boys hanging over my car, leaning against my car, sitting on my car, holding tight to my car, and I had to be ever so careful backing out not to hurt them. "They certainly like you," I said to the ladies and drove home to the quiet and my Selectric typewriter.

TRANSCRIPT: EVE HOLBROOK

CAROL: Did you talk to the guys before we went for pizza?
EVE: Oh, yeah, I forgot, Dana had connections with this one
     guy—he went to Crossroads, or Brentwood maybe, and
     they were in our grade, eighth grade, and she called him
     because she was just smashing around calling anyone she
     wanted to call at that time and she called him.
CAROL: You guys looking for action?

EVE: No, we were, maybe, she called him just to talk to a guy and you know, act cool, and then it just happened to be that they wanted to really have action and they wanted to meet us so they came to the pizza place, and they said they'd look for us around that square.

CAROL: What did you expect to happen?

EVE: We didn't expect anything to happen because we knew we couldn't do anything. Maybe you would have let us go and do something with them but we didn't really think about that, we just thought of having dinner with them, but then they persisted and wanted to come over to our house but we said no, and one of the guys knew our number and got our address and so they came over against our will. I mean, we didn't say they should come over. Well, maybe some of my rowdy friends may have told them to come on over. Well, maybe we all knew but we didn't expect them to come. And we went down the street, in case they came, and they did, and we said go away, no way, no way we can see you, and then we went back up to the house and they stayed and all of a sudden there was a knock on the window.

"Evie!" I screamed. Over the hum of the Selectric typewriter, checking the flow of my letter to Patrick and thoughts of Martin Luther and his climb to the top of a mythic mountain.

"Evie!" And my eyesight blotched and my body raged and shook spasmodically and my lungs deflated for lack of air.

I heard the crumbling of leaves, the crackling of twigs, the grate of the gate to the vegetable garden outside my bedroom where I was working, outside the window over my shoulder.

"Evie! What's going on out there! Evie! Who's there? What's happening? Evie! Evie! Where are you? Evie!" And my body raged and shook spasmodically.

136

"It's only the boys, Mommy, it's the boys from dinner. It's all right. It's all right. We told them to leave."

"Well, go outside, a couple of you, and tell them again. They're still here, I heard them, where are they? They're here. Tell them to get the hell out of here. Evie! I'm scared! Evie! Tell them now!" And my body raged and shook spasmodically as I flipped all four switches to the right of my bed, floodlighting the house and the grounds and the bushes.

"Listen, you guys!" Eve screamed into the lights from the front porch, into the night. "You better get out of here. Come out wherever you are and leave. Just get out of here!"

"Where are they?" I whispered. I stood behind her.

"They're in the bushes," Eve said. "They'll leave now, Mommy, it's all right, they'll leave."

I walked back to my bedroom and sat down at the typewriter. I heard leaves crumbling and twigs crackling and the grate of the gate outside my window. My fingers numbed, my wrists struck by lightning.

"Evie! They're still here, someone's out there, God damn them. Evie!" I ran through the house and out on to the porch. My face bones ached as I forced my jaw open.

"Listen, you guys, wherever you are, whoever you are, I don't take kindly to someone on my property, to anyone on my property who hasn't been invited. If you don't come out now and leave right away, I'll set the dogs on you and ring the alarm." I'd screamed somehow. I'd forced my jaw open. There was a silence. I closed the front door.

I sat down at my Selectric and listened to its hum and listened to its hum and sat at my Selectric. I heard them again, leaves crackling, twigs crackling, male voices whispering outside my window. I left the room and walked down the hall and through the living room to the front door and pressed the button that sparked the alarm, calling for dogs and ordering them out, but the dogs were confused and lay down at my feet.

Glazed chicken eyes peered out from the kitchen, all silent and thoughtful, bewildered, respectful.

137

"I'm sorry, ladies, for getting hysterical, but nobody's going to fuck with me," I said.

The bell clanged in the garden for five or six minutes, the boys long gone from the territory. It wasn't connected to police or patrols and no one had heard it except the kids, not even the neighbors who were home that night, whom I knew had heard and never called or walked over.

Eve visited my bedroom later that evening as I was finishing my letter to Patrick, writing of Lear and Vietnam veterans. We kissed good night. She apologized, as did I. There was no anger. We forgave each other, I for hysterically sounding the alarm, she for withholding her plans for that evening.

As she turned to walk back to her bedroom and friends, I said, "That's it, sweet baby, I'm getting a gun."

Alice revisited

When darling Alice of Wonderland fame fell down down down the rabbit hole, curtseying, I might add, part of the way (for she was well bred, a child of character) and wondering out loud its longitude and latitude (having not the slightest idea what those words meant), she landed at long last in a dimly lit hallway, and there were doors all round that long low hallway but they were all locked, and Alice despaired. How was she ever to escape her odd fate?

Lo and behold, she found a golden key atop a three-legged table made of solid glass, an old-fashioned table, an antique key, placed in the midst of the dimly lit hallway, but the key didn't fit any of its doors. It fit, instead, a teeny door of fifteen inches, hidden behind a very low curtain. A hard-to-find door. The hide-and-seek variety. Alice knelt to the floor and peered through the baby opening into a garden of flowers and fountains, a happy place where she most wished to be, but Alice could not get her head through the opening, not to mention the rest of her slim lithe body. This was not fun, this falling into a hole. This was very hard. This was a problem.

A tunnel of misery. And no one to advise.

But Alice was practical, a well-known problem solver. "If only I might shrink a bit, shut up like a telescope and, lo and behold, there appeared on the table a bottle labeled DRINK ME, and she did and she shrank but she'd forgotten the key, and she was now tiny and still unable to reach the table's surface, its legs too slippery to climb, though she tried.

(She was, after all, a child of perseverance.)

Alice wept, but only for a moment, knowing her tears would not solve the problem.

Lo and behold, she spied a tiny glass box lying under the table and in it was a cake marked EAT ME in currants and she chose to do so, hopeful she'd grow taller, or if not, if smaller, she'd creep under the door.

Whatever worked was her credo, Alice only wishing to escape her confusion.

"Curiouser and curiouser!" You know what happened. Alice grew tall, nine feet tall to be exact, and although she could now reach the golden key, she was far too big to squeeze through the opening.

Up. Down. Up. Down. A seesaw of sizes and feelings and spaces.

A tunnel of misery. And no one to advise.

Even this child of character and breeding could not control the lump in her throat, the lump in her heart, and she sat down and cried, really cried at long last, shedding gallons of tears, four inches deep, a saltwater puddle that ran down the hall.

And Alice felt Alice slipping away. Alice was in crisis, a trauma victim. (Hard to believe, but symptoms are symptoms.) For try as she did to hold tight to some sanity by questioning herself on a number of subjects, questioning her identity, questioning her knowledge, testing her memory of data and couplets, the stress of having fallen down a rabbit hole smothered sensibilities and her mind failed her. Perhaps she was Ada or her other friend Mabel, four times five might be twelve, and London was in Paris.

And all the while Alice wept gallons of tears.

There *is* magic in the world and Alice *did* shrink once more (by virtue of a fan that belonged to White Rabbit), but she'd forgotten to take the golden key with her, just as she'd forgotten all other experience, and now she was worse, far worse off than ever, she was tinier than ever and THIS WAS SERIOUS.

Alice barely had time to feel ashamed, to mourn her failure to control her destiny, to adjudicate falling into a hole in the first place, for suddenly her foot slipped and she plunged into a sea that wasn't a sea but the pool of tears Alice had shed while she was nine feet tall.

Alice was up to her chin in salt water.

"I wish I hadn't cried so much!" said Alice, as she swam about, trying to find her way out. "I shall be punished for it now, I suppose, by being drowned in my own tears! That *will* be a queer thing, to be sure! However, every thing is queer today!"

To have survived such a fall and choke on self-pity. How very odd!

Mononucleosis maybe

The name of the play was "Don Juan in Hell" by G. B. Shaw, a play within the play *Man and Superman*. I'd been cast as the leading lady, the play's love interest opposite Richard Basehart, one of America's great lyric actors, an endangered species to be sure. It was a very special project, the kind actors commit to for the love of language and the challenge of fulfilling a great playwright's intentions, and the thrill of working with an extraordinary actor.

It was not about money. There was no money or any

fixed dates for a future production when we started rehearsing in the spring of '83. We had gathered together as an act of faith in the "why" we were actors, for the play was the thing and we'd see where it brought us. If we were stageworthy, we'd find the right theater.

We all of us continued to turn a dollar doing jobs in television or film, what have you, but always returning to work on "the project," when time schedules allowed that we might meet. It was an odd arrangement, a bit unorthodox, but the players cared deeply and wished that it might prosper.

I'd spent weeks researching the life of the playwright and the smells and customs of his world in England and those of Spain, about which he had written, as well as hours of rehearsal in rearranged living rooms cleared to accommodate Shaw's fantasy desert. It was a difficult play, this play within a play, but I'd done my homework and I would be ready.

One Monday morning, three weeks after surgery, I received a phone call from the play's director.

"Carol," she said, "we've got a theater and we want to go into rehearsal next week." My arteries froze and my stomach left town as the body screamed no but the mind contradicted. Shame had made an entrance into the picture.

"Cynthia, let's meet. I have things to tell you." We arranged to do so the following morning.

Something new had been added to my daily behavior. I cried, a summer rain, at least one hour, weeping my despair at being weighed down by a lack of energy and power and terrible depression. That Tuesday morning I awoke in tears and resolved not to see friends anymore for my obsessions and vulnerability would only chase them away; or if I did see friends never to reveal the deepest truths of how it felt to be me, or of my confusion. Then I dressed real pretty and put on makeup and slowly drove to Cynthia's house.

"Cynthia, darling," and I told her the story. She was appalled but covered nicely as I chatted on about my symptoms, openly, honestly, trying to explain why I couldn't be

141

held responsible for quality. "I seem to be caught in a process that controls me. Feelings surface at awfully odd moments, and a theatrical commitment does require extraordinary stamina and emotional focus. Wobbly legs and shaky hands doth not a leading lady make!" I said as I finished my proper presentation, sipping on a glass of water over ice. Always the lady, I'd classed my way out. "The show must go on" would not trip me up.

Cynthia winced. This was very bad news. The chemistry of our play had been seriously endangered and we'd all waited so long. Must this moment be spoiled? I was ashamed of my lack of courage. Perhaps God would let me off the hook.

"Let me call my doctor, I'll call Gareth from here, and I'll tell him the situation and let's see what he says." I raised the phone and dialed his number, hoping I'd hear what I wanted to hear: Margaret had said I must let myself heal; Gareth might give my conscience permission.

"Gareth, I'm terribly sorry to disturb you but I'm sitting here with the director of a play I've been working on for almost a year, and now they have a theater and want to start rehearsals again next week, and I'm calling because I need to know what's the prognosis for returning to work." That was fair, I thought, I hadn't tipped any scales.

"Well, usually not before six weeks after surgery, and you had surgery when?"

"Three weeks ago."

". . . so you'd be ahead of schedule by ten days or so. And it takes at least a month to work anesthesia out of the system, and probably more since any medication lengthens that. . . ." Informational men set my heart beating.

"It does?" I said.

"Yeah," he said. "See how you feel at the end of the week and then—"

"I don't know if I can do that," I interrupted, the destiny lines of both palms bleeding sweat. Equivocation was not part of the plan. "I don't want to hang them up," I said. "I mean, they have to find another actress if I decide not to, and well, that's a big deal."

"Why don't you wait until the end of the week? You know, it might divert you."

"Yeah," I said.

"But then if you put a lid on all your emotions—"

"What?"

"You know. . . ."

"What?"

"They could pop up down the line and you wouldn't understand the depression."

"Right!" You bet! I knew about depression. I'd hit the jackpot. A stay of execution.

"Why *don't* you see how you feel on Friday," Cynthia said after I'd offered Gareth's opinions. A backcourt lob. Why was she pushing? "I'm sure Richard and the others—may I tell them what happened?"

"Of course! You must!" I was embarrassed.

"I'm sure they wouldn't mind accommodating your rest periods or any difficult moments you might have. It's a question of repolishing what we've worked on already. Let me talk to the others. The hard part is over!"

"What can I say? It's very confusing."

"I'll talk to them and get back to you and you see how you feel."

"Okay," I said.

"You *look* great!"

"Thank you, Cynthia. Yeah, all my black and blues faded into the night."

I knew, driving off, I must reread the play and evaluate the effort in the light of today and not imagined physical and emotional horrors, and so after lunching with Jebbie and Rags, I combed the bookcase for my copy and the reams of notes I'd jotted down. I'd lost them, it seemed, misplaced them somehow, in my bedroom, someplace, along with my glasses.

I couldn't remember. I was losing things. I'd read at the library that afternoon.

The spine of the play, if one may capsulize G. B. Shaw, is a dialogue on the will to live, the "life-force" within and its gnawing insistence, an idea whose time had clearly come for me. I'd not fully understood such thoughts before, but now Shaw's words embraced a stooped soul wandering about lost in my belly. This play might mother my state of mind if I could allow it into my life. Get on with it, Carol! I thought to myself. I can do this! Cuddled by books and the smell of reason, I had decided to stay with the project.

Two days later I heard from Cynthia. Richard and the others were more than supportive. They would do anything necessary to help me through. "They love you," she said, "they want you to do it."

"No," I said, and I turned the play down. "I'm exhausted, Cynthia. I ain't got it in me."

I couldn't work. I couldn't act in some theater in town. I knew when I stood on the stage bathed in light, and the audience filled the darkened hall, hidden from me, lost in black silence, I knew someone out there would try to kill me.

The *bitch!* I thought as I sat and then paced the TV producer's outer office stuffed with ladies who called themselves actresses. Shit! What a bitch! I'm not up for this one. It was two weeks later, time to go back to work, my first appointment since the hit on the head and I was angry, very angry, and tender and ornery having lived these weeks hangin' out on the end of a cactus branch in my very own desert of hot days and cold nights and primordial crawlies invading my bedsheets.

The *bitch!* I thought. *SHE*—another actress—was sitting in reception and *SHE*—another actress—had already auditioned and *SHE* had asked a bleary secretary if she could use the phone in a room filled with actresses who had not yet read, who were studying their scripts, preparing their minds, relaxing their bodies, while *SHE THE BITCH* called her agent, her manager, her service, and a friend. Full voiced, in tones that could fill a coliseum, she'd called her agent, her manager, her service, and a friend, distracting me and the others, mind-fucking the room, shaking concentration, misusing a work space meant for professionals. The bitch! I thought.

"The bitch!" I said in my loudest stage whisper, and retreated to the corner near an air conditioner. It was hard enough driving all the way down there, all the way from the beach to downtown Hollywood in the middle of rush hour for a 5:10 appointment to audition for the part of a lady lawyer at 5:10 my ass, I'd been made to wait, they were running late, I'd been placed toward the end of a half day of readings, asked to read for the role of a lawyer in a sitcom I liked, if you can believe it! a part for which I was perfectly suited, attractive, literate, witty, womanly, a part I'd played five billion times before (dear Christ, when did it end, these readings for everything, when did you prove you could act, you were pretty, you had a track record better than theirs).

I was hot and thirsty and perfect for the part and my hands were shaking. Why were my hands shaking?

It was hard enough finding Gower Studios:

"Where the hell is that?" I had asked my agent, pushing his patience, he was busy, pushing my luck, my head was hurting.

"Oh, you know, Carol, it's been there for years!"

"You mean Columbia Pictures, the original lot?"

"I don't know, Carol. Was that Columbia?"

"I don't know, Bob, I'm asking you!"

"It used to be Desi-Lu."

"Then that was Columbia." I hadn't told my agent what had happened to me. Why should he know? Six weeks had gone by and I was ready to work!

It was hard enough finding a place to park when there

was no parking out on the street and no drive-on pass into the studio proper, fuck the actors, let 'em walk, fuck the actors, let 'em search. Nothing changes in Hollywood. The "big boys" treat actors as mongoloid children who often create the most charming mud pies, until actors hit big and make heaps of money and the "big boys" kiss ass and send a limousine.

It was hard enough! without encountering a bitch.

I was scared. I was dizzy. I was short on breath. I had rested all day, they'd sent over the script the night before, I'd had time to prepare, if you call overnight time and I don't but who cared (this business sucked, this fast-food acting), I had parked legally, why was I hot? It was cold. I was hot.

My name was announced or rather mispronounced by the bleary secretary sitting at the desk. "Two *s*'s," I said. "The name is *Rossen*," and I made an entrance into the office.

I knew the director. The producer knew me. We chatted a bit. They were quite pleasant.

"It's been a long time!" The first line was theirs.

"Yes, it has, that's true! This is really quite a room!"

"Yes, it is, it is. What's left of old Hollywood. It was Harry Cohn's office!"

"Was it really!" I said. "Any ghosts I must meet?" My father had sat here some thirty years back.

The sun streamed into my eyes. Their backs were to the sun. The sun was in my eyes. Their ace. My move.

"Shall we read?" I said.

"Whenever you're ready."

"Let's do it," I said, and rose to my feet. "I'll nod when I'm ready for the line, my cue."

I heard the words come out of my mouth. I heard spaces of silence before lines of words that came out of my mouth. There were spaces and sounds and a garble of words. I couldn't link up the words to my mind. I couldn't force focus the story line. I couldn't remember the beginning of a sentence.

146

I considered myself the professional's professional. I would stand on my head and spit wooden nickels up and down Fifth Avenue if that was required to make a scene work. Concentration was a given. That's what I was paid for. That was *The Method*. That was *Technique*. That's what I'd been taught in Strasberg's classes, a variety of tools that allowed one to focus in the midst of disaster, in the eye of a hurricane, in the middle of a theater, or in Harry Cohn's office.

My mind flashed back to the basics of acting, the what-why-and-when of scene analysis, hoping that might ground my nerves and steady concentration and bring me back to the reading of this script:

CONTENT: a woman bantering with a man in an elevator, flirting, kidding, making a date
INTENT: connecting, dinner that night
DEGREE OF DIFFICULTY: easy, I'd done that before, hundreds of ways, thousands of times

if I could remember what I'd just thought.

I couldn't remember what I'd thought. Perhaps I could use the subtext of *this* meeting in *this* office right *this* minute.

CONTENT: an actress bantering with possible employers
INTENT: connecting, getting the job
DEGREE OF DIFFICULTY: negligible, presuming some chemistry, and they were quite charming and I felt welcome

if I could remember where I was.

I wasn't at the meeting. I'd slipped inward somehow. My body had left. I couldn't sit. I couldn't stand. False moves. Aborted. Contrived. Amateurish.

My words fell to the floor, short-circuited thrustings. I'd been fried in inadequacy. Executed. I couldn't do what I'd done all my life. I'd managed, but I hadn't. I couldn't act. I couldn't work.

"Thank you very much, Carol." We all shook hands.

"Good luck with the project." I wouldn't explain.

147

I wept my way home. Humiliated. Exhausted. Very exhausted. Impotent. Crippled. The freeways work well for self-flagellation.

Why did you go? I demanded of me.

How did I know? was the answer.

You knew damn well!

I felt fine at home!

But not with people. *Never* with groups. And not when I needed to complete a sentence. I couldn't remember the ends of sentences. I was dumb and dead and stared off into space when any demand was put upon me.

I know I know I know so what? I've got no time for these lingering symptoms. The world doesn't crave to know my excuses! The world spun on while I had a baby. The world spun on while I tripped on my marriage. The world went round and it's time to catch up! I'd whipped myself as far as the beach.

I'd lost a copy of my will I had in my hands. I'd lost a trust deed placed in my purse by my lawyer. I'd lost my favorite sweater and forgotten its color, I'd lost a pair of reading glasses and four sets of house keys, although my friend who'd been raped said that was pretty good, better than wrecking two cars in two weeks, which is what she'd done after she'd been assaulted.

Good God, maybe I've lost my mind and never never never will I know peace. And be all right.

The telephone rang as I entered the house.

"The reading was fine but they knew there was a problem," my agent reported just before dinner.

"They were kind," I said. "They were very generous. Children flunk kindergarten for that performance." And I explained to him about "my problem."

A girlfriend of mine, an English actress, had been raised in London dodging German rockets. She had an eye for bomb shelters and a flair for privacy. Her advice might be useful. I phoned her that night.

"Maybe I should have my agent tell them I'm getting over mononucleosis and I'm still weak. I don't want them to think I'm having a nervous breakdown," I said.

"Oh, I wouldn't do that," she said.

"Why wouldn't you do that?" I said.

"Why would you do *that*?" she said.

"Please, Antoinette, don't be civil."

"I would tell them that you've been mugged!"

"Why, dear God, would you tell them that?"

"Well, they needn't know the *whole* story. Just tell them you've been mugged! Everyone's been mugged. They'll understand."

"Just tell them I've been mugged?"

"Yes, tell them you were mugged a few weeks ago and it all came back at you and you're *terribly* sorry."

"That's a good idea."

"Why bother with mononucleosis?"

"Just tell them I've been mugged."

I told them I'd been mugged but I didn't want to.

"You understand, Margaret, if I give in to my tears, if I lose control, I may never find my way back to sanity. If I really relive it, if I let myself feel it, if I stop for a moment and not keep moving, this time, Margaret, he may destroy me!" Margaret had suggested we meet twice a week.

"Are you so alone? You sound so lonely. Is there no one with whom you can share these feelings? No friends? No family?" Margaret asked.

"People don't want to hear this pain! Nobody needs to hear this pain!" Margaret agreed. People *were* fearful. Margaret was blurry. Margaret a whisper. My temples burned and my face expanded and the memory of blood dribbled down my face, whenever I spoke with Margaret about it, whenever, any time, everywhere, in the market.

"Don't you see, Margaret! I can't stop this!"

One morning the next week they changed Margaret's space, moved her upstairs to floor eleven at the very end of its narrow hallway, a low-ceilinged hall, of closed doors and hidden destinies, moved her into a small windowless room, a no-exit room in a no-exit hallway, and I said to her, "Margaret, if you have to stay in this office, if I have to meet with you here, then I can't come to see you anymore. Christ, this is the center, they should know better! I can't come to this floor! I can't sit in this box! I can't, that's all!"

Margaret changed her office space.

Oh, well, fiddle-dee-dee! That's what they said in *Gone With the Wind*, but I can't remember if it was Vivien Leigh or Butterfly McQueen who has the line. It makes a difference but I can't remember. Fiddle-dee-dee! I won't think about it! Tara was charred but I'll rise again! I'd give the greatest live performance of normalcy the world had ever seen and if I convinced the world, I'd convince me. Acting is believing! (That's what they say in all of the books.)

You *are* whatever you can imagine!

I lunch with a friend in a garden restaurant, out in the sunlight and open spaces.

"It's incredible, Carol! You seem so well."

"Let's shop," I said. "Let's spend some money."

I read my books for hours on end, as pussycat paws pound my body.

"That's good," said Margaret. "Most victims can't do that."

I arrange sleep-over dates in my daughter's bed.

"That's okay, Mommy, just don't tell anybody."

I attend a concert and avoid the theater and write of the moment the man had hit me. I remembered, relived it, and I was still breathing.

Still my nerves stretched piano-string raw.

Still my body disobeyed me.

It was beginning to occur to me I'd been wounded somehow and I should lie in some corner and lick my wounds. It

150

was beginning to occur to me this wasn't a scary movie like *The Stepford Wives* or *The Fury*, movies I'd done and roles I'd been paid for.

It was beginning to occur to me these symptoms were *me*. I was a victim! That word meant *me*!

The police referred to me as the "victim" from Will Rogers.

Margaret was a therapist at the *victim* center.

My medical bills would be processed through the L.A. City Attorney *Victim*-Witness Assistance Program.

I WAS A VICTIM. It made me sick to my stomach. I wanted absolutely nothing to do with that person, which was hardly a problem, for like my keys and my sweater, I lost the thought.

A few weeks later, after my "I've been mugged!" confession, I looked up the word in *Webster's Collegiate Dictionary.*

victim /'vik-təm/ n (L *victima;* akin to OHG *wīh* holy, Skt *vinakti* he sets apart) 1: a living being sacrificed to a deity or in the performance of a religious rite 2: someone injured, destroyed, or sacrificed under any of various conditions 3: someone tricked or duped

Reader's choice: 1. a living being sacrificed to a deity or in the performance of a religious rite

Now, that was my favorite.

I couldn't work as an actress for over a year.

Black silk stockings and a garter belt

Superman was what I had in mind. Superman leaving his underground spa in Palm Springs, hands ever outstretched, reaching for me, cape flapping in a permanent press, streaking past Disneyland, topping the Bonaventure Hotel in

151

downtown L.A., circling for a moment the Music Center, and sweeping out west toward Saks Beverly Hills, crossing the fields of UCLA (and smiling down upon their football team), crossing Brentwood and Santa Monica and then into the sycamore and wild oaks and eucalyptus stationed like armies about the Palisades and through those trees gliding into my home and gathering me, like wildflowers, into his arms, plucking me out from behind my typewriter and cradling me away as he'd done to Margot Kidder except this time I'd been cast as the real Lois Lane.

That's what I had in mind, or any variation on that theme. Call me romantic, but from the night of the pizza caper, that evening of roaming adolescent boys and my terror in the middle of the night, from that evening on, for at least two weeks, whenever I had a moment, I indulged the fantasy. I would do anything to shield me from me.

For example: the letter I wrote to Patrick. I wrote the same letter to David. The exact same letter. The exact same night. I did that. I changed the beginning and the end, it was only seemly, but basically it was the same letter. And well you might ask why. Why not? 'Twas a good letter, methinks, it explored my feelings, I could not have said it better, and to be honest, I didn't think Patrick would answer that letter. Patrick was not obsessively Christian. From his point of view, it was far better to receive. I *hoped* Patrick would answer, but I didn't think he would, at least not quickly, and I needed Superman right away. He who showed up wearing a tight blue T-shirt with a stenciled red *S* across his chest was my man, within FDA guidelines, and David *had* called, the week after I returned from the hospital, and left a message on my machine:

"This is David. I just want to know if you're all right!" *Click.* That was the message, short but angry. I knew that he cared. I returned his call.

"Hi!"

"How *are* you?"

"I'm fine. Feeling better. I came home on Saturday."

152

"I've been calling!" he said.

"Have you? I never got the message!"

"I didn't leave one! I got the machine!"

"Then how can I know?"

"I hate talking to machines!"

"Nobody's listening. *I* live here."

"When can I see you?"

"Next week, at the office. Are you coming to town?"

"Only on a day when your phones won't be ringing."

"I'll call you next week when I'm sure of my schedule."

"I'll talk to you then. And I'll write you a letter."

"Just bring your body."

"I've got so much to say!"

"Say it in person."

"Okay, I won't write." We sounded a bit like a thirties comedy, all bouncy and hidden, covering the cover and enter Billie Burke.

He cared a great deal. I sent David the same letter I sent to Patrick without a moment's hesitation. *That* man wanted *me*! What he *wanted* with me wasn't clear, but hell! he might save me the trouble of drowning in pain and stop up the dike and whisk me away. And put his arms about me and let me lean a bit. I'd try to overlook the presence of his wife.

David was responsive. He called me the day he received the letter, that Wednesday after my sister had left and I'd started to see Margaret twice a week.

"I have to tell you it took three readings to understand your letter."

"Did it really?" I was a failure.

"You're some strange combination of Spinoza and Camus."

"Is that contagious? I've never read Spinoza."

"But you've read Camus."

"My obsession in college."

"I bet it was." I wasn't following well.

"You're deeper than Spinoza. It's very frightening."

153

"Please don't say that, David. I got enough problems already."

"No, baby. I'm sorry. I mean I think you're a pantheist."

"Define it for me. I can't remember."

"You find God everywhere around you in Nature."

"Yeah, I guess."

"It must have disturbed you when you read the Midas legend and each time he touched something it turned to gold."

"I wasn't thinking that well in those days," I said. I wasn't thinking well now! Were we making a date?

"I'm going to write *you* a letter."

"Please do!" I said.

"No, I'd rather hear your voice."

"I'd love to get your letter."

"Are you free on Friday? Around eleven?"

"Yeah. That's good."

"I don't think many people would understand that letter."

"I don't write that kind of letter to very many people."

"I'll see you on Friday."

"At eleven. I'll see you." The game had begun, his turf, my ball.

Now *this* was a crisis a girl could get into! This was a genuine, blue ribbon, no-kidding-around crisis! Spinoza shminoza, I had nothing to wear! Skirts and blouses and dresses and sweaters were piled high to my navel across my bed and girl was to meet boy in forty-five minutes!

This was a wonderful crisis, this silk and wool crisis, quite a bit preferable to the paper variety piled cream-pitcher high on the kitchen table of union medical forms and triplicate copies of bills to be filed with the State of California. I'd think about it later! My hair was still wet!

I was late, of course, held up by the shakes and a breathless desire to look Rita Hayworth pretty when I saw David, but my eyeliner smeared and my lipstick smudged and my hair went strange and the detective phoned in the midst of

154

dressing. They had a suspect who'd been extradited to another state. Would I look at his picture later today or perhaps on Monday? "Monday will be fine, if it's fine for you," I said to the voice over the phone.

The face of death would not pollute this day.

It seemed years since I'd thought of black silk stockings and a garter belt, a month since I'd thought of myself as sexual and wanting to be touched and trusting that intimacy.

We'd just talk, of course. That was more than enough.

David's office was located on the twenty-third floor of a black-brown steeple in an urban complex known as Century City, read Emerald City, read green for money, L.A.'s re-creation of a Greek city-state devoutly devoted to corporate services in the legal and accounting sector of the economy, with a soupçon of Hollywood thrown in for color. A studio here. A network there. And a movie house and a theater and a Playboy Club. Metropolis couldn't have sparkled better. Columns of glass, triangular, round, rectangular, square, towers of gray, of bronze, of silver steel glitterings, and the occasional liquid beige marble structure were set off by planters and hexagon plazas, wind tunnels that billowed secretarial skirts. Under the everywhere limestone flooring slept the cement-papered graveyard of dozing cars, an air-conditioned catacomb of parallel spaces, of neoned signs and alphabet levels spiraling downward and arrows pointing to the right to the left. Redford had shot his Watergate film here, here in the bowels of this anywhere complex, filmed the scenes between Woodward and Hal as Deep Throat in a half-lit deserted parking structure. Redford had been smart. He'd captured the horror. I was not. I ran from my car, mindless with fright.

I ran to the orange squared D-level escalator, up out of the darkness into the light, into the glassed-in marble spaces, into the red-runnered Hearstian hallway, into the arms of a brushed-steel elevator, through a giant oak doorway and into his office. I was safe, here in his office.

Bodies and mouths and arms and faces crowded about me and touched me gently, bodies of women, of female executives and secretarial ladies who greeted and kissed and hugged and stroked good health and sweet feelings into my soul. I stood at reception waiting for David, stood to the right of a seating area crammed with writers and agents waiting to be seen, waiting to hustle their clients and stories, wondering who was this lady being loved in their midst, the she blushing with giggles, undoing decorum in the corporate offices of this Century City motion-picture studio. I laughed and felt needed and didn't weep, laughed but felt small, very tiny and vulnerable, as a half-dozen mothers tended one wobbly girl.

David opened the door and stood in the entry that led to his office and other offices and he was oxford shirted and gray-flannel trousered and V-neck sweatered. He was everyone's kid brother who never understood how adorable he was to his sister's girlfriends. He held open the door and smiled at me and I said, quite slowly, "It's awfully hot in this room" and broke from the cluster of mothering friends. I walked through the door and into the hallway, passing by David holding the door, never looking at David but gently brushing, tracing my fingers across his middle.

I stood in the center of his office. He entered behind me and closed the door. He walked to me slowly and gently embraced me. "Be careful," I said, "my left cheek is still funny."

I sat in the seat reserved for the anxious. He sat facing me from behind his desk.

"Your office looks nice."

"Thank you," he said.

"Do you water the plants?"

"No, a service does it."

"Oh," I said, "the plants look good!" There was silence.

"Do I look all right?"

"You look beautiful, Carol."

"I had trouble getting dressed. My stockings are twisted." I looked at my legs. We looked at each other.

"I'm hungry," he said. "Where do you want to eat?"

"I didn't know we were having lunch."

156

"Neither did I. What do you want to eat?"

"You," I said.

"No," he said, and he rose and walked toward me and raised me out of my chair and we stood face to face. "No." And his hand slipped through the slit in my skirt and he was touching my thighs, touching me, and I was palming his belly, palming his hips, but we'd barely touched and now we weren't as we moved toward the door, on the run out the door to more neutral territory and the silence of crowds and more open spaces.

He cradled my arm and we ran away, through the halls and reception and down the down elevator, all the while fending off businesspeople, executives and agents who had something to say, who wished his attention talking grosses and numbers, and he nodded politely and exchanged a few words and held my arm tightly and never allowed those interruptions to impede the flow of our escape through gargantuan glass revolving doors into the beige marbled hexagon sun-drenched plaza.

I breathed deeply and anchored my arm to his back, my left hand clung to his sweatered shoulder. His arm circled my waist as we walked in the warmth.

"Glad to be alive?"

"Yes," I said. My breast crowded his side, our thighs crowded each other.

"Where would you like to eat?"

"You decide."

Wildflowers and daisies in fragile glass pitchers graced each of the pink-clothed dining tables. We stood in a room within a room of walnut panels, distinguished by archways and hidden corners and a roseate light refracting the pinkness, a pink gelled light that blended all lines of stress and time. We were in Italy. Perhaps Florence. Perhaps Venice.

David managed to charm the hostess into giving us a table where there was no table, in a room filled with tables that had been reserved. We had no reservation. We sat down at our table and smiled at each other. A less-than-charming waiter demanded our drink order and after I'd requested a white wine spritzer I said to David, "He's not very charming."

"If he bothers you I'll kill him," David said, and I laughed and he smiled and I began to recount four weeks' worth of stories. I spoke of animal instincts and Mr. Fatutto ("He said, 'This *always* happens,' I couldn't believe it!") and David spoke of the problems mounting a project and I clung to the details of my operation and we traded "can you top this?" adolescent pranks. We laughed and spun buckets of long-winded yarns and never looked away from each other's eyes and never noticed the waiter again. David mentioned two ladies with whom he was working, lady producers I had known as actresses, and I said:

"Don't be too charming or they'll fall in love with you."

"You're in love with me." The walls bent inward.

"Yes," I whispered. I hadn't meant to say that. I meant to say nothing or Don't you think you should wait until I say that to you? I was hot and frightened.

"Yes," I whispered.

"And I'm in love with you. I'm in love with your mind and how you think." He forgot my eyes! He forgot my body!

"I'm in love with *your* mind and how *you* think!" I shot through the daisies, scattering wildflowers. Such categories, hesitation, such fine distinctions! Two overeducated cowards sat lunching in pink, a man and a woman flirting with feeling, who'd never learned how to say anything simply.

There was a silence as he fed me his food, Carpaccio forkfuls off his plate. I played with my salad. We looked at each other.

"I don't know how you fit into my life."

"I know," I said. "I know," I repeated. Cosmic lunacy. Cupid was cock-eyed. "Must we wait to make love while you figure it out?"

"No, we can make love, but that's not what I said."

158

"I know," I said. "I know," I repeated. "Perhaps we shouldn't see each other."

"You'd never say that line in a movie, Carol." His eyes were laughing.

"You're right. I wouldn't. It's too on the nose." And I kissed his hand. I wasn't leaving.

"I've got so much to say and I don't know how to," he said. "Will you read a book that means everything to me, and then you'll understand and you'll tell me what to do. Maybe you'll tell me to go to Barstow and buy a bag of potatoes and bring you one every night."

I laughed. I was dizzy. "That sounds right," I said. I'd not understood a word he'd spoken.

"What will you do?" he asked. I stared. "I know," he said, "there's nothing you can do."

"You are so beautiful, do you know that, David?" I'd avoid the point, whatever it was.

"Movie stars are beautiful," he said, and paid the bill.

David's book was out of stock at the adjacent bookstore. I promised to find it that afternoon after I left him at his office. We walked the plaza as slowly as possible, reversing all systems to accommodate gravity, dragging our feet, pressing our bodies against each other, or those parts of our bodies permissible to press in such a public viewing place, his elbow to my breast, hips and thighs glued tight. He commented on the fullness of my breast and how he loved to press against it with his elbow and I commented on his elbow and how much I loved it as it rubbed against my breast, pressing it gently. We walked in silence to the elevator and up to his office where my ticket was stamped. I stood at reception as he vanished through doors. I left to find D level way down under.

Quarters and nickels and copper pennies poured out of my pocket onto the seat as I slid into my navy-blue pumpkin chariot, a handful of coins left over from lunch. He'd given

159

it to me. "I hate change," he had said. Superman would have shared the same problem, what with tights and no pockets on his hips.

However conflicted were his interests, however conscience-tortured, David had managed to transport me to my preferred destination of Neverland, to the farthest green pastures within the Beverly Hills city limits, and I rested there smelling the flowers and chomping on clover well into the next day when I was to meet up with my ranger, Tucker. We'd scheduled a trail walk for that Saturday morning, Tucker's day off, he thought that was best. We would hike the mountain up to Inspiration Point, just Tucker and me and my tape recorder. Yesterday's love mist had doused all my anxieties and ram-rodded my courage and I was fearless as I retraced my tracks up the gravel trail, memory marking the moments, measuring recollection with geomorphic fact and taping Tucker's recollections of St. Valentine's Day. Love had conquered my nervous system, with an assist, in this instance, from the gun Tucker sported, a most reassuring assist strapped to his thigh, allowing thoughts to be thought and heights to be scaled with Einstein-like accuracy and freedom.

It wasn't until we reached the rock, or the cluster of rocks at the site of the assault, that I left those green pastures of love perfuming my path, releasing armfuls of sweet peas and daffodils, rejecting the last forkful of David's Carpaccio, and was jarred into time, that time, that reality, that retelling of horror. It wasn't until Tucker pointed to the blood on the rocks, dark gray, light brown, maroonish blotches, blotches on the rocks—my blood on the rocks—that I crashed into Saturday and stood on my shadow. Bloody rocks indeed! That was me smeared about! As well as strands of my hair, fragile cobwebs of gold, still caught in the brush, the four-foot wild oak that coated the mountain he'd shoved me down.

"These are new tracks," Tucker said, indicating foot-prints leading down the incline down under the brush. "They weren't here a few days ago when I was here last."

160

"Do you think they're his?" Unbelievable dialogue.

"I'm pretty sure. No one else would know where this spot is. No one else would climb down this incline. He came back to see if your body's still here."

"Pissed off at no press? It never hit the papers."

"Yeah, these are new. He came back to check."

I took one of the rocks, a small three-inch rock, which lay on the roadside in the gully, one of the rocks smeared with my blood. I wanted to have it. I'd store it with the keys. Tucker said he thought that was all right.

The warmth of David's love had evaporated.

I had bought David's book on Friday, the day before, and called him, just as he'd asked me to, the very same day as soon as I'd read the first two pages. I'd read the first five pages.

I was hooked.

The name of the book was *Still Life with Woodpecker* by Tom Robbins and it was, by the author's admission, "sort of a love story," as much of a love story as the last quarter of the twentieth century could sustain. Love stories were not in flower these days. I could speak to that.

The heroine of the piece was Princess Leigh Cheri, a retired cheerleader, a moon-struck social activist, a tragic beauty who had sequestered herself in an attic to contemplate the meaning of the Camel pack. I immediately identified with the princess.

The hero, or antihero, was Bernard Mickey Wrangle, or he known as Woodpecker, David's would-be double, a sixties radical, a conscientious objecter who blew up draft boards and induction centers during the last days of the Vietnam War, a man intent on one last bombing, a resurrection of feelings, a revival of juicier juices. The book was devoted to their passionate pursuit of the meaningful, their uncharted meanderings in search of an answer to "the only one serious question: how to make love stay?"

I was hooked.

I possessed David's book, my weekend lover, but not

David, for David was somewhere else. David didn't call on Saturday or Sunday or Monday of that weekend, nor did he hang up on my machine. Not that I expected to hear from him. We'd arranged to speak at the beginning of the week and we would do so, I knew, I hoped, I felt sure. I hadn't *expected* him to call but I *needed* him to call. I needed to be held, I needed to be cared for, I needed in fact to be swallowed whole and perhaps piggyback carried and suckled at his breast. I needed. And his silence terrified me. I felt alone, if not lonely, at risk in the world. I was my everything to me, lover/mother/companion, and I was nothing, and there was nothing. I tossed about in that terror and pushed on with my life.

Jimmy followed Tucker in the taping order that Saturday, for he'd agreed to meet for a couple of hours. I thought *he* might know what had happened to me and if the words didn't stick in my tissue-paper brain I would absorb them sometime later. He said he didn't mind my tape recorder. We met at the house and sat in the kitchen. Jimmy had a beer. I had wine. I showed him my rock and we began.

I was shocked when I heard how badly I'd been beaten.

The interview lasted an hour and a half and when finished, when madness was recorded and stored for some purpose, I dove into David's book as though it were arms and he was with me again in a patch of green pasture, hidden in tall grasses, holding me, rocking me, tending my wounds. I read into the evening, lost in tall grasses, smoking and reading until it was midnight and I'd finished David's book. The dogs were asleep. I was exhausted.

Sunday's silence withered me. I read the mail and paid the bills and lost the day somewhere in my room.

I called David on Monday. I called him at the end of a chock-a-block day when sensibilities had dulled with daytime tedium, at that time of day when I might not cry, after viewing mugshots *chez moi* with my detective. The man wasn't my man. He belonged to another. Someone else was lucky. It wasn't my turn.

I called David at the very end of that Monday, at four-fifteen, a dog-worn hour, and reported that the answer to his question where did I fit into his life was that I didn't.

"The book's filled with passion. Where's yours?" I said, by which I meant where were you this weekend?

I did not mention my resolve, made with morning coffee, not to see people anymore as I feared my obsessiveness and vulnerability would only chase them away.

I did not mention that I could not afford the enforced silence implicit in this affair, for that silence was terrifying to me. As terrifying to me as had been the silence of the man on the mountain.

I did not mention I feared that his silence, like the man on the mountain's, might be filled with rage and I couldn't bear the pain of wondering.

I did not mention these feelings because I felt ashamed and afraid of letting any man that close. Rather, I attacked him, before he attacked me, and gave up, for the while, romantic delusions.

Mother Mary, please embrace me

My friends weren't buying neuroses that season. The unmitigated pain of my separateness was not a value they'd support no matter how many days I hid under the covers. That was not what friends were for, and despite my resolve to hold tight and fly solo, they would be known (despite barbed wire), they would telephone-catch me by the ear or know the reason why and arrive unannounced. The news had leaked, as news will do, and I was glad for the leak and glad for their friendship, and glad *they* had to make the call and begin whatever there was to say, which always began with a great sigh and "My God, Carol, why didn't you call?" And I would tell them I'd not the strength or desire to deal with reactions of horror and tears and there was nothing they might do or say except be my friends and talk to me now. And get me out from undercover.

They were there, my friends, and they were kind. They took me to movies, or they asked me to dinner, and they invited me into their home of an evening, or they sent me books that might distract, although one friend of mine, a Sarah Lou graduate, mentioned a book by Bettelheim about the nature of survival and who did and didn't in Hitler's Germany, would I be interested? I thought not. I'd get to that book sometime in the future. My despair brimmed the pot. I couldn't tolerate more.

Nothing about my condition offended. They seemed not to mind my drippy eyes and manic laughter, or shielding me from the boogeyman who waited for me all over the city and in my garage late at night. Rather, it seemed, these comings together felt creamier rich than in other times, or mine was a new awareness of texture, a new kind of sharing, a connection rooted in unseen energies, empathies, meshing, weaving, an engagement intensely felt and received that hadn't to do with neediness. I'd lived to learn to be in the moment. Those few hours were the flowers of my spring.

And there was Hal, who was there without being asked, who called almost every day while he was on the road and the day of surgery and he sent flowers, and quite often after he would phone from somewhere and we would talk family and feelings, both his and mine. Valentine violence had melted the frost that gently coated our estrangement, a joyful dividend untinged by sadness.

One day, soon after he returned and I'd refused to climb back on stage, he took me to lunch at Jimmy's Restaurant, a latter-day Stork Club minus high society but heavy on the bar and exclusivity. I was overwhelmed by its pomp and posh, and I asked if we could sit outside on the terrace out in the open since the lush beige banquettes and chinois floral wallpaper upset my sense of self—they seemed alive, as if they might eat *me* for lunch. It was cold outside, I was out of season, but the coolness lowered the heat of my anxiety. I cried as I shared my vulnerability, sure that Hal could hear it, knowing the limits of our commitment, and I sensed his tears as we hugged good-bye. I had to go home and go to bed. Exhausted again. And I needed to cry, and then cry again.

My friends had offered their love and support. I had been graced. My life was peopled and still every shadow and every sound and every space threatened my being, threatened my heart, and gobbled up trust, a cancer gone wild. The air I breathed was perfumed with violence. I lived in another dimension. Alone.

Just west of the UCLA campus, on the north side of Sunset Boulevard, across the street from UES, the University Elementary School where I had been a member of the first graduating class, right there directly in front of speeding cars bearing into the hairpin turn bending west, recessed in an alcove twenty feet high made of multicolored California stone, there He stands, there stands Jesus, fronting the entrance of Marymount High School. Giant redwoods and weeping willows and eucalyptus and sycamore trees shelter Him from the quivering heat rising up from the pavement like jiggling Jell-O, a lacy green canopy that in the sunlight serves to enhance the force of his presence. Even in darkness He isn't diminished for headlights will cause His whiteness to shimmer, hands and arms uplifted, the beckoning one.

You can't miss Him anyway, He's a very friendly Savior, erected in honor of the Sacred Heart of Jesus, King of the Highways. Did you know that? I never did till I read the plaque just to the right by the kneeling bench. He's stood there, in traffic, since the mid-1950s, arms outstretched in welcome, in love and in kindness, the folds of his robe gently lapping over and around and at the base of his body as cars skid in and out of the curve.

Actually, for years I thought He was Mother Mary, as I hurtled like a rocket in the company of meteorites down the

165

boulevard fifty miles an hour. *Mary*mount High School, Mother Mary, I thought. Word associations. My ignorance showing. Perhaps I might be excused, after all, for most of us travelers sped by so quickly that one received only the sketchy impression of long hair, long robes, and delicate features.

Ten promises had been made by the Sacred Heart of Jesus to Saint Margaret Mary Alacoque, or so it is writ beneath the statue. I WILL BE THEIR REFUGE, begins the fifth vow, DURING LIFE AND ESPECIALLY AT THE HOUR OF DEATH. I wasn't surprised when I read those words, for my instincts had whispered for quite some time that "Mother Mary" might offer a peaceful pause, a sweetpea sleep, clinging to stone.

And every day as I sped down Sunset, returning home from an evening at dinner with friends, or a ballet stretch class, or having seen a movie, I thought perhaps I'd not make the turn and jump the curb and drive straight ahead and curl up within Her concrete embrace, crawl into those arms and stay there forever.

It's amazing how little mothers know about their daughters

My girlfriend Dolores, my tried and true and good girlfriend Dolores, had flown out to Los Angeles ostensibly to see two of her four daughters who currently lived in the West. That's what she said. That was the reason given when she arrived in Los Angeles from New York City six weeks after I had been assaulted.

I almost believed her. She did fly to this coast twice a year, once in the spring and once in the fall, to visit with her daughters and tend to their bruises. They were freshly in the world, these two out of four daughters, and still needful of hot chocolate and Mercurochrome and Band-Aids. Or perhaps it was a new wardrobe they secretly desired. Whatever it was, Dolores was more than happy to comply. She was by nature and inclination a loving, caring mother.

Hence my reservations. Knowing her temperament and

character and unforgivable decency, I had good reason to suspect her mission to be double pronged, that she'd flown West to mother me as well as her daughters, to take a good look at this wreck of the Hesperus and see for herself what the madman had wrought to make sure I hadn't crumbled into billions of pieces. The how of how she might shore up my fractured psyche had yet to be conceived but never you mind. Mothers as well as children believe in kisses as magic, winged healers that bind the all of everything hurting. She'd kiss my knees and elbows if that were required.

Dolores would try another tack. First, we had lunch. Then we went shopping. It went like this:

Early Monday morning, after arriving and spending the weekend with her daughters, Dolores called and said, "I don't think I have to spend all my time with them, do you?"

"No," I said.

"I can take some time for myself, with my friend, don't you think?"

"Yes," I said.

"After all, they have their lives, they have their work and their friends, and what am I going to do, sit here until they come home for dinner? They'll only worry about me and I'm perfectly fine."

"I think you should come over here right now," I said.

"Good," she said, "because Laura can drop me off on her way to work and we can do something or nothing if you're busy with your writing. What *are* you writing?"

"I'm not sure exactly. The day it all happened. But to hell with that! Let's eat and go shopping in Beverly Hills!" Any port in the storm was the port I'd in mind.

"Fine," Dolores said, "and I'll spend the night." She'd have plenty of time to examine her patient in all the many lights of the day and the evening.

Lunch was divine. We ate Italian antipasto and drank wine and espresso and spent hundreds of dollars on clothes I'd never wear. *I* spent hundreds of dollars, vacation mad-money, as Dolores smiled on and declined the temptation as she had for thirty years while supporting Mr. Wrong. Nothing in her background promoted such extravagance, for even as one of America's top fashion models—they'd named airplanes *Dolores* during World War II—she'd worked and mothered and cooked every dinner and never splurged on clothes and indulged her fancies. And now, as the wife of the good second husband who wished to support her in ways she'd never known, Dolores demurred and sweetly swallowed her background as I spent eight hundred dollars on clothes for the closet, Dolores nodding and reassuring that "They look great on you! Not for me, I wear beige and I live in the city, but they look great on you! Go ahead and buy!"

She was a good mother. I was very happy. I felt like a girl with a prom in my future.

High on extravagance and careless hours, we drifted homeward only to find a script waiting for me at my front door, a pilot for a sitcom about a lady lawyer, my first appointment since I'd been assaulted. I'd have to audition. I'd have to dress. I'd have to drive to downtown Hollywood. Gower Studios? Where was that? The great pleasure of the day was fritzed in an instant as my body began to shake and my mind went fuzzy, rice pudding proof if ever there was one that one must grab at happiness and not wait a moment for lunch to be digested. Angst awaits on your own front stoop.

Dolores said she didn't mind at all sitting on the patio and reading the paper as I studied my script and talked to myself, locked in the darkness of my shuttered bedroom. Dinner was somehow prepared with her help for I was useless in those early-evening hours, distraught and distressed by the possibility I might not be ready for tomorrow's reading, I might not remember my words or thoughts. The idea I'd been crippled was so inconceivable and yet ever-present as I studied my script that I pummeled it senseless by three hours of rehearsal, talking to walls, propped up in my bed.

And I was great in my bed. The chandelier loved me. My mind is liquid fire, I thought to myself.

"Dinner!" cried Dolores. I felt quite secure.

168

"Dolores," I said as we sat drinking coffee, Eve long gone from the supper table, "would you mind very much watching a television show with me? It's on tonight, it's this PBS special about Bianchi . . . the Hillside Murderer? I'm sure it's gory but I really want to watch it."

"No," said Dolores, "I'll watch it with you."

"I mean, I'm scared to death to watch it alone otherwise I wouldn't ask you to watch it with me but I really want to watch it. I hope you don't mind."

"No, I'll watch it with you," Dolores said.

FRONTLINE: THE MIND OF A MURDERER, PART I flashed on the screen, followed by a loose close-up of the series' anchor, Judy Woodruff.

There was no music. She began:

> Good evening. I'm Judy Woodruff.
>
> As unpleasant as it is to hear, mass murders are on the rise in this country. The Justice Department says that in the last decade there have been at least thirty mass killers . . . and that each of them murdered at least six people.
>
> These gruesome numbers raise disturbing questions. What sort of man is Charles Manson . . . or Son of Sam? Are they insane? That's sometimes the defense if they come to trial . . . and it's one that is increasingly controversial.
>
> Tonight on "Frontline," a remarkable event. For the first time, you can journey with psychiatrists as they try to get inside the mind of a mass murderer— Kenneth Bianchi, the man who came to be known as the Hillside Strangler.
>
> Bianchi looked like an all-American boy, but he was involved in the murders of at least ten women in Los Angeles and two more in Washington State.

After his arrest, Bianchi took on the behavior of a multiple personality, and four experts concluded he was insane. But was he?

I couldn't look at the bodies. I turned away when they showed them.

When the program was over, I turned off the set and sat down across from Dolores at the kitchen table and began to cry. And I said to Dolores:

"The fucking bastard, he left their bodies, the women's bodies, in the bushes, and the world is debating whether he's a sexual psychopath or a fucking multiple personality. I wish they'd taken one of those fucking therapists who were debating the question and dragged him into the bushes left for dead. I wish they'd take one of those fucking filmmakers who show blood dribbling from a chandelier or spurting from an artery or oozing out from under an elevator door and leave him for fifteen minutes dragged into the bushes left for dead."

Dolores said nothing. Her eyes were filled with tears.

"Who gives a flying damn what he is or isn't? Fuck him. He's guilty. Kill him. Just kill him."

I got up from the table and walked into the living room. Dolores followed, talking to me. Her voice jammed the clarity of my rage.

"This isn't you talking. You're not yourself. A life for a life isn't right," she said.

"Yeah, I know," I said and shut my mouth. Maybe if I agreed she'd go back to her daughters.

I do not sleep

I was enraged. And I was ashamed of that rage, exhausted by rage hidden from me and from others, hiding, kept hidden, that wave of rage which rolled over my bed in the middle of the night and glued open my mind and glued open my eyes as adrenaline beat up my pulse and my heart.

170

I knew that rage twice, perhaps thrice, quite often, returning, as I did, to my ballet stretch class, when muscles
made slack, no longer taut and strong, jelly-buckled under a
normal workout and I knew the man had done that to me.

I knew that rage, what rage? only once with Margaret,
more often I wept and kept hidden my anger, never felt my
anger, except once with Margaret, only once, when I lost myself in the middle of her building and couldn't remember the
number of her floor or the number of her office or where I'd
put her card or any part of her phone number, and when I
found her that day I raged in her office that the son of a bitch
had done this to me, the son of a bitch had tried to murder
me and I was enraged, spilling over my friends, spilling over
Dolores and no one understood, and I was enraged for before
he had happened I'd been a little happy and the son of a bitch
had taken that from me, and I raged at Margaret for assuming, didn't she? that I was a drunk because "I drink," I said,
and I liked the drinking, damn right I liked it! It let me down
off my rage! And I was ashamed of my rage and felt what?
what rage?

My father had said to me toward the end of his life, "If
you live long enough, UCLA can beat SC." So it was with
Dolores and my liberal conscience. They won in the end, at
least for the season. The quality of mercy must be reconsid-
ered! That was the message I must digest. "Fuck him. He's
guilty. Kill him. Just kill him," I'd said to Dolores and she'd
said to me that such justice was neither humane nor tolerable, and an inner voice agreed, chanting shame and Christian
litanies disturbing my dreams: But for the grace of God go
thee! Turn the other cheek and shut your mouth, Carol.

My rage had scared Dolores. Truth is, it scared me.

Because I do not
Sleep
Through the night
I rock
Through the night

And cradle my soul
With broken arms
And scotch
And pussycat company.

Morning poetry was upon me, Hallmark card, frightened poetry, a blanket of poetry smothering fury. I buried my rage on bits of paper, shallow graves, unmarked, dotting my desk, and I took three aspirin and got on with every day. It was better to bypass that bucket of bile, better to take care of other symptoms, to bind my wounds, adjust my nervous system, accommodate fear, assimilate the experience, relearn how to go to the movies alone 'cause it's dark in the movies and a killer might hide there. It was better to opt for stabilization. Norman Mailer's epigram rang in my ears: "The shits are killing us even as they kill themselves." My lady Innocence had died. I needed time to grieve her.

I cried a great deal. I cried every day.

No, this was not the moment for vengeful rage, and I wrote out a check and joined the temple. "Stay strong," said the rabbi. How to do that? I thought. Stay with the rabbi. Live in his study. This was the moment to withdraw in peace, to write and read and rock-a-by Carol.

Rage is an anathema, a plague is rage. Rage is poison darts, the poison rays of a crisis and how will I feel in the later, in a year when my nerves soften, round, and coexist. Better, far better to spend time collecting evidence, clipping, filing, assembling the data, the proof positive, the proof perfect of what we know already, that sane or insane, temporary or otherwise, Hitler, Stalin, Eichmann, and less celebrated killers in everyday America, Messrs. Manson, Bianchi, and the guy who smashed me must die for their crimes, for the ripping of earth's sanctity. SOCIETY OWES THEM ZIP. THEY OWE SOCIETY.

I write as I sit by my faithful Selectric, a female Karl Marx from her darkened bedroom (the British Museum was too far away), rechecking the thrusts of human history and recording a slightly different conclusion to be postulated in the Pacific Palisades.

The vets understood. They'd OD'd on bestiality. They understood the aura of violence. But no one understood the vets and their feelings, and now I was a veteran of bestiality. How was I to return to this rose-tinted earth? How was I to rejoin the world in progress? How must I wrap my perceptions as one might a house gift given to the hostess before one eats dinner? In pastels, perhaps, or primary colors, but not with psychedelics and never in black. I must formulate an intelligent, rational, establishment thesis regarding the rogue, the human abortion. The world could handle a neat trendy theory that might titillate but didn't offend. Perhaps then I'd be seen as having reached a primal knowing and not as a hysteric who'd lost her cracked crackers. And we'd all live happily ever after.

With the help of scotch and Russian vodka, I spent the next nine months researching my instincts. The "Frontline" transcripts, "Mind of a Murderer," both parts, are sent for posthaste, the first order of business. All media events that address the issue of criminal responsibility are taped and catalogued on a regular basis. Newspapers are scanned for articles that deal with the death penalty in California and how the electorate feels about it. The Santa Monica library becomes a second home as I spend hours in the aisles researching animal kingdoms, how various species handle threats to their survival, how they love and kill, how creation has formed them.

And I collect every article on Vietnam vets.

The more I read the more sure my conclusion:

Human beings have strong-armed their nature in the name of evolution, moving away from their gut, away from instincts, into some distancing, heady haven. Random psychosis in the race has been dismissed as parochial among creatures who believe in their own P.R. as self-appointed demigods high on controls. If there are nut birds out there flying about, blame must be leveled at an indifferent society. If there are nut birds out there massacring the race, blame must be leveled at some crazed picture of a mother who's fashioned a "prevert" in her kitchen. If there are nut birds out there, they've been *misunderstood.* Having established THE BLAME the world is free to believe it can subdue such creatures through rehabilitation; a job, some therapy, and a peanut butter sandwich. The world cubbyholes and tags as "manageable specimens" the insatiable bloodsuckers living among us.

I retype my notes and store the clean copy in letter-size manila heavyweight folders labeled BIANCHI, ANGER, POSSIBLE OPENINGS, OTHER SEGUES, a chapter, perhaps, in the book I'm now writing. I stack them to the right of my bedroom desk and think of penguin creatures and their special sweetness and I wish I were one or could find a mate resembling the male of that dear species.

The files are useless. I would nod off when I read them, exhausted by a diet of mind-fuck and booze. It was a year and a half before rage was resurrected.

Yeah, I was lucky

TRANSCRIPT: MELINDA ANDERSON, COORDINATOR, VICTIM-WITNESS ASSISTANCE PROGRAM, MAY 21, 1986

CAROL: Okay, Melinda, what exactly is the Victim-Witness Assistance Program and how does it work?

On March 12, 1984, I made the first of dozens of calls to the office of the Los Angeles City Attorney Victim-Witness Assistance Program in order to initiate my claim against the

State of California for monies due me as a result of the assault on February 14.

MELINDA: . . . My job is as liaison for the victim with the state. I would verify all the information for the state in terms of wage loss, medical, whatever, you know, submit the claim, compile the information, submit the claims to the state. I would also work as a referral source for this victim. Usually when victims call us they have an immediate crisis. And it could be something far greater than this paperwork, and that could be the counseling referral, that could be emergency food, emergency housing, just anything. Whatever we've got access to, that's what we should try to do for these victims.

On December 3, 1985, one year, ten months, and twenty days after the assault had taken place, the claim was duly processed and I received all monies still outstanding, some seven to eight thousand dollars, due me or my doctors, the claim remaining open for any further expenses.

It had taken a long time. The case had been inexplicably logjammed, misplaced, and misfiled by the state's bureaucracy. In the process of jiggling it loose, I came into contact with four coordinators at the Victim-Witness Assistance office, two supervisors, and a staff analyst at the State Board of Control in Sacramento (them guys who authorize government checks), a man who treated me like white trash, an inferior person, in other words treated me like a victim. In all other instances, I was attended with kindness, decency, and sometimes more, sometimes less efficiency.

CAROL: Well, who do you think tells the victims about you guys?
MELINDA: LAPD is supposed to, or most law-enforcement agencies should.
CAROL: Do you find that they do?
MELINDA: Some divisions do, some divisions don't. Some di-

visions are a lot more sensitive to victims than others. But on the bottom of every crime report, you have a downtown number, Victim-Assistance Program 485-6976. And you'd be surprised how many people do not ever look at the bottom of those reports. So our information about the program is not well known. A lot of people do not know about us. You have a couple of public service announcements on TV, but they're midmorning, you know, early evenings, whatever, and a lot of people just don't know about the program.

CAROL: Yeah, well, the only reason I knew is because a nurse in Emergency referred me to a social worker who referred me to the victim center who referred me to you. I don't ever remember seeing a police report. I was having trouble enough remembering my name.

MELINDA: Then you were lucky to find us.

CAROL: Yeah, I was lucky. . . .

The monies I received were for bits and pieces of medical bills that had not been taken care of by my union insurance, as well as the entire cost of my therapy, which was in no way taken care of by my union insurance, on the grounds, I suppose, that all actors are crazy and therefore no coverage is provided. Fortunately for me, I was not without funds and paid my bills or was advised by doctors, mostly Margaret, that they were willing to wait on the state for payment. I did not receive any reimbursement for wages lost because the coordinator who took my claim did not wish to be bothered with computing that cost, somewhat complicated by my free-lance status. Fortunately for me, I was not without funds.

As often happens in situations like this, the last person I dealt with was the finest, for it was she who knew how to dig me out of the pile of paperwork manure under which I suffocated. She wrote those final letters, she made those final calls, she pushed the claim and got it done, one year, ten months, and twenty days later. She was young, cheerful, gifted, and black. I'm referring to Melinda. We never met until she handed me the checks.

CAROL: So tell me, I'm a victim, I come into your office, or I call you on the phone and I tell you I've got this problem and I don't know what to do. What will you tell me about the prerequisites for filing?

MELINDA: The first thing that I have to know is whether or not a police report has been filed, because before I can render any services to this victim the state requires that two things occur. One, the victim is cooperative with the criminal justice department, and that is to file the initial crime report. The second thing the state requires is that the victim is innocent of any of the events that led up to the crime or the actual crime itself . . . like selling drugs, or whatever. It's pretty cut and dry. You can tell when a victim has contributed and when they haven't. Most of the time victims are innocent.

Melinda worked out of the Van Nuys office, the one in the heat of the valley on Sylvan Street off the marbled ground floor of the Van Nuys City Hall, known in the neighborhood as "the old place with the steeple," Roosevelt-style Depression-Greek-Deco, my home away from home, my bar without drinks. It had been suggested I apply there rather than downtown in the central office after I'd tried, a disastrous attempt to rendezvous with a female coordinator of the downtown office whose voice had soothed me over the phone, its timbre so kindly and motherly caring that I'd forgotten the Ides of March were upon us and chanced my luck at underground parking. I'd cork-screwed my way down deep into the depths under Mayor Tom Bradley's municipal complex, into the gray-black light of the one-way ramp where air was entrapped for generations, and after hitting bottom, some six stories later, the attendants had screeched that I wasn't on their list of those special parkers for whom they made space. I began to hyperventilate and I began to break and I drove up and away over the freeways back to my home and I canceled the appointment. My lady of the phone apologized profusely and then suggested I try the Van Nuys office with the good outside parking lot adjacent. My papers would be transferred to the Valley.

It was one of those great suggestions.

CAROL: Why does this program exist under the auspices of the city attorney? To ensure that victims will speak out if they catch the suspect?

MELINDA: No, no, this is a program that originated at the state level. We don't get an awful lot of prosecutions through this program at all. We have a lot of cases with unknown suspects. Most cases that are prosecuted would be vehicular, hit and run, driving under the influence, but battery, robbery, assault, there are very low conviction rates through the city attorney's office.

I would say the state found it necessary to create this program out of grass-roots organizations or people lobbying. I think it was out of sheer concern for the victim. The victim doesn't get any consideration. Even now, if it wasn't for our program a lot of times the victim wouldn't get anything back. Restitution through the courts is often nothing, because the suspects don't have the ability to pay so the victim is left out in the cold many times.

CAROL: Not all the states have this, do they?

MELINDA: All states have a victim's program, but a lot of states don't have as extensive a victim program as California does, because California's program is the pilot program nationwide. Other states may assist victims with the application process, but they don't do all the advocating, the referral work we do.

One year, ten months, and twenty days after calmly, quietly, and courteously filing my initial claim at the Van Nuys office, and parking next door in the outside lot, I returned to meet up with Melinda and the money.

CAROL: So, how much money can a victim get, how much money does the state allow for?

MELINDA: Okay, the maximum that each victim can get is $23,000, and that can include medical and wage. For funeral and burial the maximum is $2,800. For psychotherapy for additional family members that weren't victims, $10,000. So as long as we can work the incurred expense within those guidelines, then we're fine. And say if there was a hit-and-run incident and several members of a family had been injured, then each member of that family has a separate claim.

Melinda sat jammed behind a desk at the far end of her office, a shoe-box space, sort of long, sort of narrow, framed by a large, old-fashioned double-hung window that provided the light and air and all the aesthetics. There was no air-conditioning in the office. There was no space for the three wooden desks and a legal clerk and restitutions coordinator and an odd assortment of vintage files and piles of papers and piles of more papers. Needless to say, there was no privacy. All interviews were conducted in this office. They were supposed to be private. They were not private. Most victims don't care, as long as somebody's listening.

CAROL: I had a bad-ass guy in Sacramento, a staff analyst who oversaw my claim and screwed it up, and he treated me like white trash when I called for information. Fortunately I have a big mouth and reported him to his superiors, but I can imagine a lot of people being devastated by this creep. Do you think there's discrimination in the way victims are treated?

Melinda sat behind her wooden desk, a black transistor radio perched behind her, shoved up against a corner, between wall and window, lullabying rock and sometimes the blues loud enough to cushion horror stories chanted daily, minute to minute.

MELINDA: Yeah, I hate to say this, but there is a lot of agency dumping.

CAROL: Agency what?

MELINDA: Dumping. You know, when you don't want to deal with something, dump it on someone else. There are those of us who don't like doing sexual assault or domestic violence cases because of their own personal feelings about it.

CAROL: You mean some victims . . .

MELINDA: Yeah, like celebrity victims get plenty of emergency and the other kind, well, some of us might tell the victim the service cannot be provided. . . .

CAROL: Like my first coordinator did about my wages. She didn't feel like computing the cost.

MELINDA: Yeah, that's right. Sometimes they even tell a victim to file independent of our office, directly to the state, because they don't want to deal with whatever that crime is, like domestic violence, and then they justify their attitude by the lack of prosecutions in this area, by the fact that the state doesn't get a lot of information, nor does the city attorney get a lot of prosecutions. They don't want to understand so they can't be bothered.

CAROL: No hand holding for those who deserve what they get? Is that what you mean?

MELINDA: Yeah . . . and I don't think it's fair. I know we're underpaid and understaffed and the whole bit, but why take the job if you're not going to do what you're supposed to do? We're service-oriented. And we're sitting on an awful lot of information and if we don't know how to do things, we have access to find out about how to refer people, you know?

A lot of us haven't learned to detach ourselves and not—I don't mean detach yourself in an ineffective way,

180

but you don't have to take everything so personally, everything that we hear—we hear a lot of garbage, you know. We hear all the worst crimes all over the city, but you don't have to internalize it. You don't have to turn it into a "me" issue, you know.

We gotta learn to get our own values out of our work and deal with whatever we're dealing with with the victim, you know, and stop deciding that this person they must like to be beat, so that's why they were beat. Or they look promiscuous and that's why they were raped, you know—those types of attitudes we really do have to totally put out of our interactions with the victim because it *is* happening.

Melinda cradled the phone between ear and shoulder as I entered her office for my appointment. "Mrs. Ventana!" she said to the caller as she motioned to me to sit down by her desk and riffled a file in search of checks I must sign, countersign, mark my *X* in triplicate, all the while listening to the voice on the line.

"Here!" she whispered, and handed me checks. I sat down at her desk and fondled them briefly. The first had been made out to my dentist, the other made out to the victim center. That's the way the system worked. Checks were mailed directly to "providers" after the victim signed them off.

"May I use the phone? I want to call my dentist. I wanna straighten out the double payment."

"Yes." She nodded as she spoke to the caller. "But Mrs. Ventana, how can I help you?"

"Pat?" I'd dialed my dentist's bookkeeper. "They're going to send you a check for $791, for that hairline crack, the new tooth in the back, the money I've already paid for your services. The doctor's name is on it. Will you send it back to me?"

"Mrs. Ventana!" Melinda was saying.

"Thank you, Pat, very much for your help. The whole routine's a pain in the butt."

"Mrs. Ventana!" Melinda repeated. "We don't have any cash here! Please, call the police or bring the papers I need for the state!"

I raised my hand and waved at Melinda. "Where do I sign?" I mouthed in silence.

"Right there," she whispered, her hand shielding the receiver. "Mrs. Ventana, may I call you back? Mrs. Ventana, there's a woman waiting here who has the same problems you have! Mrs. Ventana! Please! give me your number! If you're at a pay phone I'll call you back in five minutes. Please, Mrs. Ventana! Have a little patience!" Soul blew out of the corner radio. "Give me your number! Yes, I have your name. Thank you, Mrs. Ventana. I'll call you back." And she hung up the phone and stood up at her desk.

"I'm sorry," she said. That was hello.

"That's okay," I said. I was glad to meet her.

"Do the figures all match, because I wouldn't know. That's the biggest problem I have taking over old cases. I haven't looked at your case. I don't know what's in it!"

"I don't know, either, and I don't care. If I'm out a hundred bucks, then I'm out! So be it. I just want to make sure that the therapist gets paid."

"Right, I'm on it. It's being processed. I called the state personally and it's happening slowly."

"And I'm right, am I not, that as long as the state has okayed this case, officially allowed that I'm a victim, and as long as my expenses are victim related, the state will pay up to $23,000? That's right, isn't it? It's very important."

"Yes, ma'am, that's the law. Do you need a pen?" Soul had petered out and the blues had begun.

"How did you get into this job?" I asked as I signed and signed and then signed more papers.

"By accident," she said. "I never meant to be a social worker. I was a teacher! This was an accident! This was a mistake! And I'm telling you this job will drive you crazy! I'm gonna have to work my way out of this soon. I'm telling you, between the two, I'd rather be teaching! At least you

182

see the fruits of your labor. I've pushed a lot of paper in my life and look at this! My desk is stupid! I can never get it straight!" She grabbed a breath as she spilled her life.

"Now this Mrs. Ventana"—she glanced at the phone—"she calls me once a week, and I can't help her! I try to understand, she's reaching out for help, but if it's not about paper, all I can say is I'm sorry!" She sat down at her desk and rested a moment. Then she looked up at me and smiled a wide grin.

"And how are you feeling?"

"I'm fine, real good. I'm writing a book about this experience."

"You are? Well, good for you! Now, you send me a copy. They say people who are attacked are asking for it. Is that true?"

"That's a crock of shit," I said.

"Yeah, well, I was just asking because that's what they say."

"I know what they say. It's not true, Melinda. Hey, Melinda, will you do me a favor?"

"Sure," she said.

"Will you let me come back and interview you?"

CAROL: Okay, I want to know how a smart lady like yourself got into this racket and why?

MELINDA: Oh, Carol, I just stumbled into social work about five years ago, which is so strange because I always stayed away from this field. I hated it. Always. When I was in college, I just never wanted to bother with it.

. . . But I guess I've always been in human services. I'm a communicator. I love getting out information because it's always the low man on the totem pole who gets lost in the shuffle. For that matter, I'm the low man on the totem pole and I'm constantly fighting. Some issues, some calls, some something. So this is just a brief stopover, because I'm truly not a social worker, but I am very empathetic and humane when it comes to people . . . I just feel people's pain . . . The thing is, I had a brother that was killed violently, so that sometimes the whole thing is just a flood of feelings I have gone through, and I can feel people's pain, I really can, because if you live long enough, you know, my own experience or even my mother's, you know how those things can happen and how they can have an impact on the family and the whole bit. . . .

. . . I help anybody. If I have the resources to help, you got it, no big deal. I don't know anything else but to do my best, and so I'm just here, Carol. I'm just here and right now while I'm here, I will be as effective as I can. I just have to be. But I swear I cannot stay in this long. I really can't.

CAROL: Do you think because you had experienced violence in your family, that that really sensitized you to this whole thing and somehow got you, made you available to get into this?

MELINDA: You know, that's a thought. I had never thought of that. That might be, that really might be, because you know a lot of times the people that I encounter, whether it's coordinators and whatever, they really feel that we are above this. That it won't happen to us, you know? Why? You walk the streets, you know, you're not safe anywhere. I don't care if you're in the Palisades, I don't care where you are, violence and crime is everywhere, you know, so I think that might have, you know, and I would say yeah, safely, and I'm glad you made me tune into that because I hadn't thought of that before.

Tucker   Probably has. Yeah.

About varying my diet

I'd stopped eating flesh. Or call it meat. As you wish. I'd stopped eating all beef, fish, and chicken. I awoke one day in

184

April and noticed my diet had gone funny and queer behind my back. Philosophical commitment or thoughts of good health had nothing to do with this turn of events, nor had I planned to suicide and avoid my pain or recapture youth via anorexia. I simply couldn't digest a once-living creature, any other creature who birthed its babies, and the laying of eggs fell into that category. I couldn't partake in the violation. Violence is violence as a rose is a rose. Every aspect of the ritual made me sick to my stomach.

Vegetarianism had never seduced me before. I'd thought of those who partook as slightly affected, and though I relished green leaves and roots and all varieties of nuts, they were hardly exclusive to my diet, for like most California kids of every age, I ate tacos and burgers and chili dogs.

I called Les, my everyday doctor, my doctor of the all-day sucker. Protein was the worry, not absorbing enough.

"Les, I've stopped eating all kinds of meat."

"Come into the office and we'll take some tests."

"Why?" I asked. "What's there to know? This is about getting hit on the head. I need a list from you of substitute proteins, stuff that won't make me big as a house."

"Come into the office. I want to be sure. And I'll talk to you then about varying your diet."

"You're wrong," I said. "I'll come in tomorrow."

She closed the door of the baby-blue cubicle, she, his nurse, and she stood there beside me. She, his nurse, asked me to disrobe.

"Why?" I asked.

"I must weigh you," she said.

"Why?" I asked. "Why does everyone doubt me?" I took off my clothes and stood on the scale.

She, his nurse, began to ask questions. How long had I been bothered by this condition?

"How long has it been since you've eaten correctly?"

"Les knows the answers. Why do you ask?"

185

"That information belongs in your chart."

"For a while," I said. "I don't know how long." And I sat very tall on the stainless-steel table.

She asked for my arm.

"Why?" I asked.

"I've got to tie the rubber tube and take your blood."

"No," I said. "I don't want you to." My arms were crossed. I was holding myself. "I won't give you my arm. I don't want to be hurt. I don't wanna give you any of my blood." I held myself and we stared at one another. I didn't want to give anyone any of me.

My throat had jammed. My eyes were full. Tears wet and weakened my paper smock. Her face was a mask of Calvinist attitudes coated in carmel, duty bound.

"Don't you know?" I asked. "Did Les tell you what happened?" Raised needle aloft, the nurse shook her head no.

I told her my story. She was so sorry. I held out my arm. She injected the needle. She left the room. I wept in the silence.

When Les appeared five minutes later, I asked for some scotch to replace my tears. It seemed he had scotch put away in his office. He poured me a shot in a tiny white cup and made me promise not to tell anybody.

It was spring after all

Oh, my God, I wanted a moon moment of respite, carried by Neptune and guarded by Leo, I was a Leo, guarded by me. Surely, my God, the most committed, accomplished, mega-practicing masochist, needed, for a moment, at some time or another, to withdraw from misery and walk another pathway, rejecting all pain in the name of daffodils. Just for a moment? Just for a week?

I'd been sent an invitation to the twenty-fifth reunion of my graduating class at Sarah Lawrence College. I'd received a phone call from my girlfriend, Mary, my close college buddy and therapist friend inviting me to visit New York City and wander out to Sarah Lou together that weekend. It was springtime in the city. Flowers blossomed in the park. I wanted to see the flowers in bloom. I wanted to visit the Children's Zoo.

Surely this red fever of symptoms dogging my body might be doused for a moment, for only a week, in the middle of April, as I might douse my body in the heat of August, plunging into a dazzling blue-diamond-streaked pool, letting the coolness crawl up my nude body, an ice-water challenge to one's softness and center, dipped in blue wholeness, assaulted by health, until somehow the heat warmed the experience, the plunge and the challenge, and courage was the victor.

Surely this trip was what the doctor might have ordered, a vacation cushioned by friends' hospitality. I would feel safe for they were as family.

Oh, God! New York City! I was on my way, quite away from daily reminders of what couldn't be managed, fifty-percent days and forty-nine-percent failures, days that delineated stress and trauma, on my way away, flying into the sun like a female Icarus, prayerful her wings would hold tight with the glue. I was away! If I could get started.

The man driving the limousine was the problem.

I'd arranged for a limo to meet my plane at Kennedy Airport and chauffeur me into "the city," Manhattan. I would treat myself well, tender and gentle, and avoid the stress of hailing a taxi and dealing with luggage and bouncing across the Triborough Bridge in a springless carriage driven by a greenhorn to American shores who'd no idea where he was going. That experience and the ensuing aggravation was to be avoided in my condition, but the man in the limo was a problem. The man in the limo was a stranger. The driver of the limo might want to kill me.

"Why don't you think creatively about this?" Mary asked when I called to cancel all our arrangements. "Why don't you call one of the many friends you've done for in the past

187

and ask them to drive out with the limo and pick you up at the airport? I'd do it but I can't because I've got patients at that hour. Why don't you, when you're here, think of New York in other ways, and not think of the experience like it's always been. If you're frightened of taxis and frightened of the street, then tell your friends to come and get you. They'll understand." Mary was smart.

I called Dolores. Dolores was free. Dolores would assist in what I felt to be a loony and shameful request of a friend, even of Dolores who understood.

"Thank you, Dolores, I feel like a ditz," and I hung up the phone and raced off that day to a matinee movie all about Tarzan and his problems in London. Vietnam vets *and* Tarzan understood, I surmised as I wept through the film and wept on, hours later, traveling on, that day, to early temple service where the rabbi would lecture on trust and faith, how one must overcome a world of violence. He was speaking of genocide. I was thinking of me and the vets and Tarzan in London.

Hey! Hey! New York City! I was on my way! I packed my bags, and early one morning Kitty drove me out to American Airlines. Are there words to describe the thrill of an airport, of money in your pocket and a ticket in hand, flying high and away from the scene of all crimes, flying into the sun with a sherry over rocks? The plane was cool and underpeopled and my wings survived in perfect condition, strapped, as they were, into empty seats. I smiled my way over America's map, and it wasn't until I arrived at Mary's home and was asked by her husband, as we sat sipping wine, to please tell him, if I would, if I didn't mind, the details of the story, what had actually happened (for he wasn't clear and he'd never asked), that I broke down in tears, not knowing the answer. "I can tell you what happened and all the details, but *I* don't *know* what happened to me!" Mary shushed her husband while I dried my tears and made the first of many calls in search of an answer.

The journey was ostensibly in celebration of the twenty-fifth class reunion. In fact it was my miniexperiment, a fledgling attempt to examine my feelings and discover who I was in this world six weeks later; a test tube time, a fast-food measuring of my tolerance for earthlings and the pleasure they provide. Could I be with people? was the question posed. Did I wish for their company, or for my solitude? Would the companionship of friends help me to heal? What did I need? Whom had I become? I would arrange an agenda of daily operations that would push the limits of my courage and somehow discern the direction of my life. At least that was my hope, my obligation to me, to cull an order and form from my disintegration.

Wednesday, April 11

Awoke early to adventure the world. I got a ticket to *Death of a Salesman* matinee, hurray! It was only all right, not extraordinary. Any play that has as its central dramatic crisis a married man getting laid in Boston one night hardly touches the pulse of any world I know. I went by myself. I did it alone! The theater felt safe. The taxi felt bumpy. You can get killed in a taxi but not with intent. Had lunch first with Billy, and told him about the Pentothal incident, how I'd yearned for his help like when I was nineteen and pregnant. Our talk was sweet and open, without dreams or expectations, just as all the world seems sharp and hard-edged now and yet very beautiful. No fuzzy focus. No delusions. Did all right on the streets. Some anxiety with my back turned to people. Not thrilled in crowds. Not thrilled standing on corners where I would need to press up against the building, leaving no space behind me for trouble. I don't like the energy and hustle of the city. Where are they going? I've no desire to move that fast. And my makeup doesn't do well here—it runs all over. Too tired and frightened for

189

the theater at night. At night is scary. Saw Kevin for dinner.

I'd called him as soon as I arrived the first evening. He was a man I trusted with my thoughts, an intelligent man, a man of sensibilities and gentle sweetness, a man who encouraged the playful in me, the female part, the cat in hiding. Perhaps we might meet and talk and dine real swell and drink good wine and laugh a little, and talcum-coat my sensuality. If I could play with any man, I could play with Kevin.

We'd been lovers one month, the year before, when it rained and flooded the California beaches, day-and-night lovers, and then he'd returned back East to his work and a life and another woman. We'd written and met and the woman had vanished, but so had our passion and we became friends. He'd called when he'd heard what had happened to me and hoped we might meet if I came to the city. He, like myself, was cocooned in loss, a death in the family, a parent was dying, and all pleasure had been put aside for higher orders of business. He needed to play. We arranged for dinner.

I buzzed Kevin in through the five separate locks and listened to footsteps mounting the stairs as he walked two floors of the four-story townhouse. Standing in the landing of the front hall, I watched his head and then torso bob through and then out the oak balustrade edging the room. Our eyes met at the center of the Oriental rug and we smiled a great pleasure and kissed each other. He thought I looked pretty, I could see it in his glance. I thought he looked pretty, I felt it everywhere.

Mary and her husband appeared at that moment, inviting us to join them for a drink and introductions. "Of course!" Kevin said, it was only proper and polite, and we sat down together and spoke of horses. I'd no idea until that moment of anyone's interest in the subject, of Mary's passion or that of her husband, or even Kevin's ongoing interest. *I* was the person who owned a horse because my daughter loved them and I was her mother. We were speaking of horses, a safe,

190

clean subject through which to garner inklings of character. This, it would seem, was a parental conversation, that variety of talk before a date, when your daughter's going out with an unknown quantity. Mary and her husband were making sure I was safe, not really of course, except that's what they were up to.

"Well, I guess we should go," I said to the group.

"Yes," said Kevin, "we have a reservation."

"Well, have a good time," Mary said.

"And don't forget the keys," her husband echoed. "We'll be home tonight. Shall I wake you in the morning?"

"No," I said and kissed him on the cheek and Kevin and I walked down the stairs.

We ate French that evening, a fancy frog dinner, Kevin in his blue pinstriped suit, I in something I thought rather glamorous, and we comforted each other with great tenderness, allowing the other his sense of loss as we drank a bottle of vintage Margaux and ordered delicacies that melted on touch. Later that evening we made love on the couch of Mary's living room like high school kids with no place to go, we made love, a reentry, a gift mutually exchanged. Safely wrapped in Irish arms, sweetly lulled by Irish charm, soft, responsive, undefended, and yet apprehensive of symptoms popping out like a rash from the sun, trembling symptoms, tears, paralysis, I wasn't afraid and I let myself be there, close, pressed close to the body of my friend, a rehearsal perhaps for that future moment when I might wish to come close to the body of a stranger, a person unknown, of no prior history, a person I'd have to learn to trust.

I couldn't image that much trust.

Thursday, April 12

Tired out. Not enough sleep. Makeup running and my face hurting from a bearded face rubbing up against mine. Not a bad reason for a face to hurt. I hate the crowds of people on the streets and I seem to fear my purse will be grabbed. Trust. Trust. And the lack thereof! I press my purse to my breast like a little old lady. Lunch with a pal, nothing deeply shared. Alissa's not the sort who can empathize. Alissa's the sort who tries to fix your feelings and lecture you on how you'll feel in the future and talk you out of the feelings you're feeling. Who the hell needs that? There may be other friends who are no longer friends. I'm so tired. Tired. No museums today. Dinner and theater with my sister Ellen.

It wasn't the trip, the taxi trip went swell. I'd asked the driver to drop me at the corner of Forty-sixth and Eighth Avenue and because Forty-sixth is an eastbound street, and I was coming from the east, the taxi did right. It went down Forty-fifth Street, past Schubert Alley, I was shocked at Schubert Alley, I was shocked by the theater district, the theater district was terrifying, the forties, Eighth Avenue, Broadway, Schubert Alley, the streets vibrated with violence, not jazz but heavy metal, satanic riffs, in the cracks of the sidewalk, around every corner, assaulting the senses, I'm telling you I could feel the horror. I'd worked and studied in this district for years, my life as an actress was defined by this district, and now it felt like, it looked like a garbage dump, the ass end of culture in New York City, the ass end! The theater district! A hurly-burly show of rage and race, and people going nowhere except to hell, not going to the theater, pushing dope, eating dope, and hustling cars.

No, the taxi was right, it pulled right up to the corner of Forty-sixth and Eighth Avenue, the near corner I said but I wasn't sure, and I would walk the half block and meet my sister at the Italian restaurant she had chosen. It was six o'clock, maybe six-thirty, there was plenty of light, and as I walked the block I remembered St. Luke's was the next building, a pretty building from another time, and I looked up from my feet to test my recollection. There before me were two large round concrete planters, new to the church, placed at the base of the church stairway, and in one of the planters, curled up asleep around the ivy and random weeds, was a drunk, a bum, not just a bum, a drunken bum, and lying next to him on the sidewalk, alongside the planter, was his friend, another bum, a drunken bum. They weren't hurting a soul except perhaps by the force of their snores, which might disturb the nonexistent peace, but they were without question curled around church property. Suddenly the doors of St. Luke's burst open and its concierge flew down the steps, grabbing the bum planted in concrete and shaking him viciously, his head bobbing like a Howdy-Doody hat, all the while screaming "Get the hell out of here!" My pulse caught in my pearls and my head began to buzz and I crossed the street in the middle of traffic, terrified by the heat of the attack. Even his friend, the bum by the planter and a fellow, I'm quite sure, used to all forms of eviction, looked up at the concierge and put his hand on his shoulder, saying "Take it easy, buddy! You don't have to be so rough!"

I found the restaurant and went in to my sister, spewing the story all heartbeat and panting. She suggested I might like to sit inside the booth, with my back to the wall, facing outward, which I really appreciated very much. I couldn't sit with my back to the room. I needed a lookout, a defensive stronghold from which to spot the predatory.

Later, at the theater, the pushing and rudeness of crowds panicked me, those crowds *in* the theater, the intellectuals, not the crowds of the street, they were something else. During act breaks, at intermission, the flow of humanity was as a herd of cows without the soulful look in their eyes, bulls on the run for a cigarette or a pee, a mindless assault, a cultural violence. After theater, we swam with that crowd, skirmished its edge, walked in the gutter, down Forty-sixth to the corner and a taxi to drive us home, thank God, and at that corner, at Forty-sixth and Eighth Avenue, a black man's face, all red-eyed and teary and smelling bad of booze and shit, came out of nowhere, into my face just before me, and the face said, "Listen, darlin', do you need a limo?"

193

"No, I don't," I said, "but thank you very much," and the face didn't move off and then it did.

"Jesus, Carol, you'll talk to anyone!" my sister said as she waved her hand and flagged down nothing.

"Well, all I said was thank you! I think it's better to talk to a crazy and not ignore them. I think I think that. I've always thought that."

"Well, I don't think that," Ellen said. "Just keep walking. My God, I'm sorry. I should have remembered. I'm so used to the city I forgot this part."

"I don't want to keep walking. I wanna get a taxi!"

"There are no taxis. Just radio cabs."

"What does that mean?"

"You gotta call them up and reserve them before."

"You gotta be kidding. There are no taxis?" There are always taxis! New York *is* taxis!

"They won't pick you up at this hour of the night. Let's walk up Seventh. It's better than Eighth." We walked seventeen blocks before finding a cab. A fare was discharged in front of our bodies. We walked through the district dodging the crazies and their eyes and I felt I might lose my mind on the street. Midnight in a city gone mad. I thought of Tarzan.

Friday, April 13

I signed my taxes in a tall breathless building of too many people and fled the city, renting a car, speeding up the Cross-Bronx, Mary and I, back to Sarah Lawrence and the country. Cocktails on campus, dinner at the president's home. Sticky name labels pasted to the shoulder, reminders of names that fit the faces, adolescent faces wrapped in shrouds of tweed, ladies who retained with one another a vulnerability, an innocent gaze. Conversations resumed twenty-five years later, a rush of safety in friendships formed by interests and passions and no ax to grind. Some women bleached out and overdone like

194

Mrs. Astor's pet pig. But most let themselves be, for better or for worse, which was better, much better, they looked like themselves. It was a kind and warm and cheering event, a feast of friendly natures, a feeling shared by the others, I'm sure. I felt cherished and embraced by my own history and the apparent knowledge that I had been remembered and thought well of. Context. Community. An imprint in memory. Love feelings stored, retired from service. Perhaps that's enough. I got drunk. I don't remember eating dinner although I know I ate dinner but I don't remember. I was trying very hard not to spill my story but stay with the present and stay away separateness. I got very high. They asked me to make a speech after the dinner I couldn't remember, over coffee and some sort of dessert.

CAROL: "Hi, I'm Carol Rossen and I became an actress."
(*Laughter. I got the laugh.*)
WOMAN(*from the corner*): "You always were an actress!"
(*Laughter. She got the laugh.*)
CAROL: "I've been asked to speak because I was senior class president, which I didn't understand at all when I was senior class president but now I do and I think it—the fact that we are all here is so sweet and lovely and I'm glad to be here."
(*Pause.*)
      "As a matter of fact I was here at the twentieth reunion, where were you?"
(*Laughter.*)
      "It was very lovely, that twentieth reunion, you missed out! . . . It was intimate and much more personal than this gathering. . . . You should have been there. . . . Now, ah . . . to the meaning of the moment. . . ."
(*Laughter.*)
      "We were all educated to be bright, individual,

195

thoughtful striving young women and we all became mothers."
(*Laughter and no laughter.*)

I wanted to say it was a badge of honor but I couldn't remember the words I wanted. I sat down as they applauded and withdrew inside. Too much. Too soon. I'm not ready yet.

The cheeseburger and fries Mary and I ate at a roadside diner later that evening were truly memorable, never to be forgotten, something to hook a wagon to. We had stopped to eat on our way to the country, up the Saw Mill River Parkway to Mary's home in Connecticut. Thank God for Connecticut. It's so irregular.

The weekend, April 14, 15

How special these feelings. For the first time in my life that I can remember, I allowed for the companionship of silence, and of rocks and the green and of gray and blue weather and trails without compass, Nature's directions, and I sink into that silence and Saturday I watched a woodpecker's business for two hours, two hours well spent overseeing survival. Sunday I watched the rain through the window. I am happy here. I am happy alone. There is plenty of company. I don't need company.

Monday, April 16

I'm worried about how I'm going to make a living. I don't know if I can act again. I'm worried about the courage it takes. I'm worried about mind/body coordination under stress. I'm frightened. My friends say I should do something with this story. Write it down, they say, write this story. My girlfriend Adrienne said it at dinner after I returned to the city last night. My girlfriend Katya said it at lunch today, and she's a writer, she thinks I should do it. I figure the story is worth a few dollars. Or not, but I gotta do something. Katya says maybe it's the story of a victim who's no longer a victim after truly being victimized. That's a nice story but I'm not sure that's the story.

Shit, maybe I should find a real writer to help me. Katya says I must write out events by the hours, and itemize, schedule, and then on another piece of paper type up remembrances of conversations. Lists! More lists! I can't believe it! I'm going to try. Soon as I arrive home. I fly home tomorrow. I want to get back to work bad. I'm going to take dance classes and I'm going to write. Every day must be about writing. Every day alone. I never walked Central Park or visited the zoo.

Tuesday, April 17

This day was about coming home, about packing and airports and bad service and the wrong lunch on the plane, not the one I ordered. A meat-and-potatoes pass-the-salt sort of day. Kitty picked me up at the airport replete with horror stories about my darling thirteen-year-old twit of a daughter and her friend sneaking off with the truck to drive to a movie and other tomfoolery indulged in my absence. I walked into the house exhausted, attempting to deal with such adolescent pranks (chains are my choice), and with the mail and Daisy and the groceries and light bulbs to be changed and checks to be written and I felt overwhelmed and cried as I sat on the edge of my bed. And then, I just gave in to it all and I knew I must be strong, because the rabbi said so, there's a good reason, and proceed with my best version of life. And that's all there is to that. I must write in the mornings.

I'd returned to the familiar and soon withdrew into some self I'd barely met so that I might write a book I'd no intention of writing. I saw almost no one, men or women.

TRANSCRIPT: GARETH WOOTTON, APRIL 19, 1984

GARETH: . . . I'd say you've come through it pretty well, you know . . . but I still think you've got a ways to go yet. You're not back to normal yet. . . .

CAROL: No.

GARETH: And it'll be a while.

CAROL: What is your projection? It's been about eight weeks.

GARETH: Oh, I think you'll probably, it'll be a year. I mean, this is like grieving. It may be a year or two before you've really got it down to the point where you don't feel that bad about it anymore, you think about it from time to time. But you know, it's not a lot different from any kind of grieving. It's about two years before you really level out on any great loss, and in this type of thing you've got to treat it like an emotional loss. I mean, it's an emotional loss of your own self-control, of your control over your environment, over your secure feelings with other people, with strangers, that kind of thing, and you'll have to have a lot of contact with people before you start feeling real good about them again.

CAROL: Right.

GARETH: But fortunately you felt good about it before so you'll probably come back to that okay. . . . I think, you know, if someone is not in pretty good shape, at the point of something like that, it can throw him into a psychotic depression. You know, we see this now and then with people who are basically alone in this country, like an immigrant who comes into this country that something really bad happens to. I mean, they may become totally psychotic and depressed and completely detached from reality with situational psychosis.

But in your case you obviously had a lot going for you, because an assault like that, which is next to being murdered—I mean, you were this far from being killed—

is, I mean, that's about as severe an attack that you can have and come out of it psychologically intact and doing reasonably well.

But I expect you'll be okay. I have confidence in you.

GENETICS

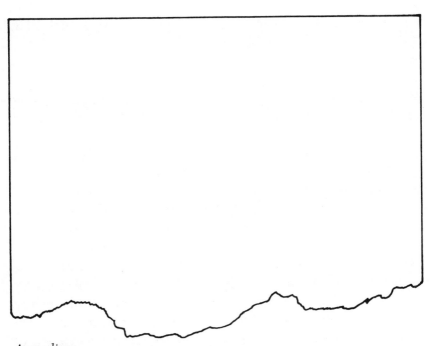

A one-liner
excerpts from the gospel
as told by Aunt Ceil my daddy's sister

TRANSCRIPT: CEIL WISHNER, NOVEMBER 1982–JANUARY 1983

AUNT CEIL: *"Ziss amoh gewein in a klein schtettela"*—"Once
upon a time in a small town," and your bubbi, [grand-
mother], my mother, would tell me a story, not a made-
up story, about the little town where she grew up, about
things that happened and people she knew. What did I
know from fairy tales, from Hans Christian Andersen,
from that kind of stuff, an immigrant kid, who's gonna
tell me stories like that! But my mother, when she wanted
to put me to sleep and I'd say tell me a story, or later
when she'd rock and I'd come home after school, my
mother would start the story always the same way, *"ziss
amoh gewein,"* "once there was," and then she'd tell the
story and she ended it the same way. In Yiddish the words
are *"a fläckele a-rhein, a fläckele a royse, the mysa iz*

203

oyss," which means "a little flag goes in, a little flag goes out and the story is over."

CAROL: What does that mean, where does it come from, do you know?

AUNT CEIL: I don't know, I don't know, but that's the way she always finished her stories, "a little flag goes in, a little flag goes out, and it's finished, it's done." Now where that comes from, or what it meant, I never did find out. But I remember when I could hardly talk, this is the way she told me a tale, always.

CAROL: So, tell me, Ceil. Tell me about Bubbi. Start at the beginning. Whatever you remember.

AUNT CEIL: . . . Her father was a rabbi and he lived in a little town called Pabroza, which was in Russian Poland, very near Vilna. And he had a family, a first family before Bubbi, with I don't know how many children, but there was a girl and there was a boy. Something happened to the town. What caused it, whether it was rains—I'm sure it wasn't an earthquake—but the little house in which they lived collapsed, burying all of them alive. It took two or three days before they dug them out and the only one left alive was my grandfather, his wife and his daughter and whoever else, all gone. He was then a man of about sixtyish.

There was another member of the family who was not there and this was a great-niece who had just gotten married, had two children, she was very young, very very young. Her husband had either died or been killed I don't know which, and she was alone and so was my grandfather. Nowhere could she with two little babies find herself another to care for them. And there was no way my grandfather could find a woman for he was old and such a very poor man. The little town was concerned about people alone, so they suggested the two of them team up together. You see, you can't marry an uncle, but you can a great-uncle because it's one generation re-

204

moved, and so they married. His wife was really his great-niece. He was forty years older than she.

So with this young wife he had two children, my mother and her brother Meyer, the one from Connecticut, and although they lived poorly, they were always learned people. He read and interpreted the Talmud to students and if he was paid with some potatoes that was a great deal, and she took in washing to make a living, a few kopeks. One of the brothers from one of the marriages educated himself and became a translator and was one of few Jews permitted to teach in the gymnasium, which would be like a high school, a junior college I would say. Another brother was a scribe, he would write Sepher Torahs—you had to be a special kind of man and live a special way to be permitted to write torahs and copy the scrolls.

Well, when Meyer was eight and Bubbi was twelve, her mother, who worked very very hard, ruptured herself in some way with the washing, and she became so ill that before they could get a doctor for her—and getting a doctor meant going to the next town for there wasn't any doctor in the town of Pabroza—she died. And so my grandmother who had always cried that she would be left a widow with young children because her husband was so old, she died first and left my grandfather, an old man, with two young kids to raise.

Now in those years what did a man know from anything in the house? He didn't know from borscht! So Bubbi, who was twelve, became the mother, and she had to raise her younger brother and take care of her father. But in that little town she couldn't make any money, she couldn't get anywhere, she couldn't do anything. So when Meyer became about ten or eleven, all they could do to keep him going if my mother went out of the house to work was to apprentice him to someone, so they apprenticed him to a locksmith. So he was taken care of. And my mother went to Vilna, to the big city, to try to make some money, to try to make a living. And she had great guilts about leaving her old father. He was a very pious man, a very good man, very learned.

She went to work in the house of a wealthy family as a maid. They may have been cousins who dealt with land, buying and selling. So she worked in the house and got together some money and then she opened a little tiny store called a *gletta rheina lofkah.* Now *lofkah,* I think, means a "small store," and what the *"gletta rheina"* means in Russian I don't know, but she sold trimmings, buttons, thread, lace, that type of thing, and it was not very far away from where the Russian army had a camp and because she was blond, with green eyes and an up-turned nose, they didn't believe that she was Jewish and they all were crazy about her and they would come and deal with her. She was able to make, for those years, quite a bit of money.

It was there in Vilna that Bubbi met Zayda [Grand-father]. He was seventeen and she was twenty-two and he drove a *droshky,* a taxi carriage, with bells overhead and pulled by horse. He met her and she was a pretty lady and had a few dollars, which most women then did not have. They went together for a while and then de-cided to marry, on May the first, 1904. My mother would say she couldn't forget the date because on that day all her friends were jailed. She was part of a group of Rus-sian anarchists who would, if they could, overthrow the czar. Every May 1 they would demonstrate, and if the government knew there was going to be a demonstra-tion, whoever they knew would demonstrate, if they knew ahead of time, they'd throw them in jail. So the day of her wedding, which was May 1, her friends couldn't be there because they were in jail.

Meyer her brother was also involved. When he got older and came to Vilna to work, he got mixed up with a bunch of kids who were revolutionaries. He was very young then, seventeen or eighteen. And they made up a plan in which they would bomb a train and on the train were generals from the czar's army. The plan was aborted, somebody squealed, but they were all caught and he was sent to Siberia. Meyer spent eight years in Siberia in chains. But I'm jumping ahead. That's a different story.

First Bubbi met Zayda and they got married and made up that Zayda would go to America. The Russian army was reaching out for him and Jewish men were badly mistreated in the army. By now Jews knew Russia was no longer their home. He would go to America and she would follow when he got there.

Now, Zayda came from a little town called Zossel, a tiny place, a *shtetl*, a village, and in the first week of his life his father was killed by Russian *mujiks* who stole his wagon and everything in it. His mother remarried a man with rafts of children and Zayda became the youngest of the crew and he was treated like a baby, they liked him very much, but like any child in those days he had nothing, and he would do anything for a piece of bread or an apple. He slept in a drawer. It was a very very poor childhood. When he got to be sixteen, he felt he could help his family by not staying home and going to a big city to make a living. So he went to Vilna and became a *droshky* driver and then he met Bubbi and they got married.

When they decided to go to America, he went to say good-bye to *his* zayda, his father's father. He was the only grandchild from his father, there were no more youngsters from that side of the family, and Zayda knew that once he left he would never see him again. So he went to say good-bye to his zayda, who was then about one hundred. He was still sewing, he was a *schneider*. The zayda felt so bad because he had nothing to give him, he wanted to give him a going-away present, but he had nothing, he had absolutely nothing. If they had a little piece of bread they were lucky. So he gave him a piece of sugar, chopped from a lump, wrapped up in paper or whatever and said, this should be for his journey so his journey would be sweet, and then he gave him a little pouch with tobacco. The pouch was his own and it was all he really possessed and he said, this is so life would have a flavor, and then he gave him his good wishes for a good life in a new land. That was his bequest. That's all he could give him.

So Zayda came to America via steerage. He crossed borders at night—he had no passport—from Russia to Poland, from Poland to Germany, ending up in Glasgow, Scotland, with relatives, although in those years if you came from the same town you were a relative. They were so poor the best that they could give him was a place to sleep on the floor in the kitchen. He worked helping them make brushes or something to do with brushes until he got together just enough money so that he could come out to America steerage.

And when he got here, he had uncles here, these were his father's brothers and their name was Rozzin. Later your father changed it to Rossen. He came to New York and went to his uncles, they were all *schneiders*, like the zayda, but they all had large families and there wasn't any room for him. And Zayda wasn't trained for anything special. So a cousin suggested he work with him for a man who made house dresses—wrappers they were called and they were nothing to make—and sell them in the little towns in the rural areas of New England. So he would sew at night, he learned to work on a machine, and in the daytime they'd pack them up in a pack, put them on their backs and go out to the farms.

Zayda spoke no English. Zayda knew from borscht about anything English. So when these farmer's wives saw this good-looking young immigrant, and he was good-looking, nineteen at this point, they thought, hey, he's cute! and they would teach him English, how to say good morning and when they said how much, what the numbers were. They taught him whatever little English he learned at this point. But the man he worked for didn't pay what he was supposed to, he cheated him on the wages, so back he came to New York City. And one day he was sitting in the park on a bench, and another cousin mentioned someone needed a painter—a paint*ner* as they used to say in those days—and that's how Zayda became a painter.

Now my mother, Bubbi, waited for him and waited for him and of course time went on and he never got enough money to send for her, he had hardly enough to sustain himself. It was a question of waiting and she didn't want to wait. She wanted to come, and she came, like a lady. She'd been in business, so she sold the store, came out with a few bucks, and she came like a lady. She came with a passport, steerage of course, but she came with a passport and paid her way. She had a regular passport, a Russian passport with the imperial eagle on the front of it, and inside it said *die kleinbürgerine Yochbed Zukier* in German, and Russian and French, "Yocka Zuker from a small town" and the date and stamped with the Russian seal. She came with her cousin and she paid for *her* ticket, on a big white ship, one of the better ones.

So when she came to this country with a couple of dollars, she didn't come empty-handed, the ones that came to meet her at the boat were my father and his aunt, his mother's sister, and she was quite a lady, she was here many years before Zayda. She had lots of friends who thought my father was handsome and she couldn't see why he'd bring somebody from the old country when he could find himself a girl here in America. His Nona he used to call her, they came to the boat, and whatever Bubbi brought she said to her, you don't need it here in America, the samovar, the brass candlesticks, you don't need it here in this country, the feather pillows that she

209

brought, you don't need it, you don't need. She had a large family. She needed it herself. She talked her out of a good deal of things. And Bubbi and Zayda went to look for a place to live and the only one they found was in back of a butcher shop. They had a rough time, very very rough. I was born a year later on the Lower East Side, but your father was born uptown, after we moved.

I was a baby when we moved uptown to East Seventy-fourth Street between Avenue A and First Avenue. We moved into a tenement in Yorkville they called it, four stories high and this was real primitive, with bath-rooms—toilets! there were no bathrooms. Bob was in a crib and I slept on a "lunch"—well, they called it a "lunch" but it was really a lounge, it was a leather chaise lounge, and I was lucky. Some kids slept on two chairs pushed together. I remember the poverty, people very very poor.

Zayda was a painter and around that point he de-cided he didn't want to work for anyone else and he'd take little jobs in between the other. Bubbi was frugal, she never bought things on time. Most of the people had the peddler come and you'd buy something and pay, say fifty cents a week. The neighbors worked in the sweat-shops or took in piecework and when it was slack time, when times were bad, these women never put anything aside for those times, and they had to go *schnorring*, to ask their families for help. Bubbi was very proud, she wouldn't do that, even if it meant she never had a new coat, and she wore the same coat for as long as I remem-ber, but we always had food. And she fed the other chil-dren. Mama couldn't stand it if they didn't have to eat. She didn't care about the parents because she felt, don't buy that piece of rug for five dollars or whatever! That was an extravagance she just did without. But *we* never did without, there was always food for us.

Soon we moved downtown to Second Street, where

the folks bought the candy store, or that's what they thought. I mean, they put up a good deal of the money but Ellstein from the Village, Bubbi's cousin by marriage, put it in his name and they didn't know it. They had decided to buy a small store, a business, Zayda was still a painter but they weren't making a living. So he thought Mama could run the candy store and he would help when he was there, they used to work twelve to fourteen hours a day. Any heavy work that had to be done, he did. I was five and your daddy was three and I remember they made seltzer themselves. They would get barrels of carbon something, and they were on rockers, and then they would use water and then attach it to the fountain. And all the kids would come in and for a penny you could buy, it took you half an hour to decide which jawbreaker. Everyone who had a store lived in the back, and we lived in the back on the street level, not up a stoop or in the basement. We had one large room, the kitchen or whatever, and then a small bedroom divided by a window. And one little toilet and that was it. It was just like it was in Bob's picture, *Body and Soul*, even to the way your daddy set up the set. And Bubbi had one blouse that she washed every night and ironed every morning and put it on, one change.

Now, the store didn't fail but it wasn't making very much, nobody had anything, it was so poor. And Ellstein said he was going to sell it, and he came to tell the folks that they had to get out. It's our store! my mother said. What do you mean get out? Well, it seemed that when the papers were drawn, since neither one of them could read or write English very well—very well! not at all! my mother could read printing but my father nothing—they found out that it was in Ellstein's name. He had bought the store in his name with their money.

It was just at that time that Bob was very very sick and it turned out it was pleurisy and he got so sick my mother was scared to death and she called the doctor who said he must go to the hospital. In those days we were all terrified of hospitals, you went to a hospital, you never came back! And my mother had all kinds of doubts about sending him, but the doctor said he must go or he would die.

So Mama called the hospital to send for an ambulance, and that's when Mr. Ellstein arrived for the money—he wanted the money which wasn't there. I think there was something like five dollars in the kitty, they had these little drawers that pulled out for the money and he wanted that money but she wouldn't give it because she needed to pay the doctor with something. As far as Ellstein was concerned that wasn't important and there was a fight and Bubbi pushed him out the door. She picked up a knife and threatened to kill him if he didn't get out. Then she paid for the doctor.

We only lived there a year when they moved out of the candy store, back to Yorkville, on Seventy-sixth Street, 426 East Seventh-sixth Street, and we stayed there until I was twelve and Bob was ten. They moved back to a tenement but this was one step better because there were two toilets and four tenants on each floor, so the two on the left used one toilet and the two on the right used the other. The La Guardia family, which you know Fiorello came from, lived upstairs on the top floor.

My father was still a painter and my mother, in order to supplement the income—if things were rough you didn't ask anybody—she became the janitor of the building. She used to scrub the floors and take out the ashes, and the coal for the furnace, whatever was needed. It was not a job for a woman and Mama wasn't too well but she didn't know it and she didn't care, she did what she had to do.

My father began to get work on his own. He'd a faculty for making friends that was uncanny, some very

212

wealthy people who owned tenement houses. One in particular, a Mr. Offner or Hoffner, was crazy about Pop and was giving him work, and one day he told him, look, he said, you're never going to get anything unless you own property. I've got a house on Seventy-second between First and York. I'll lease it to you and you can make money. He didn't want to bother with collecting the rents.

So Pop took the money meant for something else— he needed one hundred, two hundred dollars, a fortune at that point—and Bubbi got angry but he leased the house. He started to go on his own more and more and they heard of a paint store that was for sale and Momma decided they should buy it. 762 Second Avenue, Forty-first and Second Avenue, around the corner from Murray Hill. So we moved into the store and we lived above it in a cold-water flat that was long and narrow. Business was so bad—I remember it was winter—that my father, who hadn't my mother's stick-to-it-iveness, was all for walking away and just forgetting it. Bubbi, on the other hand, refused to let it happen, so whatever they'd take in on Monday she would put in the cash register on Tuesday, so whatever came in on Tuesday, see! twice as much as Monday! and since she was taking care of the books he didn't know the difference. He thought, well, gee, it's really picking up!

And he got into the habit of going to auctions, paint stores that were going out of business, he would buy up wallpaper for practically nothing and that's how he started to make a little money. Plus the store was near the Murray Hill district, all brownstones cut up into singles and apartments. The landlords never did anything with them, so you had to buy a gallon of paint or a pint or a roll of paper and do it yourself. The folks started to get business from the tenants, and that's when they began to make a little money.

213

One day a Yankee came into the paint store, somebody new from around the corner. Bubbi was alone in the back, it was a long narrow store, like a candy store, and there was a long counter that ended halfway, and then shelves all around with the wallpaper. You had to have a ladder to get the paper and some of the paint was high as well, and there was paint behind the counter and in the back. Bubbi would have been forty-two at that time, with green eyes and fair skin and a round, stocky body, her blond hair knotted at the top of her head, stuck with combs that held it off her face.

So the Yankee came in and he said to my mother, I want a gallon of blue and Bubbi said yes and climbed up the ladder to get the paint and brought it down the ladder and set it on the counter.

"How much?" said the Yankee.

"A dollar forty-five," she said.

"A dollar forty-five?"

"A dollar forty-five."

"A dollar forty-five? Who do you think you are?"

"Go to hell!" she said. "Dets who I yem!"

Oh, she was a toughy, but very well spoken.

A YEAR
LATER

FEBRUARY 14, 1985

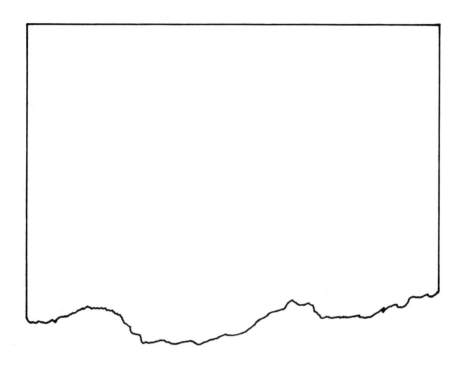

Walk II, Jaws III

Writing had kept me from madness, if madness is depression, and perhaps it is not when so well grounded, the madness of alienation and fragility, a natural consequence of my experience. (Had Lear gone mad? I think not). Rather, writing had given me God-like status as I ordered the insanities of life on this planet, thereby gifting myself with a sense of control. For four to eight hours of every day I re-created events on a piece of paper and in the doing made them mine, a part of my system. I slowly fitted together all the slivers of violence so as to grasp the whole picture and acknowledge a chaos "full of sound and fury" signifying naught. The rest of each day was spent in tears. I wrote, and I cried, and then I wrote some more.

There were no men in my life but a few old pals and

husbands of friends and quite casual acquaintances, like the gardener I thought I might trust in the yard, but no one with whom I shared a real intimacy, no one new in my life, no one of the world. The passion to paper pain with sexuality, drugging my hurt into twilight sleep, had fallen off the planet and down a hole. Life was a meat and potatoes affair.

And soon it was almost a year to the day, Valentine's Day 1985, and I couldn't afford to write that day and miss the occasion to walk the walk. Salvation might lie in the confrontation. I knew I must hike the mountain again and relive it "as it was" the year before and meet up with the *him* I was sure would be there and change the outcome of the day. If I could round up the courage to face the bastard. If I could hire a gun to murder for me. I felt terrified and I'd felt that too long.

I called Gary, my detective, and presented the thesis.

"I don't think Valentine's was an arbitrary date. I've checked it with several South Americans I know and they say Valentine's is very big in South America and as you know I've always thought this guy was South American." There was a silence.

"That's interesting," he said.

"Yes," I said, "I think so, too." There'd been no suspects, no similar crimes, a twelve-month goose egg filed at headquarters. "I think there's better than a sort of maybe chance that this guy will return, that he'll come back that day. I don't mean he'll come back looking for *me*, I just think he'll come back looking for *someone*, and if he doesn't come back to Will Rogers," I said, "he'll come back someplace else but he's gonna come back! That's my instinct!" I breathed, fending hysteria. "I don't know why but that's what I'm feeling!"

"Stranger things have happened," the detective said.

"You think so? You really think so?" Christ, I was right!

"Yeah, that kind of thing sometimes happens," he said.

"Well, if you think so, if you think that, do you think

218

you might go up there that day? I mean, I want to go up there that day! Do you think you might want to go up there, too?"

"My lieutenant won't go for the idea," he said.

"Oh!" I said. Screw the lieutenant!

"Carol," he said. My mind was drifting. "If you decide to go up there you let me know and if anything happens we can be there quick."

"Oh," I said. "Oh! Okay!" How might I phone if I were dead?

Killers on tap were scant that winter. The rangers had scattered and could not be found. Cal, the head ranger, had been bumped up the ladder and no longer roved that particular mountain. Tucker Ranger was off on a midyear vacation and "He won't be coming in for any reason" was the message relayed by his girlfriend to me. I'd the distinct impression he was nailed to a bed.

The day would be midwifed alone in my room.

Why my six-foot-five journalist friend John should call the Monday of "memorial week" was one of God's mysteries and a numerologist's delight. He'd remembered the anniversary only after dialing the last two digits of my telephone number.

"What does that mean?"

"I don't know," he said. "How are you, Carol?"

"Rotten," I said. "I feel real shaky and I've hurt my back just the same as I did last year at this time and I cry a lot."

"Are you going to go up on Valentine's Day?"

"Yeah, I want to. If I can. I want to," I said.

"If you need someone to go with you, *I* will," he said. And that was that! Without the help of an agent! My blond, blue-eyed, gentle giant always-friend had committed to battle and challenged my dragon. I'd no idea if he could throw a punch but I figured his height would command attention.

"Thank you. I accept. What if the creep is up there waiting?"

219

"I don't have a gun."

"I didn't think you had."

We'd meet at my house at 7:30 A.M.

I couldn't remember my name. I'd awakened at 6:00 A.M. that Thursday morning not knowing who I was or where I was, which wasn't a surprise, not once I'd remembered my name.

Stress, Carol. This is called stress. What are you going to wear? And I grabbed a great breath and considered the options. The same outfit, perhaps, bloodstains and all.

The idea was mediocre and melodramatic. Whatever the day, it wasn't B-picture tacky. Sweats would be fine but the clean variety, my jewelry would be my current passion, leg warmers to be cued by the color of the sweats, and pink tennies given the same assignment.

My name is Carol and I'm no longer married.

The day had begun. I would get dressed.

I've made up my mind.
You're my Valentine.

said a black penguin waddling into a snowy-white background, a heart-shaped lavender balloon grasped in one hand and a giant heart-shaped red candy box squashed under his flipper. I angled the card up against Eve's orange juice, next to her vitamins, in front of her egg.

"Come along, sweet baby, your breakfast is ready!" I blared through the house via intercom.

"Good morning, America!"

"Good morning to you!" Eve laughed at my jokes and wolfed down her egg as David Hartman keyed in to our kitchen proceedings. Diane Sawyer had left. I missed her badly. In all other respects the day was the same.

220

"Have a good day, Mommy!" Eve rushed to the door. "What will you do?" The car pool was waiting.

"I thought I might walk the mountain today." Eve kissed me good-bye. Her look was pensive. I sat down at the table and rocked my terror.

I was tight. My back was hurting and I was tight at the base of my spine and up and down my neck and around my mouth and my stomach hurt me. John arrived at precisely seven-thirty, a perfumed Gary Cooper minus the pistol, and I felt tight and shy and very grateful.

"You want some coffee?" I tried to smile.

"Sure," he said, as he ducked through the passway into the kitchen.

"I think I'm almost ready!" I stood by the chair hunched forward slightly, holding my stomach, deep-breathing as deeply as fear permitted. "I've got a tape recorder and a pad and pencil and *now* is when I wish I had a gun, goddamn it! I never got one, you know, I didn't think it was me. Still don't. Do you?"

"No," he said.

"I thought maybe we'd take Rags if you don't mind holding him because if *I* try holding him I'll never walk again." My eyes averted his. He'd not known me this way.

"That's fine," he said. "I don't mind." He leaned against the sink as he sipped his coffee, smelling of cologne at breakfast time.

"Why are you doing this?" I asked and wished I hadn't, just wished I could trust any man's intentions.

"It just seemed the right thing to do," he said.

John finished his coffee. We drove up to the park.

The stables were empty. I'd suspected they might be. Jimmy and Teresa no longer trained there. They'd left last summer, and Eve had followed to other auspices and better management.

221

My life at Will Rogers had diminished considerably.

Change was in gear. My fear was old news.

The day was hot and clear and crystalline blue, just as it had been the year before. A siroccan wind brushed through my hair, stifling bird calls and trail gravel crunchings, denying me access to future forewarnings of footsteps pounding down upon me, out of a bend or up from below.

The wind was high. That was dangerous.

We had parked. Rags was leashed. We started the climb.

As we rounded that part of the hiking trail that hangs low but well above the horse paddock and rings, that part of the trail from which I first saw him, I looked up at the point and scanned its perimeter shrouded in light and jabbing the blue. I looked up in search of that dash, death's sentinel, posted against the Technicolor sky. Sun-washed stillness rose above me, the virginity of morning not yet shattered. My man was nowhere. He'd not yet arrived. My man was elsewhere. He was not to be seen.

I quickly glanced back, over my shoulder, through the dust and down gravel, down into the bend. Perhaps I might catch him following our threesome. The hour was early. He might hang behind. He might wait for the sun to shift its position, wait for time to edge closer and full-circle the year and so sanctify the moment by precise reenactment.

I glanced at my watch. It read eight o'clock. I'd made an early entrance. My timing was off. I wasn't meant to *be* yet. He might lag behind.

The road was deserted, excepting our presence. No one had trailed us. At least no one seen. I looked off to the west out over the Pacific. Catalina was clear.

"I'm scared shitless," I said. I snapped on the recorder. "Everything is stunningly beautiful, just as it was. The lavenders and the blues and greens of the chaparral and sage and wild oak are as vibrant and lush as ever and the smells of wildflowers and eucalyptus are overwhelming. I can see Catalina and the wind is very high, making it absolutely impossible to hear a goddamn thing and that's scaring the shit

222

out of me. That, and other things. More later." I switched off.

Twigs crackled in the wind. My heart froze in my chest. A remembrance of that moment when the man had left me and broken the silence and crawled out of the brush.

I'd forgotten that moment. It, too, was now with me.

John was silent. I was silent. Rags was silent but tail-fanning happy. He seemed to hear nothing. We marched on at pace.

"There's someone ahead."

"Where?" I said.

"Ahead. The next bend. He's walking a bike." A Yuppie-like creature sporting an Afro appeared out of a deep twist in the trail, a Yuppie wheeling his bike down the road.

The distance was shrinking. The creature enlarged. He would pass on the left, on the outside lane.

"Good morning," I said. He was by my side.

"Good morning," he said, and he passed without nodding. The day was on replay, the words recycling.

"He's not my man," I whispered to John. My head was buzzing. Perhaps I was wrong. "But I think it's very odd to wheel a bike up a mountain."

"Not really," said John. "People do do it."

The sun baked the brush. The wind was still high. Wood crackling and crunching masked the sounds of birdies and snakes playing canasta.

"There's somebody else," John announced. "A man with a dog walking ahead." Man and dog were pointed toward Inspiration Point, walking, it seemed, just to be walking. Blotted against the blue horizon, they'd blocked the infinite, smudging perfection. My eyes refocused the thirty-yard blur, to further police and inspect the male person. He appeared to be stocky and in his fifties.

The dog, of course, might be a killer.

They vanished to the right. A road cut had grabbed them.

We were ten yards into that twist in the road where I'd passed my man and said good morning, where we'd suckered each other in a casual glance and peanut butter stuck at the base of our souls. And now baggies of pain burst over my head, stink bombs that skunked the mountain's beauty. The greens had turned gray. My eyes were all smoky. The wind was high and twigs were crackling.

I glanced over my shoulder and then looked ahead. Both directions were clear but the Y was before us.

"This is it, the Y, where I turned right," I said as I weaved to the center of the bend, bumping Rags and then John, jumbling our order. I no longer knew where to walk, my instincts had tangled, nerve fibers detached. If I followed my natural inclination, I'd shoulder the road cut, the easier distance; if I shouldered the road cut, I couldn't see what might be coming above or below, jogging out of a bend, dervishing toward me. I'd be trapped inside where escape was not possible.

The rim of the mountain beckoned me, the ledge where the mountain falls into the canyon, the rim over which he had dragged my body. I veered to the left, to the lip of the road, mulling the invite to trail its perimeter.

I would tightrope the ledge to the X in my brain, to the spot up the road where he'd smashed my skull. I'd hike the crooked line of crumbling soil and tweak my courage and not sail off and slide the ravine where he'd left my body. The odds were with me, if odds still existed. A forty-yard climb, Roger had said when I'd taped his recollections the year before. Forty yards from the Y to where he attacked you.

"A forty-yard climb from the Y to the spot," I said into my tape, and began the hike.

We were there. At the spot. I couldn't stand still. Jiggling in place. Hot-footing a dance. I knew *he* was there! I knew *he* was with us! I knew *he* was watching and gauging the moment. I knew *he*'d climb out of the brush below, rush out at me now, and drag me down with him. I knew *he*'d drop out of the clouds to my right, pinned to the sky, high on the rise, sledgehammer in hand draped down his spine.

I paced and I rocked. I weaved as I spoke. The brush was crackling. I was on fire.

"*This* is the spot. *This* is the place. *This* is where he stood," I said to John. "*This* is where I was. *This* is where he dragged me. The brush is high now. It was all bent."

John said nothing. Rags wagged his tail.

"Are you scared?" I asked John.

"No," he said. He stood with his back against the mountain. He stood where I'd stood the year before, he stood in the ditch and looked up at me. *I* was on the rise. *I* was on the rim. *I* was where *he*'d been, where *he* was in my brain.

"But I know how important it is for you to do what you're doing." John spoke very slowly. "To come back and find out it's no longer here."

"Let's go," I said. "Let's get to the top." I hadn't the nerves for an overview.

Man with dog was seated on the second park bench, a slice to the right of where we were seated. We had reached Inspiration, a pancakelike round, Will Rogers's stubbed point, the thumb of the mountain. My eyes scanned three hundred and sixty degrees of empty, open, flat-footed space. *He* had no where to hide. I almost felt safe.

Our bench had been angled to accommodate a view of the Pacific Ocean and the southwest coastline. I sat next to John, Rags at my feet, my back to the trail, to the east, to the sun, to the moon-shaped space of nothingness. I sat facing the sea, my back to *him*, my back to death or to that possibility. Like a toreador, I'd turned my back on the money.

Rags will bark if someone comes close, I thought, peering around at nothing at all. I would dare the moment. I would dare for I wished to give in to the peace, to my body's insistence I give in to the peace, sink into the peace and embrace the moment, the peaceful pinkness of that morning moment.

I'd leave it to Rags and withdraw my surveillance.

I slipped out of my body and climbed up a cloud and gazed down on two guys and a girl and two silly dogs on top of a mountain overlooking the city, a sleepy L.A., just awakened

225

and washed, a sparkling Pacific, chest breathing and stretching, Catalina bruising the white-blue horizon, clean, unpolluted, winking with pleasure, its yellowy crust shooed away by warm winds.

I gave in to the craving, "the chocolate almond fix," a two-minute respite, a pause in the action.

Softly, gently, I reentered me, my body gone soft, its knots unknotted, smothered in smells and the heat and the beauty, soaked by the morning and chairing the world from papal ceilings of cotton candy, immersed in God's rainbow, whole and at peace.

I sat alone, on a bench, together with a friend.

Man and dog had left. I hadn't noticed.

John sat beside me, Rags at my feet, talking of drugs and booze, of other obsessions, crutches and death and confronting one's pain. John had been talking. I was somewhere else.

"We should go," I said, not knowing why. I wished to live life on top of this mountain.

"Okay," John said, and uncurled his body. We stood for a moment facing the sea, devouring vistas and staying the silence.

"Maybe you've got this wrong," John said, taking the lead as we crossed Inspiration. "Maybe this isn't about Valentine's Day. Maybe this guy likes to kill people Wednesdays!"

Perfect! I thought and my kidneys gave out. "Maybe this guy likes to kill people Wednesdays!" I said to my tape.

The wind was still high.

We retraced our tracks down into the bend, into the hook where the man had smashed me. My palms and my pulse still warned of his presence, warned he might yet be stalking the moment, the uneven moment descending the trail, the moment his body claimed mine as its target and fractured my skull, stopping my heart.

The gully of the site was spotted with rocks scattered about where I'd stood and fallen, mates to the one stored at home with my keys. I had a passion to kneel and gather each one and stare at their surface of mineral mirrors, hopeful to capture my bloodied image, curious to know if my blood marked the spot, if I'd lettered the earth à la "Kilroy was here." I had a passion to stop and play in the dirt.

Yet I walked through the bow of the sightless bend, passing the rocks that had traced my body, never pausing to caress even one stone for fear of the man and the killing moment, the one I'd not guarded, giving in to distraction. I never paused and bent down to collect one specimen, for I was embarrassed by John's bearing witness to an archaeological dig in the name of conceit, to my infantile pleasure, my two-year-old joy at fondling my leavings, discovering me.

I walked the bend and passed the site.

The lilac-green brush that had canopied me, that sage-dotted brush rocked in the wind, mothering hidden lives as we walked its border, descending forty yards to the intersection.

I arrived at the Y. Unbloodied. Breathing.

"Which way should we turn?" John was speaking. "Which way do we go?" he was saying.

"To the right, the short way, the way the old people came."

I was cheating. I was tired. I was still afraid. I'd chosen the path *he* never traveled, the trail I'd not used the year before, the shortcut off the mountain, a fire road. My watch read eight-thirty. There was still time. *HE* might *hold* on the killing until nine-fifteen. He might be entering the park at this moment, or rounding some twist in the lower road, and if I walked to the left, as I'd done before, we'd pass in reverse and Rags could kill him. If I stuck to my plan and repeated each action.

"Yeah, to the right, the short way, let's get out of here!"

Fuck the pain, I thought. Fuck the confrontation. I've done my best. I've finished this morning. Let him come! I can't wait! To hell with the bastard!

I'd call the shots. I'd make the moves. I was in control of this scenario.

We were down off the mountain in six minutes flat, Rags pulling John over sliding gravel as I held his hand and skied through the dust.

We walked to the car and then drove to the house, the number-one errand of the day completed.

John left for work immediately. He hadn't the time to stay for breakfast. I made some coffee and rewound the tape and sat myself down at the kitchen table to replay the morning's odyssey.

The tape was blank. The words hadn't stuck. All that I heard was wind whistling hard, crackling and crunching the brush at Will Rogers, masking all sounds and erasing my voice.

Let's get the billing right

I had a dream on Friday, one night later.

I was sitting in a theater—it was also a movie house, one of those houses used for both purposes—and I was surrounded by people I'd never seen before, never met or seen, which was odd since I knew we were all of us there attending an event of common interest, a celebration of something, which normally meant we'd know each other. But we didn't.

We were strangers.

I was there to receive an award. I was sitting on the aisle. I had chosen the seat so I might rise and run fast down the polyester runner just as "they" do at the Academy Awards. But this was happening in Oxnard, California, a town you drive through to get where you're going. A not-glitzy town. Away from Hollywood. And I was by myself. And Patrick was with me.

Patrick was on stage standing stage right, he was a part of the awards presentation group, and I knew he was there because this celebration, this confirmation of worth, had everything to do with something he'd told me and I hadn't heard.

The men on stage seemed very disorganized. There were four or five men, there were no women, just guys on a stage checking their notes, shuffling their cards and shuffling their feet on a Winter Garden stage, quite wide and bare, lit by white light, stark white, untinted.

None of the men wore a tuxedo.

Everyone was talking. The people on stage were talking to each other and the people in the audience were talking to each other, everyone was talking and nobody cared.

I wasn't talking. I was waiting to receive my award of merit.

Finally a man announced my name, he said my whole name, Carol Eve Rossen, but he got it wrong, he mangled the words, he'd sieved the vowels like mashed potatoes, he had no idea *who* I was but *I* knew it was me he was mispronouncing. *I'd* get it right when I gave my acceptance, I wanted to get my name right very badly.

He announced my name and I jumped from my seat and ran down the aisle, ready with thank yous, managing the high-heeled flight without falling, dancing my way along fibered potholes.

I arrived at the stage, at the foot of the theater, but there was no ramp or staircase to climb, there was no way to get onto the platform except to shinny up a black tree ladder abutted against the lip of the stage, a black plywood board with horizontal wood strips that were very steep, straight up and down.

I didn't mind the inconvenience. I monkeyed the ladder and walked onto the stage.

Everyone was talking. And nobody cared.

Someone, not Patrick, gave the award. A man turned to face me, his back to the audience, and said to me, "Carol, this is your award. It's a black Cadillac convertible and you don't have to thank anyone. We're running late on time. Just leave the stage."

No, I thought, I want to say thank you! (I wasn't feeling in the least bit shy or nervous and I wished to say my name

229

right and to thank the people.) I walked past the man to the microphone and introduced myself, I said my name clearly, I got my name right, I said it slowly, and I thanked the audience for the black Caddy.

"I really deserve it but still," I said, "it's so pretty and just terrific to be given an award! It means a lot, I love it a lot, and even though it's something dead and gone, a death, a memory of another time, it will be cherished. It will be honored. It has great style. It was a classic."

I'd finished my speech and walked off the stage and ran up the aisle. But someone, a stranger, had taken my seat.

I didn't mind. There were other seats. I found one in the middle and took my place.

SIX MONTHS LATER

AUGUST–SEPTEMBER 1985

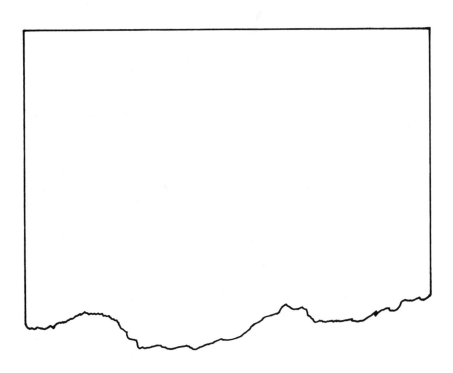

A no-popcorn gig

What a great dream, right? Fabulous! Just fabulous! Talk about cooling out an experience! So positive. So clean. So existential. I loved it! I'd dreamed it! I'd wished it into being! Margaret said she thought it would be incredible to end the book with a dream. All the analysts would go nuts if this book ended with a dream. I thought so, too, I liked the idea, but in truth, the dream was just a touch premature by at least six months and more like a year. Life simply isn't that neat, would that it were, and I wasn't *that* comfortable wearing my skin around L.A. for months in the future.

True, my tears had been bottled by sixty percent and I'd managed to do an acting job and I'd plans to give myself a party and thank all the people who'd been thoughtful and kind and to celebrate the idea of friendship. Paranoia had lapsed and given way with most of God's creatures, if not

233

with strange men. Time is a healer, that proved to be true. I was doing quite well for a girl who felt numb.

Now it was summer of '85, a Sunday in Hollywood, a day of worship, a day many in Hollywood go to the movies at the Academy of Motion Picture Arts and Sciences, if you're a member of the academy or you've a friend who invites you. It was a day to visit our temple of commerce, which housed a grand theater and its perfect sound system, to view an immaculate print of the newest release in the company of peers in the entertainment business. It was a "say-hey!" day, a day of communion, particularly for those who were not working and felt isolated by freeway systems. It was an alive and well day, a reconnection. If you can get to the church you ain't dead yet!

I found that reassuring. I'd been numb for some time.

It was Sunday, August 11, 1985, a Sabbath by the sea and the day before my birthday. I'd neither read the papers nor bought bagels and lox but rather filled in the particulars of my unemployment claim to be mailed on my way to morning yoga. The afternoon would be spent with a pal at the movies, the three o'clock show at the academy, ensconced in cut velvet and lost in darkness viewing Michael Cimino's *Year of the Dragon*, a stylish mystery à la *Chinatown*, rumored a winner by the "they" who know, a no-popcorn gig but a kick and a giggle. It was a Hollywood ending to a nebulous week, a touch of fun to temper a sadness. But first I would tend to physical fitness.

Early-morning yoga rarely seduced me. Mornings were for writing before my mind became cluttered with shifting patterns stenciling the day. Words, however, had flown the coop. I was blocked. I hadn't written in three months. I'd managed three hundred pages of a manuscript, of a book, THE BOOK, THE ASSAULT STORY, but now, since May and the heat of summer I'd been stuck, wordless, unable to touch that part of the story having to do with Bianchi, having to do with my rage and feelings I'd stored and forgotten where I'd left them, didn't wish to remember, didn't wish to feel. I'd given up on the book, my files quite useless, perhaps all it had been was a therapeutic exercise and that's fine, I thought, that's good, that's helpful. I'd turned outward again, to the world of hijackings and repotting geraniums and lunching with friends and firing my agents and looking for work and feeling a numbness, a sad indifference, haunted every moment by the lack of completion. I'd hoped yoga would help overcome the imbalance.

The matinee performance of Cimino's *Dragon* was a mob scene of cohorts kissing and waving. All 1,106 seats of the academy were occupied or reserved and not a Hershey for sale. Hundreds of *New York Times* Sunday sections rustled in breezes of air-conditioning, brought there by the membership as previewing reading matter, but no one was reading, not *really* reading as pages whooshed and whirred like windshield wipers. There was too much electricity, too much buzz, too great a rush of sparkle and shimmer and great expectations of intent and quality to concentrate on the word as writ from New York. We awaited a *GOODY*, this would be a *FLICK*, this was *THE REASON* we were all in the business.

The overheads dimmed, the screen filling with light.

Twenty seconds into the film, after a musical fanfare under the credits reminiscent of Cleopatra's arrival in Rome, the screen was drenched in blood. A few minutes later it happened again, and then again it happened, and I knew then the drenching would be endless, I knew the film was about the drenching.

I was electrocuted by a rush of blood, a river of blood pouring down on my head, boxed in my seat by surrounding seats filled, unmoving, mute, drenched, mesmerized by blood drenching the screen, drowning the theater, pounding my head. I looked away from the screen and stared into the dark and I thought to myself, Well, I really can't leave or I'll disturb the whole audience and I can't ask my pal because she wants to be here and I know he'll stop he's got to stop he can't be serious he's got to stop. I raised my hand to my eyes and scrunched down in my seat and tried not to watch the picture at all.

I stayed the two hours. I gave in. I went limp. I submitted to the beating, to Cimino's beating, as I had to the man on top of the mountain and I cried and I cried and I didn't make a sound.

I was his victim. And I was enraged.

When the screening was over, some of the members of the academy applauded the film. Others hissed. I was among them.

Every ounce of anguish suffered that day I'd not regret. The vileness and violence of the film had undone my rage, releasing my wrath. The hotter I burned the better I felt. Electra in mourning knew no more passion. The son of a bitch had ravished sensibility and who now would be his executioner?

I could not stop talking about the film and exploring each perversion. I could not stop *thinking* about the film and its violation of every decency. Cimino was a killer and I wanted him dead. I wanted revenge as the Greeks understood it, and Zeus heard my prayers and granted permission that I might follow my heart.

There were critics out there who had missed the point, mindless, it seemed, of the public trust, more interested, it seemed, in the celebrity fuck. Ten days later I wrote this letter:

August 23, 1985

Gene Shalit
N.B.C. The Today Show
30 Rockefeller Plaza
New York City, N.Y.

Dear Gene Shalit,

As a victim of a violent crime, and let me be specific since Michael Cimino's bloodbath, The Year of the Dragon, *in no way seemed to offend or nauseate you, as a woman who while taking a walk was hit in the head seven times with a sledgehammer and pretended to die and lived to write about it, as a victim of that violent* crime I must ask how dare you dismiss all criticism of Mr. Cimino's flick as "everyone still getting on his back" while interviewing Mickey Rourke on "The Today Show" August 21st.

Surely you have noticed that there is a great deal of difference between an exploration of violence and the ways in which it dehumanizes society, i.e., The Killing Fields, and a film which victimizes its audience in its excesses, drenching it in a bloodbath which can only be understood as its creator's misdirected masturbation.

Yes, Cimino is an artist. Yes, he is visually seductive. Yes, he creates images which are original and often breathtaking. But as John Powers wrote in L.A. Weekly, he is an "artist from the retina out"—he is a man suffering from "moral myopia." He is a pusher of rage, a hustler of violence well groomed in sound marketing strategy, and let us not forget his artistic origins. Madison Avenue—the ad business, where merde almost always passes for dessert.

The world is too much with us. Loony tunes abound out there. We all must take responsibility for that violence dousing American life these days. If you think someone out there didn't leave Cimino's film well stoked for the killing he would soon commit, then you are out of touch with the street Cimino deifies.

Cimino cannot be excused from that responsibility, if there are any controls left in him to exercise.

Critics cannot be excused from that responsibility.

I cannot be excused from writing this letter. And I would like to be. It would be ever so much easier.

As an artist, as the daughter of a great filmmaker, and as a victim of a violent crime, please reassess this film and all others like it.

Most sincerely,

Carol Rossen

cc. Howard Rosenberg, Los Amgeles Times

I finished the letter and I began to shake and I began to weep and I breathed tiny breaths of no air at all. And I sat at my desk and was paralyzed.

The Feds would come and get me, I was quite sure. The Feds would come and get me as they had my father for expressing feelings contrary to the NBC News Division. One never forgets the lessons of childhood.

Shalit would come and get me, I was quite sure. Shalit would get me by critically destroying whatever was left of my acting career; if you stick your neck out they cut off your head, axiomatic if one lives in Hollywood. One never forgets the lessons of childhood.

If I revealed myself publicly as the lady from Will Rogers, the one who'd pretended but hadn't died, *he* would know, *he* would find me, *he* would come and get me, of that I was sure.

That was the reason my hands were shaking.

I held my own hands for two days and nights and then called my friend Joyce and read her the letter and spoke of my shame and my lack of courage. I hadn't been able to send the letter. Joyce didn't think anyone would hurt me for writing that letter and expressing my feelings. And I believed Joyce because I was ready.

I sent the letter. And I sent lots of others.

Shalit never answered me, which was neither a surprise nor a disappointment. We were not destined to become pen pals. Very likely the letter got lost in Johnny Carson's mail. Shalit. Carson. What's in a name? What mattered to me was that I had the courage to write him and others like him, critics, newspapers, a scattering of executives. I'd found the courage to rage and to hell with the consequences. I'd come out of the closet and I was hot.

I wanted Cimino strung up Western style; that is, I wanted big bucks not to flow in his direction. If he had the right to make flicks of his heart's desire, I had the right to despise them in word and in print. Rumor had it he'd signed for another, this one about serial killers. I wasn't surprised at the choice of material; he was very like them, furtive, on the prowl, leaving his mark project to project. All of my energies would now be directed against those I felt were deranged, working in film.

A few days after I'd sent the letters, the Los Angeles police leaked through the media that our town had been graced with the real thing.

Cimino would be scalped by the Chinese community while The Night Stalker terrorized southern California and I got off on the genuine article.

A paranoid jig

The temperature was in the mid- to high nineties, weather-persons predicting no break for a week. Every paved surface of massive urban sprawl radiated steam heat by 8:00 A.M. each morning. By evening the air that bedded the county oven-baked God's creatures like Thanksgiving turkeys. Dogs and cats, indoor sleepers when the moon appeared, dug in under shade trees in search of the cool. Impatiens and petunias and the last of the summer's sweet-smelling gardenias cocked their heads earthward and despaired, the ground cracked and parched, unabsorbing of water. It was hot in L.A. The city was cranky.

Water on the ankles, knees, in the head afflicted every-one. Daily chores were put aside as taking too much effort. Playing Russian roulette was a great deal safer than driving freeways or inland routes known as the flats; even-keeled men and women, car owners for years, were mysteriously trans-formed into giant wasps behind wheels, darting every which way, stopping and starting, preying on each other's territorial boundaries. It was best to submerge in the nearest swimming hole, or in an air-conditioned office if that was one's fate, or shop a chic mall newly built and enclosed. If there was hope for relief it was late in the night, past midnight, early morning when a maverick breeze snuck through the layers of yellowy smog, sifting window screens and sliding over the sashes.

That was the problem. That's how *he* got in.

We'd lived with his presence for years, it seemed, although it wasn't until midsummer that the newspapers and television were saturated with the drawing, a composite of the killer. It was reported to have been an ongoing story, the details of which were stored somewhere in memory with other atrocities that graze our lives over coffee, horrific events in Glendale and Monrovia, bloodlettings in Whittier and Monterey Park, minimassacres scattered about the Southland, unrelated, unrelenting since 1981; for it wasn't until the spring of '85 that the police first suspected at least four unsolved murders had been committed by a creature hiding in the dark.

The *Los Angeles Times* would later itemize the diversity of troughs he had fed from, sparking recollection of those wonders past:

> Prowling the freeway corridors of Los Angeles and beyond, the stalker preyed upon businessmen, Asian immigrants, grandmothers and retired couples. He kidnapped children off streets and sexually assaulted them; he dragged one woman from her car and shot her repeatedly. Most often, he crept into tidy tract homes through unlocked windows and doors before dawn, cut telephone wires and attacked his victims while they slept.
>
> In serene middle-class neighborhoods, he killed men first, then turned to their women. He bludgeoned, slashed throats, raped, sodomized and shot his prey, using .22 caliber and .25 caliber pistols—easily concealed weapons that make relatively little noise.
>
> Wearing soft cotton gloves, he also killed and maimed with a tire iron and a claw hammer. Some victims were handcuffed to door knobs or bound with electrical extension cords and brutalized.

Afterward the stalker casually snacked on leftovers in the kitchens of some victims. He raped one woman and then ordered her to cook him a meal. He gouged out the eyes of another victim.

He . . . stole their jewelry, television sets, cameras, and . . . their suitcases.

Now, in the ripeness and wet of late summer, a core of panic had lodged in our collective belly, an indigestible morsel that defined this happening, that informed the fucker as quite different from Bianchi or New York's Son of Sam or other serial killers mucking about. This creep was indiscriminate, he didn't play by the rules, he liked to kill all kinds of people, every way and anyplace. He hadn't a preference for brunette collegians with their hair neatly parted down the middle, or Hollywood streetwalkers or youthful black males.

He didn't conform, that was the bitch. For a moment it was reported he liked sleeping souls in one-story yellow houses near freeway on-ramps but that didn't stick, that didn't hold water. He'd just shot a man point blank through the head in an adobe house out in Mission Viejo. Everyone was "it" in a gory game of tag, black and white, yellow and brown, rich and poor, the Yuppies. Tremors of victimization shook all the people, inklings of what it felt to play war for real. Life was on edge, a paranoid jig.

The case had become a law-enforcement obsession, investigators abandoning their family lives to sixteen-hour days, seven days a week, circling the stalker and chasing their tails. Neither hook nor focus nor viable stakeout offered itself anywhere in the county. That's why the leak, the supersaturations, the composite face, the eyes staring out from television tubes and newspaper print, a five-week haunting by skinny Big Brother, this month's pin-up freak, the nameless capped weirdo. They were begging for help from the greater community, hoping for the loan of our eyes and hearts and instincts for survival, our animal selves. The police understood the nature of the beast. He would not be sated by or-

241

gasms of blood. He needed sex and fresh meat more and more often.

It was hot and my head dripped and throbbed. There'd been nerve damage to the left side of my face from the sledgehammer pounding and cracking the cheekbone. The nerves hadn't been severed but they had been weakened. Those strands of nerves hooked over my ear, somewhat like Victorian spectacles, and trickling down to the left and the base of the cranium just above the neck where hair starts to grow, they bunched and met, a coming together. That meeting was called a reference spot, and if there was tension astray in mind or body, the spot beat and pounded and flashed with pain, a warning light that had found its way to the weakest point in the nervous system.

My sweat glands, as well, at the left of my face along the hairline no longer functioned properly. The heat of the sun or the heat of anxiety induced sweat to pour forth like a faucet without valves, that side of my face and hair totally drenched, the other only damp with beads of perspiration. Sometimes I cried from these random attacks of soggy salt water rolling down my left front.

It was hot that week, in the upper nineties, and my head dripped and throbbed of the heat and anxiety every day of that week before they caught the Night Stalker.

Pasta primavera radical chic

"Do you think the Night Stalker could be your man?" my brother asked me. Lots of people were asking. They called to ask about it. "That composite picture looks a hell of a lot like him, like your composite picture," my brother said. I kept my composite on my desk in the bedroom next to the Polaroid of Eve as a baby.

"Yeah, it does," I said, "except it doesn't. The cheekbones are the same but the face seems thinner. And they say he's tall and has curly brown hair. My guy wasn't tall and

242

his hair was straight. Although hair can be changed. I guess. I don't know." I barely remembered his face anymore, except if I stared into a corner where two white walls came together and conjured a vision, a particular moment. It wasn't clear, this comparing composites.

"Well, I think it could be him," my brother said.

"I never saw his teeth, he smiled a crooked smile, they say the Stalker's teeth are all gapped and disgusting."

"Do you ever talk to your policeman?" he asked.

"Sometimes," I said. "Not for six months."

I'd clipped and collected the Stalker's face and stacked it underneath my composite drawing. Every day all that week I cut out the story, for every day there was a story with a picture in the paper, Frank's picture of him, my friend Frank who liked Rags. The sketch was by Frank. The style was the same. Every morning I'd cut and staple and stack and focus feeling and feed my rage, a perversely ritualized "hands across the seas," a special connection known only by the few, an intimacy nourished by horror and violence. I cherished the obsession and found it repelling.

That Saturday morning of Labor Day weekend, the police made a move that shook my fixation. As was my wont before putting up coffee, I turned off the lights that had burned through the night, hanging from trees and hidden in bushes lighting the night like a Hollywood opening and protecting me and mine from The Stalker. Jebbie accompanied me down the drive to the street where the newspaper lay haloed by a rubber band. Where will he be, I thought to myself, on the front page or in the Metro section? I reached for the paper and rolled off the band and lifted the folds that unveiled the first section.

He was there, of course, staring at me, but he wasn't *he*, he'd been replaced, he wasn't a composite, he had a real face in a photograph and it wasn't the face of my man, but he might be my man, I'd never be sure. I stared down at the face of Richard Ramirez.

Jesus Christ, I thought, the cops must be scared, they

243

never release this kind of stuff. Now if they catch the son of a bitch some goddamn lawyer will say his case was prejudiced in the paper, that his civil rights were somehow obstructed, that they named the killer without proving it first, the legal system's hopelessly fucked.

Richard Ramirez stared at me.

Richard Ramirez. I'd make him my man.

Later that day I brunched in Malibu, at Saturday noon of Labor Day weekend, for I'd been invited to the home of friends. We sat out in the sun under striped umbrellas.

"Who?" he asked, he another guest, he a producer of movie magic.

"Cimino," I said.

"Why?" he asked. "Why doncha like him?" Pasta primavera dribbled from his mouth.

"If you'd seen his film I'm sure you'd know why. They oughtta string him up and auction him off like Garland's red shoes in the *Wizard*, you know?"

"Oh," he said, reaching across. He needed more cream cheese for his bagel.

"Carol was hurt, almost killed last year by one of those people like the Night Stalker," my hostess announced in explanation.

He said nothing. Put an olive in his mouth.

"How terrible for you," she said, his wife, slushing sun oil over blond thighs.

I said nothing. My head throbbed. It was hot.

"They got him, you know!" My host was speaking, a dear treasured friend of twenty-odd years.

"Who?" I asked.

"The Stalker," he said. "Found him and beat him in East L.A."

"You're kidding," I said. "When did that happen? I just read this morning they'd released his picture!"

"This morning," he said, "in East L.A. The early edition didn't carry the story. They saw him and chased him and

244

beat him with a steel rod after he'd tried to steal someone's car."

"The people. Not the cops."

"Yeah, the Latinos."

"He's a poor soul, a poor tortured creature!" The lady of the house was ever charitable, devoting her life to social causes, helping her friends in every which way, averting her eyes and avoiding vulgarians who wheedled their way into brunch invitations.

I said nothing. I loved her too much.

We moved into the house to escape the heat.

The sated producer was semiconscious, deep-breathing grosses and puppy-dog tails, collapsed on the divan that faced the palms and a stretch of sand overlooking the sea. His wife had withdrawn and would return shortly, lost, for the moment, in a jar of cream. The rest of our group had been struck by the lulls of late afternoon of a day at the beach.

"Capital punishment can't be justified." My host had spoken, interrupting the silence.

"Killing is a sin," my hostess said. "Killing is a sin no matter who does the killing."

"The statistics show that no execution has ever deterred another from murder."

I supposed that were true but it wasn't the point. I said nothing. I loved them too much.

We sat in silence, staring at dunes wobbling in heat, and the sand beyond and then the sea.

"I really want to see him." I spoke in the pause, addressing the view as well as my friends. "I really want to see Ramirez hurt and bleeding. Can we watch the news? I'm sure it's on cable." The living room boasted a giant screen that made watching television like watching movies. Bigger than life. No one objected.

Just as my host rose from his seat to adjust the big screen and balance the sound system, the doorbell rang at the front gate out on the street way away on the highway.

"Who's that?" my host said.

"Who's that?" a voice echoed. The sleeping producer had awakened from dreams of sharing world profits with Dino de Laurentiis.

"I don't know," said my hostess. "No one's expected."

"Don't open the door!" My host was speaking.

"I won't," she said, "I'll talk on the intercom. Hello!" she sang out as she pushed the button.

"A package from the shelter," an accent staccatoed.

"What package from the shelter?" One of her charities?

"A package, Señora!"

"I'm not expecting any package from the shelter. Just leave it by the gate!"

"Where, Señora?"

"Right there, by the gate."

There was a silence.

"What package could that be?"

"Don't answer the door," my host had hissed. His face was rigid.

"No, I won't darling, please! Oh, the package!" she said. *"Now* I remember."

"Wait till he leaves before you go get it."

"Yes," she said.

"Yes," we chorused, the producer and I, as we both turned back to the screen and the image of Ramirez being led to a car, the cops having cuffed him, his head swathed in gauze.

"Damn! We missed the beatings! We missed the crowd! I wonder if they've got it on film?" I said. "I wonder if CBS will show that tonight?"

No one spoke. I continued:

"Jesus, I'm glad he was bludgeoned by his own, that the people on the street beat the shit out of him and not some tight-assed white guard standing in a shack checking out the entrance to Malibu Colony. That would have been bad. This is really great!"

And in that moment I remembered another, a moment high up on Inspiration, a moment I'd lost, a moment I'd eaten and crammed down my gut and left there to block my life, a moment between the third and fourth bash when I realized someone was trying to kill me, *the* moment I wanted to kill the bastard, to smash him and claw him and tear him apart, *the* moment of rage at the violation, *the* moment before I gave in to survival, becoming his victim and praying for mercy, betting on the scam that he'd believe my lie: that I'd died and that he'd won, that I was his to do with: the moment before the will to live conquered fury.

Now I could feel. Now I was strong. Now I wished he was dead. I wanted to kill him.

"Yes," said my host, "it's better this way. It's best that his own found him out on the street."

"Yes," I said and stopped my head. I was in Malibu with my friends and a movie producer and his lovely wife, Blondie. My host turned down the sound and put on his music, Puccini arias and thirties' ballads.

We listened and smiled; both were so beautiful.

The bureau was closed on Labor Day. It wasn't until Tuesday, three days later, that I phoned my detective and told him my thought that perhaps the Night Stalker was my man.

"I'd like to be part of a lineup," I said. "What do you think of the possibility?"

"I never forget you, Carol," he said. "Whenever anything comes in I think of your case. But this isn't it, it just doesn't fit, not his height, not his weight, nothing about it. I'm sorry, Carol. I won't forget you."

"God, I wish it were him!"

"I know," he said.

———

I was left with my rage. I felt whole again. I may have been scarred but I had survived. Like Jacob's struggle with the angel, I hadn't let go until I was blessed.

Oddly, I'd learned to love life all the more.